THE SEC

THE SMILE

ELLIE MASON

Editing, design, typesetting and publishing by UK Book Publishing

www.ukbookpublishing.com

ISBN: 978-1-915338-60-0

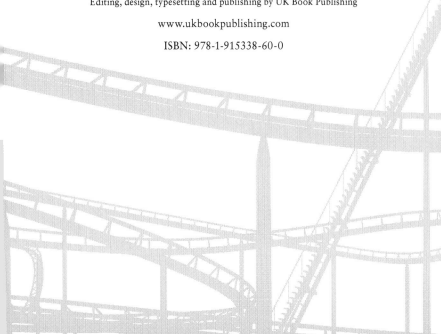

CHAPTER 1:
THE BEGINNING

Some things are best left forgotten. One of these things was the Tragedy of Magic Land. It was once a grand theme park built upon the legends, fears and fantasies of the people that made and visited it. One of these people was a younger Samuel, who was in love with the Perfector, a newly opened roller coaster and the crown jewel of Magic Land. Even though he couldn't go on the ride himself, he still adored collecting all the merchandise he could. This love of the ride, however, would commonly leave him alone and bullied. But, he would always keep his head up in the hope he would one day experience what he loved. However, life had other plans.

It was a warm and sunny day, and nothing seemed amiss. He was watching his favourite cartoons, when the news flashed on the TV screen, but instead of the average stories of new inventions or celebrity gossip, the screen only displayed tragedy. It was The Perfector, swarmed with paramedics and police like moths to a flame.

"Breaking News! The Perfector has been found to be the location of a group of murders, with the bodies being discovered this morning. The victims were a group of park guests, with their autopsies revealing how the killings must've been committed late yesterday. So far, there has only been one victim found alive, an adolescent girl. We will keep you up to date on this ongoing story once more information comes to light," the news reporter said.

The camera zoomed in behind the reporter, where a girl on a stretcher was being taken off site by two paramedics. While they were moving, the girl tried to say something to them. She began with incoherent crying about her mother, before trying to alert the paramedics to someone above the track of Abyss, as if something was floating in the air. However, nothing was there. Believing she was delirious from the pain, they gave her anaesthetics, and she fell asleep.

Samuel felt his heart shatter, feeling both his dreams crumbling in front of him, and shock for the victims. His parents tried to comfort him, but all they could do was make him stop crying. Weeks passed, with the situation turning grim. The only survivor had vanished from the hospital where she was healing from both the traumatic event and having to get her hand replaced with a prosthetic. The only hint of her abductor was a coded note that, once decrypted, read: "She is now one with The Perfector. Do not search for her, it will be pointless."

The note's advice was ignored, and a search party gathered, but she was never found. Distorted CCTV footage of the day was uncovered, showing the victims being beckoned by what appeared to be a staff member of The Perfector into the staff area of the ride, where they never exited. An interview with the manager was released that stated that she didn't recognise the staff member on the footage and that she was unnerved by the figure, with its height and almost calculated movements being a defining trait. But it was too late. No amount of evidence that pulled the blame away from the ride mattered.

The entire park was soon shut down and left to rot, with people hoping they could forget the tragedy. People feared and avoided the area around the park, believing that the local legend of the Oakwood Curse was real, and that the land was now not only cursed, but haunted by the ghosts of the victims of the killings. Many even swear that they have seen humanoid figures walking near the gates, with inhuman attributes like unnatural eye colours and strange powers. However, those people usually end up being seen as strange or mad by their peers.

Soon, it became a joke or a rite of passage for teens and kids around the area to dare each other to venture into the abandoned land, or even stay the night. Those that returned were seen as an equal to even the best in the group, and were respected by others. However, there had been numerous cases reported where those that dared to enter the park either never returned, or came back 'wrong'. They'd be emotionally distant, quiet, and showed signs of trauma despite never having experienced anything traumatic before their visit. But to many, the rewards of going into the park and returning outweighed the risks of death, disappearances or emotional damage.

One of these people was the now teenage Samuel, who was a common target for bullies for his enjoyment of The Perfector. He would be jeered and taunted, his brown hair constantly pulled and tugged. Some would even say that he should've been one of the victims, or the killer themself. One day, the bullies came up to him with a deal. He would go into the ruins of Magic Land and stay there for the night. If he returned, he would be allowed into their friendship group, and the bullying would stop. He quickly took the deal, tired of being shoved around. However, when the day came to enter the park, he soon realised that what he had chosen may've been a mistake.

A cold breeze was blowing in the air, making the dead leaves of September rustle and shake. The sound of crunching could be heard, as Samuel was pacing back and forwards on a patch of damp grass, crumpling the dried-up leaves under the soles of his shoes. He sighed, and started to think. "Why am I doing this? This is just some game the others play. I should just go back home. They'll stop pushing me around eventually, right?..." he said, trying to think of what to do. He looked down, rubbing his pale hands as he was pacing to warm them up. The breeze blew in his face for a moment, blowing his hair away from his face and making his eyes water. He brushed his hair back, and sighed again. He was wearing a polo with the Perfector logo sewn on the front, similar to his old jacket. The moonlight was reflected in the logo, highlighting the colours with its silvery glow. A pair of brown coloured trousers was secured onto him by a tough leather belt, and scarlet trainers were worn securely on his feet.

"Stop being a chicken! If I do this, I'll finally be accepted! Things will be great!" he said, knowing he was alone. He ran across the road. He stopped at the gates, which once signified how the park was a fusion of the past and present: both the site of an ancient palace, and a modern and thrilling theme park. However, it now stands like the ruins of the palace, woven with fallen branches and brambles. Samuel put his foot into one of the gate's intricate patterns and climbed it like a ladder, twisting at the top and landing on the ground with a thud. He held in the pain, before getting himself up.

Just as he turned to follow the trail, he caught something in the corner of his eye. In the thick of the trees, a pair of violet eyes were staring into his, with a calming allure. Then, a feminine voice spoke to him. "You shouldn't have come here! The Perfector has taken over, since the days we were open. They'll capture you eventually. I'd try to help you out, but I fear if I do, they'll get worse. You'll have to find your own way out," said the voice, revealing herself to be a woman with cool, sky-blue hair. She was wearing a dimly glowing futuristic set of armour, like something you'd imagine in a Sci-Fi novel. On the armour's back, a slot that seemed to be for a pair of geometric wings to come out of came into view.

He looked at the woman. "Who are you?" he asked, taking a step forward, before the woman gasped and ran off. "Hey!" he yelled, before sighing and continuing to walk on.

He walked for a few minutes, looking at the surroundings. The buildings and fencing were plastered with weird posters of a creepy man wearing a white lab coat with small golden shoulder pads. His eyes were weird, swirling yellow and black, probably a stylised representation. He was smiling chillingly, his mouth curling at the ends, while a black top hat sat on his head. "Smile, and you'll always be happy!" ran in black and yellow text, with hints of red and white on the picture. "That is super creepy, looks kind of dystopian," he spoke.

He sneakily pulled out a pen and doodled a funny face on the psychopathic-looking man on the poster, giggling while doing it. He suddenly felt like he was being watched, but only saw a little plush toy of a cat, with big googly eyes. He shrugged and looked away from the plushie, not noticing how the plushie's eyes were following him around. He spotted a newspaper stand, taking a glance at the papers there. Surprisingly, they were mostly intact, except for a few smudges, rips and crinkles. After a few seconds of glancing, he realised that all of the papers were dated 2018. The year of the park's closure.

Samuel walked away while passing multiple vendor carts, with snacks still in their cases, preserved for the ages. He didn't know why they could still be edible, as the power should be off, but didn't want to think too deeply about it.

He left the park entrance that he remembered was called Fantasy Lane. This used to function as both the hub of the park, and the shopping area. At its peak, there would be people bustling all over the street, with food and merchandise being sold like snowflakes in a blizzard. However, the years had degraded the lane into a ghost town. Samuel followed a path that winded to the left, which was now rough and unclean.

He glanced up and noticed he was standing in front of a large, dystopian-style gate that was dotted with security cameras and warnings. Above him, a large sign was stuck to the gate. The sign read 'The X-periment Facility' in a unified, scientific font. Two posters had been stuck on the gate in order for anyone inside the park to see them. They all seemed to be in a cartoon style, reminiscent of the 1950s.

The poster to the left depicted a wacky operating room, with a smiling person sitting in the chair getting an injection from an equally cheerful nurse. The nurse had perfect makeup and a cute uniform, while the person in the chair was wearing some normal-looking clothes. The message: 'Ask one of our friendly doctors to get perfected today! Join our joy!' was written in a bouncy, animated font with the same colour scheme as the one with the man, but in more pastel shades. Another poster was showing a sad, lonely girl sitting with chains and handcuffs that seemed to have things like hearts and swirls drawn onto them to make them seem unthreatening. 'Sadness is madness, Gloom's your doom!' was plastered onto the poster, in italics.

The dominating gateway had yellow and black striped police tape stuck onto it from the park's closure to keep the public away from the area. However, the tape had been torn apart, and now lay limply on the pavement. The towering drop of Abyss stood tall like a prideful ruler, dominating the dystopian fever dream of a winding track that was The Perfector. Somehow, the alien and electronic sounds of Abyss and the distorted, creepy tune of The Perfector still bombarded Samuel's ears. Perplexed, he turned around and saw something that puzzled him even further. A cart from the Perfector was hurtling through a loop, filled by a group of identically-dressed people. The boys were wearing black surgeon masks with a yellow hypno swirl, pale yellow lab coats and a pair of swirly hypno goggles. Their hair was all dyed some combination of yellow and black, and was mostly spiked. The girls were dressed similarly, except their lab coats looked like dresses and were light violet. Their hair was long and flowing or bunched up in ponytails, and also coloured yellow and black.

The things they had in common, besides their strange attire and hair colour choices, were their expressions. They all had a long vacant grin, and yellow-hued irises with a hypno swirl instead of pupils. Every one of them was staring blankly in front of them.

"Why was I obsessed with this thing? It's freaky!" he said, his subconscious flashing back to the adverts shown on TV when the park was still open. They were frantic fever dreams, filled with flashing images of needles, smiling faces and the maniacal roars of laughter that the ride's insane mind control process, dubbed perfection, inflicted upon those that undergo it.

In the corner of his eyes, he noticed that there appeared to be a separate entrance, themed to look as un-eye-catching as possible. It couldn't be the staff entrance, since he knew from research that the staff door was on the other side of the building, painted in a glossy chrome colour, a far cry from the bleak, grey door that was in front of him. The door was open, swaying back and forwards, in a way which looked beckoning, like something wanted him to enter. He strolled towards it, eyes glued to the people, but convinced himself it would be fine. He creaked open the door, and looked down onto a spiral staircase, before a scream echoed through it, hitting him with full force.

Samuel winced at the volume of the echo, before cautiously starting down the cold metal stairs, a metallic sound echoing from each step. After a few minutes the stairs stopped, and he entered a large, sprawling hallway. Its walls were a pale cream shade, with black streaks running along the top and bottom. A yellow exit sign tightly clung to the ceiling, an image of a person running was placed next to it. He walked through the left corridor and peeked around the corner where two workers were standing.

The smaller scientist wore a similar attire to the rest of the scientists, except for his mostly black hair and a simple necklace hanging on his neck, while the other scientist looked to be more in power, with a badge saying 'Co-Head of Testing' pinned tightly to his shirt. "You better have good news, Jay, or your job is at risk," the Co-head said, sternly looking down at the worker, who didn't return his stare.

"Ok, sir. The latest test of the gas was a failure. There were traces of Carbon Monoxide...All of the subjects expired. Please don't fire me..." Jay said, quivering.

"Ugh... Just put more Nitrous Oxide, and up the joy hormones... don't put too much in though, or people will laugh until they die!" the Co-head growled, before walking off.

The other worker followed him, and when it was safe, Samuel ran quietly to the drawers, pulled one slowly open, and revealed a bunch of files. He opened up the first one, and started to look at what was on the file. There were a few reports on the project and what had happened during testing, with the tests that were described making him feel his nerves rising. But the thing that caught his interest was a blueprint for the proposed attraction, tucked behind the reports.

The blueprint was a rough sketch of what looked like an indoor roller coaster, that seemed to be a blend of Abyss and The Perfector, in all but name. The title of the project was most likely Project Madhouse, as it was written on the top.

Before he could get any proof of these designs, he was taken aback by a bright light shining from behind him.

"Sir, you're not supposed to be here. Please cooperate and look at the light," the doctor said, holding what appeared to be a small flashlight-like device. Samuel had been spotted. In a panic, he closed his eyes and ran past the man. When he again opened his eyes, horrific experiments unfolded in front of him. There were people suffocating in thick purple gas and thudding helplessly at the glass for help, but nobody came.

There were people getting electrocuted or being injected with substances. Large lights flashed in the cells, making Samuel shield his eyes. From behind him, he could hear footsteps getting heavier and louder, as the scientists slowly caught up to him.

Briskly, he diverted himself and ran back towards the stairwells where he had entered from, dodging the puppet-like people swiping at him to grab or inject him. He thundered up the stairs and banged on the door, but it didn't budge. From a speaker in the wall, multiple jovial voices came through. "They are coming for you, new friend! Soon you'll be able to join our happy family... So happy! There's no need to fight it," the voices said, the speaker sound laced with static buzz.

"You were the people riding, weren't you?" said Samuel. "Well let me out, please! I don't want to be like you!" He asked again, but the people didn't seem to care, continuing to hold the door shut. The footsteps got louder and louder.

"You've made us unhappy...If you fight, you'll make it worse for yourself..." A voice echoed up the stairwell, in a singsong-like way, but still chilling. A woman shuffled up the stairs, her pale skin making her look like a zombie or a vampire; her yellow and black eyes were sharp and pointed, and her stare like daggers made it worse. Her hair was a dark brown colour and scruffed up and messy, with some parts torn up, making her look more deranged than the other scientists and workers.

She smiled crookedly, as if she was planning to plunge a dagger into him. Her face had a deep scar across her eye, making her look more like a psychopathic monster than a person. Her lab coat was stained yellow and red, and torn from struggles with the test subjects. Yellow leggings clung onto her legs, and black slip-on shoes covered her feet.

She was gripping a syringe with a translucent white liquid, before pinning Samuel to the door. "Don't struggle... It'll be easier for both of us!" the lady sang, joyfully.

"Get away from me!" he said.

She became enraged and while he was kicking and struggling to get away, she plunged a syringe into his arm. He yelled, trying to get away as the lady injected the liquid into him. He tried to fight the effects, but he soon felt himself slipping asleep. "I must stop her...I can't...give up..." Samuel groaned, before falling under the medicine's effects and slipping slowly unconscious.

After what seemed to him like a few minutes, Samuel started to wake up, but he couldn't move. He saw shimmers of light fly by above him, and patches of colour, like people to his side. He heard voices, people talking about things, but he couldn't understand or decipher. "Get...Cell 19a...Miss Swirls..." before he faded away again, for what could have been hours. He was awoken by a blazing light, with an extreme headache, and slight grogginess. He was in a room, with white walls, hypnotic swirls painted all over. The walls were plastered with Perfector propaganda posters; some had the same man from the posters up above, instead saying two words 'JOIN JOY'. He pounded at the door, to no avail.

He was trapped, and he would soon be lost in their crazy ideals. He sat on the end of the bed, which was surprisingly comfortable, before spying a TV remote. He pressed a button and the TV, a wall mounted flat screen, flickered on.

He navigated a menu on the screen and movies appeared from a selection. To his dismay, no movies that he liked were available, only bootlegs and what seemed to be propaganda videos for the facility. Samuel then flicked to normal channels, seeing cartoons about happiness and friendship, a bunch of localised channels for foreign subjects, a channel which had hypnotic swirls and smiles flashing rapidly, and an information channel. The information channel contained information regarding news broadcasts, feeding times for subjects, and other special announcements, with an upbeat tune in the background.

It was quick, but occasionally a cheerful female voice would sing along to the tune. "Smile, Smile, we want you to play! Join our Smiles forever and a day! Come play, come play, Join the Perfector today!"

Samuel flopped onto the bed, before dread filled his mind. "What happened...Why didn't I just leave and go home?..." before sitting up and hugging himself. Flashes of smiles appeared in his vision, before he blinked and they vanished. "Samuel! Stop crying and do something!" he said to himself, before standing up, determined.

CHAPTER 2:
THE ESCAPE PLAN

When Samuel calmed down after his confusing experience, he assessed his surroundings again. Just like always, the ceiling lamp, which looks like one you'd find at an operating theatre, was shining down onto his bed, which was white like the rest of the room. He had torn the posters to find any hints of an escape route, so what used to be idyllic phrases like 'Smiling all day keeps the doctor away', now say things like: 'Stay away'.

"It's just like a prison cell, but more technology." He chuckled to himself. "Heh...Who'd believe that The Perfector, of all things, is real? How'd they make all this? Surely at least somebody would hear the drilling! Yet The Perfector, and everything around it, is perfectly stable... Knowing the logic, it might as well be magic!" He assessed in his mind, before getting spooked by the TV changing to an image of a lady in a cloak, smiling cheerily.

"Good morning, everyone! Today is the 3rd of October 2028, the temperature is 7° and the time is 6:00AM! Today we have a new person that will soon be a part of our happy little family! Isn't that just great? His name is Samuel and I bet he is so excited to be here. If Mr Miles would be so inclined, maybe give our new recruit a tour once he's properly adjusted. And Samuel, your soon-to-be best friend Hypna will take you soon to get your procedure done!" The lady smiled and laughed, her tone tipped with the type of sickly sweetness you would use to a child.

He looked at the woman in the video, his heart burning with anger, after being kidnapped and trapped. "This lady has the nerve to treat this nightmare like some sort of daydream? And to act like I loved this place? Never!" He threw his fist into the TV, smashing it, a giant crack appearing on the screen. Pain shot through his arm, making him grip his fist. Luckily, it was only slightly cut.

"Have a good day and stay smiling. This is the Minister, signing out!" The distorted image of the lady cheered, then the TV broke.

Samuel had a moment to calm down, before a voice behind him made him flinch. "Mr Samuel, I presume?" said a female worker. Her face was that of a doll, with pale sunset yellow eyes, skin like porcelain and perfect, blood red lips, her dark hair in pigtails, ending with yellow Highlights.

"I am Hypna, a staff member of The Facility. I am here for your procedure." Hypna giggled to herself, but her laugh felt like daggers being plunged into his back.

"Procedure? What procedure?" Samuel spat back, keeping his guard up. "Oh! I see you've not heard about our Perfection? Ha! It's simple. We influence you into the correct way of life…" Hypna said. Her expression was frozen in a doll-like state. Just as she paused, her irises started to swirl, slowly gaining speed. "The way The Ministry wants you to live." She tried to swipe at him with a syringe, but he dodged out of the way.

"Not this time, Psycho!" he said. He ran and ran, then closed himself into a room. It was as dark as night, with the faint sound of liquid splashing on tiles, echoing and rebounding off the walls. Suddenly, the room flooded with light, blinding him.

When he finally opened his eyes, he saw he was standing inside a sterile white room with yellow posters, charts, and other memorabilia stuck perfectly on the walls.

All the drawers were neatly pushed in, and the desk was tidy. A dentist's chair was standing in the middle of the room, with small latches at the armrests and footrest. Above it, a device hung from the ceiling, which seemed to be part-light and part-machine. There were things like syringes connected to the device, which Samuel could tell was the source of the dripping. It also seemed to be able to move.

His attention soon turned to a glass screen in the wall, where he could see Hypna, looking down on him. "Get on the bed, Mr Matthews. I don't want any problems with your procedure," Hypna requested, with Samuel promptly shaking his head and trying to open the door.

However, when he tried, all that happened was a faint clunk from the door. "How has it locked so fast?" he talked to himself, now panicking. But before he could find a way to unlock the door, he felt a tug from behind him. He glanced down for a moment, seeing that a metallic, claw-like device had latched onto him.

The mechanical arm tugged him onto the chair, before the shackles prevented him from moving. The machine whirred to life, making buzzing noises as it moved. When the machine stopped, one of the small arms, which had a needle attached to it, inched closer and closer to him. "Don't worry. It will only hurt for a moment. Then you get to join our organisation!" Hypna smiled like a doll, her shark-like teeth showing. The syringe was so close to Samuel that the serum was dripping onto his skin.

The serum felt warm to the touch, though it was actually cold. He clenched his eyes shut, fearing that he could not escape, but a sharp bleeping stopped the machine. He opened up his eyes and heard the fire alarms screaming.

"Oh, it seems that Tom's burnt breakfast again! Hehe! Wait here, I'll be back in a blink, so we can finish this procedure. Maybe we can go out for food later?" Hypna muttered cheerfully, practically skipping away.

When she had left, Samuel found a way to loosen his arm.

He pushed away the needle with his head and rummaged in his pocket. A glint of metal shimmered in his hand. He looked at what he found, recognising it as a bobby pin. He quickly undid the locks, and shuffled off the dentist chair.

To blend in, he changed his clothes from his usual shirt and jeans, to a smarter looking lab coat and black and yellow pants that were neatly piled on the side, clearly meant for him if the procedure had continued. He sneaked towards the door, trying to not trip any alarms. When he opened the door, a bunch of scientists and workers with the same swirly eyes, sang in unison. "Welcome to Joy!" Behind the impromptu choir, a tall figure of a man cleared his throat, alerting the rest of the workers to his presence. They all bowed slightly, before stepping aside as the man walked out from behind them.

The man wore a peculiar black top hat, with a lemon yellow coloured ribbon that wrapped around its base. The hat sat on his golden yellow hair with coal black tips. A pair of yellow and black swirl goggles was covering his eyes, and a slightly stained white lab coat was wrapped onto him, trailing into two tails. The man smiled, his voice sounding much less false than the others.

"Hey there! My name's Doctor Smiley! You probably know me from all the posters. I'm the Head of Morale and the face of this place! It's customary for new people to have a tour to get accustomed, then we test you to see how skilled you are, to assign you a job. Who knows, you could be an assistant head, maybe even to me!" He tipped his hat, bowing as he did.

Samuel awkwardly mumbled. "Uhh...ok?... also, you're embarrassing me..."

Smiley looked like he was about to frown, but stopped himself, sheepishly smiling. "Erm... sorry for making you uncomfortable! Heh..." he said.

Samuel politely shrugged it off, even though Smiley felt a little off.

"These are Project Comply and Project 17. They are our latest projects in the facility! Other than Project Perfector, of course!" Smiley rambled on, his voice bouncing up and down cheerfully. Samuel looked around, noticing how in the rows of doors leading to different rooms, one seemed to be blocked off.

"Hey, Smiley, what's that door for?" he said.

Smiley paused for a moment, stopping the tour. "Oh! It was the old Project Abyss Section! It had a few labs, as well as the... holding cell for the only surviving subject. We prefer to not discuss what happened there, it makes our organisation look...cruel. Let's just say that we used the abyss to create life, and things went terribly wrong. Turns out that poking a metaphorical bear with a stick doesn't end well. I wasn't around at the time, so I can only imagine the containment breaches. On a lighter note, the debatable success of the project led to the creation of Yours Truly! So, I guess it's not that bad," he explained with an ever-present smile. Smiley continued to mutter about the other projects, but Samuel could only think about what could've happened in that section.

Whilst the tour was on, he noticed Hypna walking by cheerfully, her dress-like lab coat and her hair bouncing as she walked and hummed a chipper tune. His fear took over and he persistently asked Smiley if he could leave.

"Why do you want to leave the tour? I thought it was fun..." Smiley asked quizzically.

"You... don't want to know," Samuel said.

Smiley gasped slightly, then giggled and let him leave. He bolted towards the bathroom to escape Hypna, beads of sweat dripping from his face. He found the bathrooms and locked the door. The lights flashed on, this time, with no crazy towers or needles. Safety, at last.

He flipped on a tap to make it seem like he was busy, then started planning on escaping. "I need to get out of here, or they'll make me a freak, like them. I could use the ventilation, but it'll be like a maze, and I would make a lot of noise… maybe I could hide out until they forget about me? No, they're crazy, but they're not stupid."

As he was talking to himself, a girl's screams rang through the hallways. Instead of an enraged howl from Hypna or another scientist, it was a cry for help. A teen's voice. "Someone, anyone, help me!" echoed the voice again, and again.

He slammed open the door, and bolted to Smiley.

Samuel grabbed Smiley by his shirt, his face filled with surprise. "What are they doing to her?! Tell me!" Samuel glared at Smiley, anger in his eyes.

Smiley gulped, trying not to frown. He stuttered, afraid for his life. "I don't know…they're probably going to perfect her. Maybe she's no longer useful to the facility? I wouldn't expect it though, as she's perfectly average for the tests…Well, more resources! Now, could you get off my lab coat?"

Samuel let him go and ran to the cell, where a scientist was looming towards a girl, probably 15 in age, doing the exact same thing that Hypna did to him; stating their name, monologue about what they were doing, then attempting to swipe at them with a liquid. Only, he yelled at him before he struck her.

"Hey you! Don't you dare touch that girl!"

The scientist, a man with black, spikey hair and the same eyes and smile, looked at Samuel with surprise. "And who are you to tell me what to do? I'm told my orders by either The Minister, the Heads or Smiley. Now let me do my work." He pushed Samuel away, and walked off.

Samuel grabbed the scientist and pushed them to the corner, stunning him. "Run!" he yelled to the girl, who ran for her life, her dark brown hair swishing back and forth while she ran.

"Thank you" she mouthed, as she turned a corner.

Hypna tapped Samuel on the shoulder, smiling to herself. "Aww, such compassion...Such a shame that you'll soon see her as nothing more than a test subject, a lab rat, per se." She grabbed him by the arm, before getting it shaken off.

"Never," Samuel said softly, before galloping away, nearly tripping over, looking for the girl.

Hypna looked toward Smiley, who was shocked at Samuel and the girl's quick escape. Hypna's face was full of venom and rage. "Smiley, you know the boss needs more test subjects, seeing how this entire place is empty. So, why would you let him go? Was it out of self-defence? Was it...Pity?...You know we can't have remorse for our test subjects," Hypna said. She circled around him like a lion to its prey, her grin turning malicious.

Smiley glanced down, noticing Hypna was holding a yellow taser in her hand, small sparks coming off it every so often.

He panicked, throwing her against a wall in self-defence. Hypna managed to catch herself, and shoved him back, causing his goggles to fly off his face and smash into the wall. Without his goggles, his eyes were in full view. They were more vibrant than the others and were spinning, making a hypnotic effect.

Smiley's smile shattered, tears forming in his eyes. "No! I'm always joyful! I won't do it again! I'll do whatever you say! I'll even go after him! AGHHH!!" His pleas were cut short with a zap, before falling to the ground with a thud, lying limply, a look of pure terror frozen on his face.

"And just like that, knocked out...tsk." The other scientists nodded, so as to not have the same fate as Smiley. "Hehehe... such weak behaviour, he needs.. motivation." Hypna's necklace, which was usually hidden by her dress, started glowing and the unconscious body of Smiley started levitating off the ground and floated around Hypna. The only sign of life was an occasional shudder, as they both vanished into a room, for a very long time.

While Hypna was monologuing, Samuel chased after the girl. "Hey! Miss? Wait... up," he said, gasping for breath, stumbling and fumbling, before the girl saw him and stopped.

"Why are you following me? They'll capture us both!" She looked behind him and pulled him into a room, locking the door tightly and barricading them in.

"I'm Samuel. Now who are you, Miss, and why are we here?" Samuel questioned, clearly hurt from her grip.

"Ugh... It's Eliza, and I'm here for the same reason as you, kidnapped and nearly brainwashed. Now, stop questioning me and shut up," she said in annoyance.

Samuel looked at her for a moment; the fact that she knew how he got here made his head spin. She looked to her feet and sighed.

"I didn't mean to be, well, mean. This place brings back memories that I'd rather forget," she said, taking off a pair of gloves. When the gloves were off, Samuel saw that the girl's left hand was a prosthetic. It was made of a mixture of steel and plastic, with yellow highlights to add a touch of colour. "...A few years ago, me and my mother came here for fun. That was, until a staff member called for us and a few others to...come into the Staff area for some sort of tour. I didn't want to, but my mother made me. Fear of missing out, and so on. You know the rest. I managed to survive by fighting the killer off, but they really damaged my hand. When I was finally rescued, my hand was found to be a lost cause, and replaced with a prosthetic. I'm lucky to have survived, but I still miss my mother," Eliza said.

"I'm sorry for what happened to you," he said, feeling sympathetic.

Eliza smiled, trying to change the subject. But then, a scream echoed through the hall to them. They looked at each other.

"What was that?" Samuel said, puzzled. "It wasn't Hypna, she's a girl. It couldn't be the scientist who was trying to hit you, as his voice was too growly. Which means…" He spoke out loud, figuring out who the scream came from. "Smiley…" Samuel said, with a twinge of sadness in his voice.

"Is he the man from those posters that The Minister put up?" Eliza questioned.

Samuel gave her a thumbs up, and stood himself up. They both looked towards a vent in the ceiling, and plotted a plan.

Samuel pushed Eliza into the vents, then jumped in himself. They made sure to be quiet, so as not to alert anybody. The vents were dark and dusty, a slight breeze blowing through. They slowly shuffled their way through the metallic maze, until they saw an opening in the floor that was connected to the room where Hypna entered. It was a mirror image to the one which Samuel entered with yellow beams lining the walls, with the difference that there was someone lying still on the bed. A familiar top hat was placed onto a tool table. A glint of light appeared on one of the persons' badges, and it became visible. On one side, there was a shimmering golden hypno swirl and on the other side, engraved on the grey and yellow badge, in golden writing, was one name: Smiley.

Smiley's eyes flickered open and closed, before he awakened fully with a sharp breath. He moved to sit up, but his arms kept him chained down, before getting pulled back to the chair.

His eyes flickered back and forwards, looking for an escape, but the door was locked and he was stuck tight. He then looked to his right where a shadowy figure loomed above him.

Hypna, like always, was smiling, while talking darkly to the now aware Smiley. "Oh, you've awoken, just in time in fact! Your special procedure is about to begin!"

Smiley looked fully to his left, seeing himself in the mirror. His golden hair was now fully visible, gradients of black down the tips, ending in an almost inky black.

There was a purple bruise on the side of his face, evidently from his fall, and there was a group of wires connected to his chest. "Oh god no...please... Hypna, you don't need to do this!" Smiley said, sobbing his eyes out, not knowing what she was trying to do to him.

"Never. You broke the rules, you get the punishment. Unless you want me to throw you into the hole of Abyss, without the cart!" She laughed, maniacally this time, and pulled a switch, causing the power to the lights to turn off. Screams of terror rumbled in the room, then stopped. The lights slowly returned, to a horrific sight. Smiley was lying limp on the bed, face frozen in a pained expression. In the corner stood Hypna, doubled over in laughter.

Samuel had seen enough. He jumped down, which surprised Hypna, who squealed in shock. "What are you doing here?!... No matter! That means I get to see if it worked." Hypna smiled, before speaking calmly.

"Smiley." Quickly, Smiley's eyes opened; they were spinning to the point where anyone who'd look at them would be entranced, with a smile on his face. Whatever happened, Smiley snapped. "Smiley, this boy doesn't want to smile! What do we do to sad people?" Hypna questioned.

Smiley smiled psychotically, sliding off the table while snarling at Samuel. "We force them...OR ELSE!" Smiley answered, rushing at Samuel, who rolled to the side, a moment before Smiley caught

THE SECRET OF THE SMILE

up to him, making Smiley collide with the metal door which opened it, and dazed him.

Eliza hopped down, before running with Samuel through the door, and sprinting down the corridor, as if their lives probably depended on it. Smiley picked himself up. He started to glow with a golden hue before his wounds were healed. He grabbed a knife and a pair of syringes with Smile Serum in them and walked out the door.

CHAPTER 3:
SMILEY'S ATTACK

"Eliza, do you know how to get out of here?" Samuel asked her, worried.

"What? Oh, kind of, I was half awake when it happened, I saw two scientists putting in a code to open a door. Then we entered a few hallways which all connected up to here. I also felt like we were going up, like an elevator of some sort. There was also a stairwell." Eliza blabbed on and on, before Samuel cupped her mouth.

"Hush, We're on a breakout mission, not a chat-off." Samuel giggled, before stopping quickly and ducking under one of the hospital beds.

He grabbed Eliza and pulled her towards him before they were seen. A group of scientists walked past, their shoes clicking off the floor, leaving red footprints that quickly disappeared. They then heard a familiar muttering, before a pair of smart, black pants with yellow stripes on the sides, with a yellow liquid dripping on the floor from the air above them. Suddenly, the legs started to move, bending.... kneeling, a white lab coat with tails coming into view...Smiley.

They only had a few seconds of time to escape, before he would see them.

"Samuel, Eliza… I know you're there. I can feel you breathing."

Samuel looked down, and saw a yellow gloved hand below his face. It tickled his chin, so Samuel had to laugh. Eliza glanced up, seeing a hand sized gap between the hospital bed and the wall. She smiled to herself, before pushing the bed towards Smiley with all her might. Smiley screamed before getting thrown towards the wall with a thud. He quickly grasped the hospital bed, but he still was hit, going to the floor, luckily alive. However, his nose was clearly broken.

"Go!" Eliza yelled, before both teens stood up, quickly rushing through the remainder of the corridor. Smiley's eyes flicked open while he was sitting himself up. He laughed darkly, looking at the damage then gripping his nose, before a glow shimmered from his palms.

A few seconds later, he stood up, chuckling. Where damage used to be was now perfectly healed. Smiley looked towards the end of the corridor while his eyes glowed yellow, before going back to normal. He grabbed his knife and put it back into his hat, while firmly gripping the Smile Serum syringes, before the needle tips both sharpened, with a quick glint of golden light.

Samuel was struggling to keep up with Eliza, who practically flew through the corridors. They passed many corridors, before finally stopping at the door, as they didn't know the code. Samuel gripped his head, flashes of swirls and phrases like 'Join Joy' were whizzing round inside his head.

"Sammy, what's going on?" said Eliza, worried for him.

"I think the serum's starting to affect me, I'm running out of time!" Samuel cried, thinking about the thought of him losing his free will.

"Wait… doesn't The Perfector have its own code, numbers to letters or something?"

Samuel grinned, smiling for the first time in forever. "Joy?" He thought. The red bulb flashed red, with a shrill beep signifying that he had got it wrong. "Hypno?" tried Samuel.

The bulb glowed again, the beep getting louder, as he continued to fail. The footsteps behind them grew louder, as Smiley was quickly catching up. "Abyss?!" Samuel burst out, frantically. The door screeched its beep, as Smiley's laughter echoed closer and closer. "Last try before it's useless...Perfection." The little light bulb shone a bright green hue, signalling a correct answer. "Yes! Eliza, follow me!" Samuel cheered as the stairwell door unlocked and they were eventually allowed access to the outside. He bashed the door hard, opening it.

The sunlight blinded the two teens, as they hadn't seen natural light for a day. The towering tracks of Abyss still stood tall, over the pit of The Perfector. Freedom. They were safe. Samuel tried to turn left, but Eliza told him otherwise. "If we leave, they'll just replace us with other victims, we need to stop this at the source. We need to destroy The Perfector. Destroy the queen bee, and you destroy the hive."

Samuel thought for a moment, then nodded happily.

They both started to run to The Perfector's controls, before The Perfector's theme echoed towards them, followed by a static hum. The two children turned themselves around rapidly, before their faces became hard. A familiar doctor was starting to appear on what remained of the TV screens placed on The Brainwasher, as through the years, items were broken and stolen, like the logo of The Perfector. It was Smiley with his eyes swirling rapidly, chuckling at their misfortune while his pointed teeth were showing. "Hello again. I don't exactly like being nearly crushed by a hospital bed. So, I've changed my mind! Instead of trying to perfect you two..."

Both teens were suddenly snatched from the ground by an unknown force, and were hovering in the air. A cloud of yellow gas revealed Smiley, swinging on the pole in the middle of The

Brainwasher. He laughed, before his voice became weird and distorted. "I'm going to kill you…" His voice came back to normal, almost like magic.

"Not you, Samuel, you're ok with me! Though it was you who caused me to get hurt, I forgive you. I may even name you my Co-Head of Morale! Wouldn't that be swell? I'd even perfect you myself, so you can have freedom, unlike those half-baked tactics they think works. What do you say?" Smiley held out his hand for a handshake, but Samuel refused. "Hey! That's not a way to treat a friend! Ah well, I'll ask later. But first, I'll need to deal with her!" Smiley pointed at Eliza, teeth bared. "I've got an idea. Come with me, bestie!"

He grabbed Samuel's arm and pulled him from the power's grip onto the platform. Just as Samuel was on solid ground, Eliza was whizzed towards the Loading Bay.

"Eliza!" Samuel yelled.

The ceiling gap closed, with Eliza trapped in the cart. "Sorry for the drastic split-up, but dealing with her is really necessary. You're free to watch!" he said. Smiley pressed a button, making the cart launch forwards.

It narrowly missed colliding with several walls and soon burst into the daylight. To Eliza's surprise, the restraints suddenly unlatched. Fortunately, she was still being kept down by the forces of gravity. As long as she held on for an upside down section, she was fine. Angry, Smiley pressed his hand onto the console and carved it with a glowing yellow energy. The vapour-like, translucent gas erupting from the yellow gas canisters connected to The Intoxicator became honey coloured, and the yellow syringes on The Injector squirted some smile serum.

Soon, all of the legs started moving around, like they were extensions of Smiley himself. Samuel looked to the cart that was running towards him, before taking the leap. He landed squarely on the second row of seats, the speed making his hair rush back. Eliza grabbed him and made sure he was okay, and after a few seconds, the arms started their assault.

Eliza and Samuel simultaneously ducked under the Injector and The Exciter and jumped above The Perplexer. Eliza jumped over The Intoxicator and the Mesmeriser, while Samuel ducked under both. Smiley pulled a lever, and the cart suddenly slowed down to its normal speed, nearly knocking Samuel off, and tripping up Eliza.

"What happened?" Samuel asked while looking at Eliza, who was looking up at Smiley.

"I don't know, but I think it's Smiley! He seems to have a mix of technology and…I hate to say this, but maybe even magic under his control."

Eliza looked up at Smiley whose eyes and hands were glowing, as well as two control boxes, which were controlling the movements of the arms. "We need to get off before he notices–" Eliza explained, before being cut off by a bout of insane laughter.

The injector leg was hovering above them, dripping with some smile serum. Smiley was standing on one of the metal bars, looking at them, his eyes twinkling with twisted joy. "Well, that was rude! It's kind of hurtful that you go with her over your friend! But, I'll not take it personally. Sorry for being blunt, but it's better to give in to me. She's trying to destroy The Perfector. If this device goes down, you would not only be leaving a bunch of people with no memories in an unfamiliar place, you'd be killing me! I would have some time to fix things, but the point still stands. I wanted to have a peaceful compromise, but I guess we have come to violence," Smiley explained, while leaning over the edge of the leg by hanging on a wire. His face bore a wild smile, like an insane clown, before he jumped off the top of The Injector's metal frame, the large leg swinging back into its normal position. A thud rumbled the cart, and Samuel and Eliza stumbled for a few seconds before regaining balance.

Smiley was perched on the bottom edge of the cart, staring at the two teens. He slowly got up, wiping the dust off his coat, before grabbing a scalpel from his hat. "Checkmate. I control the coaster, so I can't fall off. You can. Give up, and I'll make it quick!" He laughed chaotically, his face more horrifying up close. Despite sounding psychotic, Smiley seemed not to notice how mad he sounded.

"NEVER!" said both Samuel and Eliza in sync.

Smiley laughed so hard he cried. "We're nearing halfway, and we're going quite fast. Sammy, you might want to brace yourself. Ignore me, Subject!" he said. He waved at the boy, before he started to levitate above the cart. On the bottom of his shoes, a golden glow lit up like a lantern, and left a streak of yellow whenever he went. The two kids looked at each other for a split moment. Eliza had already braced herself, but Samuel didn't realise what Smiley meant until too late. The cart rapidly slowed down like it had hit a wall of water. He was thrown backwards, but quickly grabbed the back of the seats and gripped on for his life while the cart climbed up the track. The cart was about to twist down into a drop, when the wheels jammed and trapped the cart on the top of the drop.

Samuel was holding on as tight as he could, feeling his hands slowly start to hurt. His legs were turning from the tingling feeling of pins and needles into numbness, as they were being whipped and blasted with the cold wind. After a few seconds, his vision and hearing cleared, blobs of colour turning into solid shapes. He thought he saw Eliza smirk at his pain, but when he blinked to clear his vision completely, it was a look of shock.

Smiley was chuckling darkly. "Now, who's on the receiving end!" He walked carefully over to Samuel, then slowly bent down to kneel on the backrest of the seats, moving Samuel's face to make it eye-level with his. "You look like you had a rough landing. Don't worry, this actually makes things smoother! You now require medical help, which I can provide! I may be a little strange, but I'm still a doctor! Of course, joining our little club is usually a requirement. I wasn't being misleading about what I said earlier,

I can actually keep people's minds intact! If you just let me, I'd be overjoyed to show you."

Samuel was starting to panic, as he felt his grip starting to fail. Just as he fell, he felt a hand stop his fall. Smiley. The man helped him up, and put him down on the seats. Just as Smiley started to summon what appeared to be sleeping gas from his hand, Eliza grabbed him by the shoulder and pushed him. The shock made him stumble away, as he dropped a syringe that was in his grip. His moment of weakness gave Samuel enough time to get up. He joined Eliza's side of the roller coaster cart, making sure to not fall.

"Augh...You annoying girl!" Smiley was kicked by Eliza, who laughed at him mockingly. "Nah ah ah, you shouldn't attack people!"

The insane man wobbled at the edge of the cart, arms flailing, trying to grip onto Samuel. Every time Smiley attempted, however, Samuel just took a step back and Smiley lost more balance. The man glanced back, looking down to the floor. As soon as he looked down at the height of the fall, he felt his chest tighten from fear. But, he needed to fall for what he had planned. "I'll be back!" Smiley screamed, voice dripping with malice. He smiled creepily, before taking his right foot off the cart, making him plummet down into the pit while laughing like a madman.

A loud thud thundered, as well as a loud snapping sound. When the teens looked back, they saw that the form of Smiley was lying on the track with a dark smile on his face, looking right up at the duo.

"That should keep him," Samuel said. He jumped off the attraction with Eliza and landed onto a soft patch of grass, checking to see if the other was okay, then running to escape. "I can't believe that Smiley was a bad guy! He seemed so..." Samuel looked behind him at The Perfector, one of Smiley's syringes shattered on the dark concrete floor. "Kind..." He finished his sentence, before he sighed slightly.

"He may have been insane, but he felt different to the others... like he genuinely cared." Samuel was about to stop, but Eliza quickly pushed him forwards. "At least we're okay, he'll probably heal. If he's able to heal a nose, he can heal a body. That also means he'll probably be back, and if a broken nose and possibly a cracked skull gets him trying to kill us...I hope we're not on the receiving end of that outburst!" Eliza laughed, before continuing to walk.

They were barely a few buildings away when a loud creak of metal rumbled through the track along with more sickly snapping. Screams and laughter thundered around, before morphing and changing until it was glitchy and autotune. A group of grey, metal pincer arms gripped the sides of the pit, making an ear-piercing screech so loud that Samuel and Eliza had to duck and cover their ears. The arms pulled themselves up, revealing the figure of Smiley.

He started to laugh dementedly, the spider-like arms keeping him from touching the ground. His left eye was hollow and black, a small yellow dot in the place of his pupil. His mouth was filled with sharp, dagger-like teeth. The spider-like arms were spread around him, with some revealing Smile Gas sprayers and bunches of syringes. With the way he was moving with the mechanical legs, he looked like a creepy, animatronic amalgamation of half man, half spider. "Hahaha! Do you like my other form? I hope you don't have Arachnophobia! Then you won't smile!" Smiley said. He bared his teeth at Samuel and Eliza, breaking into a sprint.

"Yup, RUN!" she said, then the two children started to bolt for their lives. Just as they left the Facility, a whistling sound flew towards them. A pinching pain jolted through Samuel's neck and made him trip up. One of the spider legs snatched Eliza off the ground, as she was struggling and screaming. "Samuel!" Eliza cried, before her screams were muffled.

Samuel's vision blurred and spun, with bursts of colour shimmering everywhere. The faded figure of the creepy, spider-like form of Smiley was looking straight into his eyes, before jabbing Samuel with a metal rod. Samuel felt a zap, like static, with drowsiness setting in soon after. Samuel's legs gave up, making him start to fall to the hard ground. A few moments before hitting the ground, Samuel faded into sleep, not feeling the impact, or anything after.

CHAPTER 4:
REVEALING THE RULER

He awakened to the sun in his eyes, and a perfectly clear sky. Samuel looked around, to see that he was in the entrance of Magic land; however, it was like it had never shut down. He could hear birds chirping in the trees, as well as the triumphant and magical music coming from the speakers dotted around. He had a cone of pink, cloudlike candy floss in his hand, and was smiling cheerfully. Samuel walked around for a few minutes, having an absolute blast, before everything went wrong. Everything became distorted and glitched, before he was plunged into a dark abyss. He couldn't see anything, except a version of himself, standing about nine metres in front of him. The doppelgänger was taller than him, with significantly altered features, but he could recognise himself anywhere. He didn't have any control of himself, instead seeming more like a bystander. The copy started to talk about things that he did not know about, all linking to the coasters and rides of the park. When he finished, he broke down into tears.

Samuel went to comfort the version of himself, but phased through them, showing that he could not help. The tears and crying slowly morphed into bitter, dark laughter. The figure turned around, before disappearing into glitch-like yellow particles. White flooded his vision, as screams and pleas for help bombarded his mind. The only thing he could see through the white was a discarded knife, soaked in some inhuman, black liquid. "I'm sick of all this weirdness!" Samuel screamed, before pain spread across his body. Then... everything stopped.

He awoke with a jolt. His first feeling was a metallic taste in his mouth, and his breath against his face. He gradually opened his eyes to adjust to the blinding lights, and slowly got up.

"Ah, look who finally awoke! The Boss will be wanting to see you soon, so don't misbehave. Also, here, for the wound," said a guard, who, even though she was hard, she still had warmth in her eyes. She threw a box of plasters into the cell he was in, and he stuck one on, and spat out the blood in his mouth, which must have clotted, as nothing else came out.

"Thanks?" he whimpered, slightly scared. His cell, a circular bubble-like structure with the strength of steel, floated above a small, coil-like pole, with the occasional flicker of gold and honey coloured jolts flashing around; it was like he was in a huge tesla coil.

Suddenly, a hole opened through the substance, with the guards beckoning Samuel out. "Come. They want to talk to you. You should feel lucky, not many advocates come here with their mind intact," said the female guard, a smirk on her face.

A cold voice echoed towards them through the hallway. "Bring him in, and then leave. I want privacy."

The two guards pulled him out, when he noticed the metal collar around his neck, with the codename '4B-725' inscribed onto it. "It must be from a past experiment. The code looks familiar... Anyways, it looks a bit worn, like they used it a lot. Whoever it was containing must've been quite dangerous."

They walked into the room; it was a huge, rectangular room, with the roof coloured to look like a syringe.

"Samuel. I was told about you, trying to escape with...them," the voice continued, beckoning Samuel over. Where the needle of the syringe would point out, a platform rose from the floor, with Smiley, now fully humanoid again, and Hypna on each side, perfectly symmetrical. On the second platform, there was a throne-like chair, with a cloaked figure of a woman perched upon it. Her hands were in front of her, with one being a jagged, robotic replacement.

The chair dominantly stood on a podium, making it look taller than it was. The chair was metallic, cold and crooked, like it was made from the scrapped pieces of an old cart. On the sides of the chair there was a pair of monitors connected to the chair by some metallic arms. "We need to talk, alone preferably. Smiley and Hypna may stay," she said. Her voice had a cruel, yet happy tone. She shook her hand and the guards left Samuel with these psychopathic monsters, their grins ever present and their sharp teeth bared. "Samuel, I believe you know whom you are talking to?"

"Yes. You're the Minister. The person that everyone mindlessly praises, but I can see you're just a monster! You make your own members torture others and even each other to please you!" he yelled.

The Minister twitched her finger towards a button, before stopping herself. "Well... would you say that to... Eliza?" she said mockingly.

"What does she have to do with you? Just let us go!" Samuel said.

His anger provoked The Minister further.

"Oh no... you've angered her! Run!" both Smiley and Hypna gasped.

The Minister stood up from her throne. She was a long and slim woman, wearing a lab coat similar to Hypna's, but longer.

She was draped in a long and black hooded cloak that hid some of her features.

Her face was, since her long, brown hair was covering most of it, with only a pair of black lips visible. The click of high heels followed the figure before stopping above Samuel. "Why do I have anything to do with her?... Do you want to know why?" she said, a dim glow of yellow shining through the cloak, growing brighter with every word. Samuel nodded, determined. "Well...Here you go!" the Minister yelled, before she burst into a glitching, static light. After a few seconds, the light died down, then started to morph and shrink and change, before disappearing completely.

When Samuel opened his eyes again, the shock of what he saw made him step backwards. There, in front of him, was Eliza, with the same eyes as everyone else, smiling, sharp teeth and all. "I was her all along! Learning your tricks and your secrets! Everything and more. Isn't that right... Samuel Matthews?" She smiled, joyfully.

His face was a mix of shock, terror, and rage. "H... How do you know that!" he screamed at her.

"Simple, when we knock anyone out for the first time, we implant a microchip so we know what they are up to." She laughed.

She smiled, before tapping Samuel's neck. "It's right here! Though, it'd poison you if it was attempted to be taken out by a non-ministry worker." Eliza smiled, then pulled Samuel up.

"How... why?" Samuel fumbled on his words in his shock, before Eliza put a finger to his mouth and started to speak. "Well, it was all an act. All high-ranking ministry personnel have robotic enhancements, but everything else was fake. We were trying to see if any of our new advocates had the guts to try and escape; only you tried. Smiley never even got shocked, he was acting! Well, except for the part where you fought him off the coaster. But, you'd be surprised with how much a Ride Spirit can heal! For the snatching, we both switched back as soon as you were knocked out and the guards picked you up. But now, you've reached the end of your journey...and the ending is a choice," Eliza said.

She clicked her fingers and she glitched back to her Minister form, before brushing her hair and hood back. She had clear pale skin, and her eyes were cruel and as sharp as razors. She flicked her hand and Hypna nodded, before walking towards Smiley, giggling creepily. A glint shimmered in her belt, a knife. Both Smiley and Samuel saw this and gasped. The Minister clicked her fingers, before Smiley's face went blank, and he fell to the floor.

Quick as lightning, Hypna grabbed Smiley, clutching the knife, before placing it against Smiley's neck, and looking at Samuel seriously. "Here's the deal, sugarplum: the ministry's running out of members, as not many advocates are fit for perfection, some too tall, some too short, some too young, some too old. You, on the other hand, are perfect! You're smart, athletic, brave, determined... everything we need, as well as great at making people happy! You're the magnum opus of the ministry! So...you will let yourself get perfected, and we will let your little friend go, completely! A life for a life. Do we have a deal?" The Minister put her hand out, a yellow, firelike glow shimmering around her hand.

Hypna pressed the knife harder onto Smiley's neck, forming a cut across it, blood starting to trickle out. Anymore, and Smiley would risk bleeding to death.

"Fine. But this is for Smiley!" Samuel yelled, before reaching out and shaking the Minister's hand, accepting the offer.

"Great! Now, follow me, and we'll get this sorted with!" she sang, pointing her hand towards the exit. "Guards, help Hypna contain Smiley, and follow me."

Two guards picked up the limp form of Smiley, a bandage wrapped around the scar on his neck. The Minister was holding Samuel's hand, taking him to an unknown location. Samuel thought about what would happen next. He would have to have those injections, he'd be forced to breathe in the Smile gas and more. Smiley would probably have his mind fixed, and his colours returned to normal, whatever his normal was. Samuel looked back at Smiley, touching his hand slightly; he could feel a pulse, luckily. A weird tingle crossed his forehead, before he heard Smiley's voice, but no one was speaking. "You should have denied," he said, but somehow, only he could hear him.

"I'm not a human. I am a spirit. I can only fully die if my coaster, The Perfector, is destroyed and I cannot link to another ride or role. If they didn't have me, though, they couldn't perfect people. They also would never purposely kill a high-ranking ministry personnel unless they rebelled. I haven't," Smiley explained in Samuel's mind, before sighing, and ending his explanation, the tingle faded away.

"We're here!" the Minister chimed.

In the dark room, there were two metal beds with shackles and metal helmets.

"What is this room for?" Samuel questioned, puzzled.

"It's for... permanent perfection and anti-perfection," mumbled the Minister. Smiley was awakened with a snap of the Minister's fingers, like she was controlling him.

They were lying on the two metal beds, looking at each other. Two guards walked towards them and shackled them into place, and fastened the helmets tightly. "... Sorry."

Both Samuel and Smiley sighed to each other.

"Ok... 3...2...1!" Hypna and the Minister said in unison. The machine roared to life, making a thunderous growl like a ferocious beast.

"AGHHH!.." Samuel screamed, feeling as if he was being slowly ripped apart, before going silent as an icy blue glow emanated from his helmet and went into Smiley's, and a golden glow from Smiley to him. The lights flashed and flickered, before finally giving out and going dark, slowly returning to normal. The grips that kept both Samuel and Smiley on the beds unlocked, and both boys fell to the ground with a thud. Their clothes were singed from the electricity, and there were burns on their skin. Their hair was spiky and messed up, with hairs poking out, from static charge. The guards placed two fingers on Samuel and Smiley's necks to check for their pulses. They nodded to signal they were alright, and sent two of the squad out to gather a pair of hospital beds.

Eliza looked down at her arm prosthesis, morphing it into a flashlight. She shone it into their eyes to test their reactions. "Not glazed, and can subconsciously still react. Good, they've only fainted," she said to herself, as her arm shifted back to normal. She perked up again, signalling the guards to remove them both. Following her commands, the gathered guards placed Smiley and Samuel on separate hospital beds, rushing them away.

CHAPTER 5:
TWISTED TRIAL

Samuel felt a warm tingling sensation. He felt comfortable, like he was at home. He imagined waking up in his bedroom, to his family, and forgetting all about the freaks of the ministry. Was this all a dream? Was he waking up from this nightmare?... He then thought of Smiley, and Eliza, and the strange woman in the bushes. "No... This couldn't be fake..." he kept repeating in his head, the thought getting louder...and louder... As he was thinking of this, a shrill beeping noise woke him up, Followed by an automated voice. 'You have 2 pieces of mail. Press 1 to op–' the message was cut off by Samuel pressing a button, to open them. The first message abruptly started. "Rise and shine! The procedure was a success. Welcome to the Ministry! Also, it took your energy out of you, you fainted. So, we gave you a place to stay! After all, you're one of us now...There was a problem?... Check in the mirror, then open my next message. Thanks!"

Samuel felt groggy, as if he had just had no sleep at all. He glanced around the unfamiliar room, filled with confusion.

The room was immaculate and pristine, with lemon yellow swirls painted on some of the walls, and blank white on others. The lights looked like security cameras, blending almost perfectly with actual cameras. It looked like an expensive hotel room. Samuel sluggishly walked to the kitchen, throwing open the fridge, finding it half full of weird ministry branded knock offs of actual drink and food brands, like French Fries and chicken.

He grabbed a carton of Smile Milk and poured himself some cereal. The weird milk turned chocolaty, and a little smile formed at the top. "Chocolate milk and cereal... At least those weirdos have good taste," Samuel thought, smiling. Five minutes later, he went to the bathroom, brushing his teeth. When he'd finished, he lifted his head up, and noticed how the mirror was caked in condensation. "Well, might as well clean it," he mumbled to himself, before he picked up a cloth and wiped the mist off. He first spotted the signature hypno eyes, the twisted smile, and the pale skin. "Yeah, Perfected." His eyes then trailed towards the black and white blurs around him, and in one swoop, rubbed it all off. The person reflected on him had blonde hair, a white lab coat with tails, and a most peculiar black and yellow top hat. He was looking at Smiley. Samuel screamed, only for Smiley's voice to rush out. He and Smiley had been body switched. "Oh god... oh god... What in the world is happening?!" Samuel ran towards the bed, before starting the next message.

A slight hum rumbled from the answerphone, and Eliza's voice came through. "I'm guessing you saw. Yes, we swapped yours and Smiley's bodies, now he can live a normal life, while you're stuck with us!" Samuel gasped, both confused and enraged. "I'm guessing you want to change back, but we had a deal. You get perfected, Smiley gets free! I didn't say how. Anyways, we'll be coming soon to check if you're okay and ready for a briefing of your new job as our Head of morale! PS: don't take this to heart, I just want the best for ya! Love, Eliza... or the Minister, depending if we're meeting formally or informally!"

Samuel sat down on the bed, gripping the hat. "I guess this is me now... At least I'm not dead. Smiley gets free too... Maybe I can text him or something, I did see a mobile on the desk!" Samuel picked up the phone, its case a shade of bright yellow, and scrolled through the numbers. Smiley wasn't there, but The Minister was. He pressed the button, before a shrill beep repeated three times. A message came through. "I'm sorry, I'm a little bit busy at the moment. Say the message after the bee–" Samuel switched off the message and placed the phone in his pocket, zipping it in. He walked towards a water cooler, and poured himself a cup of water. He drank it and swallowed quickly.

He suddenly felt a wave of happiness, as a smile spread across his face. "Well... that was a particularly joyful cup of water..." Samuel grinned, before looking at himself in the mirror. "Huh, I guess looking at Smiley in a happy light, he does look quite cool." He quickly grabbed the top hat that was placed on the bed, placed it onto his head and straightened it up. Suddenly, a knock came from the door. Samuel ran towards the door, opening it. "Eliza?" Samuel smiled, eyes closed.

"No. This is Hypna! We need you, Smiles." Hypna winked, before grabbing Samuel's arm and dragged him away from his room.

After a labyrinth of corridors, they arrived in a courtroom-style room, with multiple people sitting about a surgery bed, sat below an Injector arm. At the back of the room, a line of chairs stood tall, with signs on the base, saying things like 'Head of Experimentation', 'Head of Kidnapping', 'Head of Technology' and Samuel's new role, 'Head of Morale'.

"Samuel! I see you've awoken from our little... test." The Minister giggled, walking down a flight of stairs.

Samuel yelled, angrily. "You! You better tell me what's going on here!"

The other scientists gasped in horror. "Calm down; he's new here, he doesn't know our mentality yet!"

The Minister smiled, holding Samuel's hand. She leant in and whispered inconspicuously into Samuel's ear, "Call me the Minister for now, and after, we'll have lunch and a chat, sounds nice?" The Minister showed Samuel to the Head of Morale's seat and told him to sit down. Not to anger her, Samuel sat down, trying not to damage his new tailed lab coat. "Now, we need to start this trial." The Minister waved her hand and a light shone down onto the surgical bed, a small boy trapped onto it by brown bands. The boy had dark hair, aqua eyes, and crimson trainers. It was Samuel's body, with Smiley inside.

"Killing two birds with one stone? Smart." The boy laughed with a hint of sarcasm.

"Yup, that's Smiley alright," Samuel thought, grinning slightly.

"Now, Samuel, this person is Smiley. Since you accepted the deal, you have his life, and he has yours. But, we didn't say that his life would be long. He is no longer useful to the Ministry and needs to be dealt with. He simply knows too much. Since this is your first day, we decided to let you settle his fate. I know it's a bit much, but I thought it was a suitable welcome to your responsibilities!"

Samuel thought about what had happened, about what the Minister said. "Smiley nearly brainwashed me…and it would be cool to be in power for once. And you said he was acting… yet again, she could be lying. It depends on what the options are." Samuel finally started to speak. Samuel was about to give his verdict, but was stopped before he could by a loud yell.

"Samuel! Please…I don't hate you. All that stuff I did…I was not in control! That little pest Hypna was controlling me. Please don't kill me!" Smiley cried.

"Minister, who's controlling the machine?"

"Look down."

Samuel looked down, and a big glowing button was on a console, reachable by only him. Smiley was doomed, and he was being forced to pull the trigger. Samuel frantically looked around, only finding decorations.

On the right wall, there was a picture of a lady, with the same smile and eyes, wearing a pink lab coat, with the name 'Dr Mason' inscribed on a metal plate and some plants. Samuel had to do a breakout, or they'd both die here. "May I do it manually?" Samuel pretended.

"Ooh! It seems we may have an early adopter! Go ahead, Sammy!" the Minister said with excitement. Samuel walked down the stairs, smiling as creepily as he could.

"Samuel? What are you doing? Did they tell you to do it yourself? It's a trap!" Smiley cried, before stopping suddenly, smiling and winking. "Check my hat, there's a screwdriver, push the top and pull the metal piece," Smiley mouthed.

Samuel grabbed the hat and put his arm into it, his arm feeling like he'd dunked it in ice water. He fished through the hat, coming upon a screwdriver. Samuel pulled his arm out, and there it was, a screwdriver themed to the injector leg. He pressed down gently, and felt the metal piece loosen. "Hey, Eliza, you really think I'm joining your dumb game?! What a joke! Thanks for the room, the phone and my new friend, but I'm going to say no." Samuel, in one fell swoop, broke the bands trapping Smiley, who immediately sat himself up and slid off the bench.

"What are you idiots standing there for! Get them!" The Minister screamed, burning with rage.

"We'd love to stay and chat, but we gotta go!" Smiley mocked their pursuers, before grabbing his hat while fixing the screwdriver and placing it back in. "Great, I've got my hat back!" Smiley smiled mischievously, before both of them ran through the door and out to the hallway, while being chased by Hypna and the other Heads.

With the room empty, the Minister looked at her robotic hand and clicked her thumb and middle finger together, forming a projection screen. She flicked through the menus, before starting a call with a long silent number.

"Hello again, S. It's been a while, hasn't it?... Yes, I know this call must be a shock, but you are the only person who can distinguish the targets from each other in their current state. It's obviously clear now, but I have a contract for you. Just a return task, with a loose tie to fix... The pay will be higher than your normal ones, for loyalty reasons and such. You may also do what you deem necessary to the target we need out of the picture. Just keep the one we want back alive... I'd prefer for it to be finished in this month, but as long as it's done, it doesn't matter... It's a deal then, Nightstalker. Don't disappoint!" She ended the call with a press of the screen, which dissipated with another finger tap.

Meanwhile, Smiley pulled him and Samuel to the side, and stopped, panting for air. "How do you humans...do sports?!" Smiley gasped, out of breath.

"I thought you were joking when you said you weren't human!" Samuel whispered, confused. "Nope. I'm spiritually attuned with the Perfector. That's why I have a magic hat, it helps me with my weapons and stuff like that. It also has syringes, a laughing gas tank, my eyes are hypnotic, etc. I'm a spirit. The Perfector itself, per se," Smiley answered. He took off his hat and plunged his arm into it, pulling out random things.

Firstly, a pack of plasters. "Nope, not hurt." Then, a small vial of a red liquid. "Save this for later, as it's the only one." He chuckled. He shuffled through his hat, but he couldn't find anything else of use. "Alright then. Plan B! Kid, put your arm straight across from your chest, like you're going to chop something with it. When those guys get to the end of the hallway, slice your arm through the air and say 'Protectus Balencia!' – got it?" he commanded.

Samuel gave him a thumbs up, having no other options. Announced by the fanfare of their thunderous footsteps, Samuel did as Smiley told him. As his hand cut through the air, it started to spark to life like a flare, sending a streak of flickering gold torrenting through the hallway at the unsuspecting group. With a sound akin to both electricity and laser blasts in Sci Fi films, the streak collided with the group, knocking them all into a pile like an avalanche of bodies. The now adult teen gave Smiley a high-five in achievement, and then returned to running. The duo stopped at the door, before Samuel spoke up. "Computer, open! It's...Smiley!" he lied. A flat scanner came from the door, requesting something. "It's looking for your handprint!" Smiley pointed towards Samuel's hand, and Samuel obeyed.

The device scanned his hand for a moment, before it beeped and unlocked the door. Smiley opened the door to the outside and closed it after both he and Samuel had left, locking it tight. The sun was low on the horizon, its glow dimming as brilliant reds, yellows and oranges filled the sky. Samuel's now golden hair was shaking slightly in the breeze.

"What a view," Smiley gasped, the sun reflected in his eyes. "I've never seen something this beautiful... I never really see the sunset often."

Samuel sighed, turning towards Smiley. "We should go now," Samuel said, before strolling out.

The two boys were just about to cross the gate out of the X-Periment Facility when a voice startled them, almost like it knew they'd be there. "And look who we have here. Greetings Smiley, I thought you'd never leave that place. To be honest that would be better..." The deep voice greeted the two from behind their backs.

Both Smiley and Samuel turned around to be greeted by a tall man with a smirk on his thin face. His skin was peach and his hair was ebony black, with amber crawling up the tips. A curl of hair was hanging in front of his orange eyes, which were highlighted by a pair of rectangular glasses. If Samuel squinted, he could see something on his face, but he couldn't get a clear view. When he looked into his eyes, he somehow felt as if the man's stare seemed to pierce into his soul. A black top hat was placed gently at the top of his head, standing tall like the coaster that the man seemed to be linked to. The hat itself was quite similar to Smiley's, except for how the band was a deep hue of orange, and the different symbol embroidered on the hat. Instead of a radiant yellow hypnotic swirl which could be seen from a mile away, it was a capital 'Y' with the stick ending with two points, like an arrow.

The man was smartly dressed in a crisp, black suit that fell into two tails, and an orange tie. He wore sleek, black gloves on his hands, and a clean pair of black pants. A grey belt was wrapped around his waist, secured by a crimson buckle. Finally, his shoes were a pair of polished boots that were worn in slightly from use. Altogether, he looked like a gentleman.

The man looked down at the two of them, stunned by the lack of a response. "Smiley, you didn't respond?" he said.

"Err... I'm not Smiley, he is!" Samuel pointed towards Smiley, who grinned. "...I see. I knew you weren't him, but I couldn't resist to test you. I can assume that you and Smiles got body swapped, or something similar? The Ministry and their creative solutions," he said. His tone was dark, yet somehow still managed to be lighthearted. On his face, however, his expression showed a knowing stare, as if he knew who was who from nothing more than a glance.

"How did you know that?" Samuel asked. He inched away, hesitant of his knowledge.

"I'm good at reading people. You learn that around here. My name's Void, and you are?" He held his gloved hand out for a handshake, which Samuel cautiously accepted.

"His name's Samuel, since he clearly isn't responding," Smiley said as a joke.

"Come on, let's get a shortcut to get you both fixed back up. We should be able to get to the place I'm thinking of in two minutes." Void chatted for a moment.

"Void... we kinda need to go now." Samuel said, pointing to the door that had a growing sound of footsteps echoing from it.

Void nodded in agreement, a plan formed in his mind. "I have an idea, though it may be embarrassing. You'll understand soon," Void told him, with an uninterested tone.

He stretched his shoulders, preparing for something. "Samuel. Since you're technically a Spirit right now, you can do things that you couldn't before. One ability that you have is a Speed Rush, which basically makes you run insanely fast. You're ever so slightly slower than me, but it won't be worse in the big picture. You just need to focus on speeding up!"

Samuel agreed with a thumbs up. He glanced upwards and noticed how Void was looking at him with a serious expression.

"...Samuel. This may sound weird, but one of us has to carry Smiley, since he isn't exactly able to run at our speed right now." Void spoke sarcastically.

Smiley immediately pointed to Samuel, whose eyes widened in reaction. "Samuel! He kinda saved my life," Smiley said with a grin.

Samuel nodded in agreement, trusting Void. He nodded, before speaking to Samuel in a clear voice. "Okay, you need to pick Smiles up, but don't hurt him. When we get this reversed, anything that happens to him will happen to you," Void said. His hand glowed, before Smiley started to levitate. Samuel grabbed him, making sure he wouldn't drop him. Smiley smiled a bit and looked away, as the idea of him being held by a 16 year old in his own body was very embarrassing.

"Wow...I'm extremely light...or Smiley is extremely tall and strong. Probably the latter," Samuel thought, before rushing off with Void.

CHAPTER 6:
THE SHORTCUT

After a few minutes of running, Void threw his arm out to make them both stop. Samuel stopped in his tracks and placed Smiley down, before the spirits deactivated their speed boosts.

"Smiles, why can't you just remove the microchip? We wouldn't need to overwork this person that you're talking about then," Samuel inquired, before Smiley and Void looked at him, confusion in his eyes.

"As you probably know, only a ministry member can remove the chip. Since you ran off, you basically resigned from the job. Unless you go back and prove your loyalty, the job will be put in limbo, per se," Smiley explained, twirling his hand. "A job can stay in this state for about a month, then if you don't go back to it, someone else gets picked. To try and stop this, anytime a high-ranking Ministry member goes AWOL, security surges, to try and get them back." Smiley looked at Samuel sternly, before sighing.

"Samuel... Why did you save me?" he muttered, sadness in his voice.

"Why did I save you? You're a friend! I can't leave a friend behi–" Samuel was explaining, before he was interrupted by

CHAPTER 6: THE SHORTCUT

Smiley, who flung his arm back, hitting Samuel in the leg, making him take a step back in response.

"NO! No, I'm not!" Smiley yelled, tears forming in his eyes. "Samuel! I tried to murder you! I would easily have succeeded too, if you two didn't fight me off! I'm a monster! Anyone I touch gets hurt!..." Smiley looked down, stamping his foot down slightly, a small cloud of dust coming away from the path before settling again. "...Or worse..." Smiley then broke down, crumpling to the ground, whimpering and sobbing.

Void seemed unfazed, but bent down, trying to calm his sibling down. "Smiley. Why are you crying? All those things are in the past, and you couldn't refuse a command. Besides, if any of us is the villain, it'd be me. We just need to focus on fixing this whole mess," Void said, gently rubbing his hand on Smiley's chin. Smiley laughed a bit, but still continued to cry.

Samuel kneeled down, before wrapping his arms around Smiley, hugging him. Smiley wiped his eyes, but a frown was still on his face. Samuel pulled up Smiley, before tickling his neck, where Smiley immediately burst into uncontrollable laughter.

"How'd you do that, Samuel?" Void asked, still slightly monotone.

"He's in my body, I know my weak spots," Samuel replied, smugly.

After Smiley had finished his laughing fit, they then continued to walk for a minute, before stopping near a shadowy manor, the wind blowing through its windows, making a moaning sound.

The sun had now set, with the remnants of the sunset outlining the derelict manor. However, Void seemed focused on something only he knew. As he went to take the two deeper into the forest, a group of bushes started to rustle. For a second, he looked mad, as both he and Samuel summoned their weapons. Void had a pair of ebony blades, which gradiented into a shade of orange, while Samuel had Smiley's signature Smile Serum syringes.

"Eek! Please don't hurt me!" A young girl, probably 13 years old, was looking like she just saw someone try to hurt her. A single flowing ponytail was lying on her shoulder, before going to her elbow.

A silvery dress, with blue lace on the straps, was tightly lying on her shoulders, and a golden necklace hung on her neck, with a ruby cartoon soul swirl attached to it. The trio, who were all taller than the girl, all sheathed their weapons, with Void's blades vanishing into fire like sparks, while Samuel placed his Smile Serum syringes into the top hat.

"I'm Sally! I'm the only living person in this place, if you don't accept that annoying fire hazard, Blaze," Sally said with an eyeroll. She tugged on Void's sleeve, trying to show them around her home. Void roughly flicked the girl's hand off his arm with a smirk, before sighing and following the others.

"This is my ride! Well, the ride's under it. I'm the spirit of Poltergeist!" Sally smiled, proudly. She stood in front of the door of the mansion and flicked her arms out in a T position. The doors opened, with a creak. "This way! It's the safest way around the park! Well... unless you want to have to deal with The Ministry." Sally chatted to herself, while she walked the trio through her house, with weird gems, crystals, and other oddities littered around. The four of them stopped at a bedroom, which was decorated with purple and pink. "This is my room! It's where I rest and stuff. Sorry if I am a bit chatty! I just don't have a lot of people visiting this place. Most people go straight to The X-periment Facility, or Florette's Crypt, or Fawnia's Palace...I'm going to go get the teleportation pad working. Wait here!" Sally skipped into her room, closing the door behind her.

"Well, isn't she hyper!" Smiley chuckled to himself, arms on his hips.

"Still, she could've said hello. Guess we're doing a different short-cut," Void complained, while his face displayed a faint sign of annoyance. He shrugged briefly, before turning towards a bookshelf brimming with different crystals, gems and metals that were being put on display in an ornate fashion. Though the crystals were beautiful and glittered in the light, the only thing which he looked at was a polished bar of silver. Samuel was boredly daydreaming in a chair tucked to the side, while Sally was making a mess in her room, looking for something. She started to speak to herself, muttering cheerfully. "It was here last time I used it…This thing is more problematic than The Perfector!… Still wish that only it closed. Maybe we wouldn't be dealing with The Ministry's meddling then." She spoke out loud.

Smiley opened the door and went in. "Sally! I heard you say that!" Smiley yelled, offended by her comment.

"Huh? You're not from The Ministry! You may be dressed like them, but I can tell from your entire demeanour you're not with them. If anything, you look like you'd be running from them," Sally replied, before Samuel walked in to try and calm down Smiley.

"It's…him." Sally whimpered, seeing Samuel.

"You've got it all wrong! He's from The Ministry, not me." Samuel rebutted.

Void came in, and sighed. "Long story short, they got body swapped. That's why we're going to Fawnia's Palace," Void explained.

"I thought you said we were going to Florette's?" both Samuel and Smiley replied, pushing their arms out in front of them.

Void levitated the two angered people, walking towards them. "Calm down. She didn't mean to say that. Did you?" Void spoke, calmly, before looking at Sally, who rolled her eyes at him, and went back to searching. "She's rude," Void mumbled, before going to take Smiley and Samuel outside.

"Wait! It's right there! Teeheehee!" Sally pointed to a black tube with a silver button on the top. The tube levitated over to Void, who grabbed it hastily. "Just press the grey button, say the location that you want to go to, then press down the silver button at the top!" Sally smiled, showing Void the teleportation pad. Void dumped the two on the ground, letting themselves get up. "Step here." She giggled, before Void, Smiley and Samuel stepped onto the pad. "Happy travels! Bye bye!" Sally waved, excitedly.

"The Crypt!" Void spoke to the coordinator, before pressing the silver button. The door closed, and Samuel felt like he was being spun like a spinning top, but both of the brothers were seemingly unfazed. Suddenly, the spinning sensation stopped, revealing them to be in a forest, but with leafless trees. There were gravestones with silly puns like 'Paul Tur Geist' and 'Vann Pyre' engraved onto them.

The speakers, hidden in the trees, were playing scary music, like haunting nursery rhymes, mixed with the sounds of birds, the howl of the wind, and ghostly whispering. A grey tomb lay in front of the trio, with a pentagram-like star built as a logo or symbol above it, with a fake tombstone made to look like it had been ripped from the ground with 'D3M0N' clawed on with flickering green LEDs engraved in the letters.

"We're at Florette's. Happy?" growled Void, annoyed at the fact he had to be here. Suddenly, the Crypt door, which looked new, due to the fact that it was not overgrown with the greenish-brown vines that were tangled and overgrown around the area, opened.

On closer inspection, however, some of the vines were fake, added for the theming of the area. Samuel felt a warm tingle in his face, before two beams of bright yellow light shone from his eyes. He shone the light in the doorway, revealing a ramp, going down in a square like pattern. "Finally! Somewhere WITHOUT stairs!" Samuel burst out in a chuckle, before starting down the ramps.

"Florette? Anyone here?" Samuel and Void said as their voices echoed through the tunnels.

"Smiley, Void, come in! You really didn't need to ask!" a gentle voice said.

They were suddenly at the bottom of the ramp, as a gust of magically summoned wind blew away. At the side of the room, a brown-haired lady was sitting on a stool. A pale green dress was wrapped across her, draping slightly below the knee. The dress itself was detailed with a faint shimmer at the skirt, and hemmed with pink summer flowers on the top. A beige bow was tied around her waist, with two spare ribbons trailing down her back. On her feet, she was wearing a pair of sandals that seemed to shimmer like water in the ocean. She had brownish tanned skin, with a few freckles on her nose bridge. Her eyes were a lively green, shaded with faint black eye shadow.

"Oh! You seem to have brought a friend, someone new to talk to. What's your name?" She questioned who she didn't know was Smiley, only for Void to laugh in the background.

"You're talking to the wrong person, Florette. He's the new kid here," he said, pointing towards Samuel.

"Really? Or is this a prank? Alright, I'll check," Florette said, as a flower bloomed from nothing in her hand. She pinched this flower, turning the petals into a magic aura. The magic channelled to her fingertip, with a faint shimmer radiating off the tip.

"Let me see…" The woman placed her fingertip on Samuel's chest, as her iris started to glow. After a few seconds, she removed her finger as her eyes returned to normal. "Aha. I see a reason for this problem, Smiley and this new child's souls have been switched! It makes sense why you knew all along, with the whole seeing souls thing," Florette said, nodding quickly.

"Yes. I know. Their name is Samuel, by the way," Void piped in, sarcasm in his voice.

Florette glanced at him, a hint of annoyance in her eyes. "A soul swap spell is what you need. I just wish you gave me some warning. I was researching if perfection can be reversed enough for the subject to remember themselves. Also, you still haven't repaid me for the countless energy potions we use for you!" Florette groaned, before flicking some locks of hair away from her eyes, the light radiating from Samuel's eyes adding golden shimmers to her long, brown hair. "Follow me. I'll take you to my home." Florette shook her hands, and as the crypt lit up, Samuel's eyes stopped glowing. The four people walked in the catacomb-like pathways until they were at two hallways. "Don't go to the left, come to the right! The left is where the roller coaster is. Though, if you ask politely, I might be able to get it working for a ride after you're both back to normal!" Florette laughed, before letting the trio of boys in, finally walking in behind them.

They were met with a doorway, which Florette said the password for. "The Spirits have awoken!" The door creaked slightly then swung open, revealing a room with bookcases filled with multicoloured books, with potions and equipment placed neatly on benches. "Okay, boys, stand still... This may feel weird." Florette pointed towards the centre of the room and the two boys stood there, making sure to stay absolutely still. Florette's eyes glowed with a green colour, before two shimmering lime-coloured beams went into both Smiley and Samuel's chests. Samuel and Smiley groaned, as they started levitating slightly, their eyes glowing, changing from blue to yellow for Smiley's body, and yellow to blue for Samuel's. They both were placed back on the ground, wobbling around a bit.

"Woah... That was weird..." Smiley muttered, before looking down at his hands. He was in his own body; same with Samuel. "Yeah! Finally! Whoo!" Smiley cheered, little yellow sparks coming from his hands.

Samuel laughed, before grabbing Smiley then Florette in a hug. "Thanks! I can be me again! Aha!" Samuel smiled, before looking at Void, happily. "So, what now?"

The two looked at each other, before Void shrugged with disinterest. "We could have simply gone through with the removal process. But, since Smiles isn't a Ministry member anymore, for now at least, we're kind of stuck. Plus, I'm not good at borderline surgery," Void said, glaring at Smiley. "Unfortunately, it looks like our only tie to the Ministry has been cut. We'd have to either try and get the chip out and remove any toxins, or try and befriend a Ministry member. You can see why that isn't really possible. So, for now, you're microchipped. The most we can do is either confuse the chip enough to break tracking, or hope the Ministry hasn't sent someone out for you. They haven't done that for nearly 15 years now, so I'd say it's not likely." He sat down on a chair, with his head leant on his hand and his focus on his phone.

Smiley glanced at Samuel, before noticing that he was still wearing the Ministry's outfit. "Oh! Here, let me help you out!" Smiley flicked his hand, before a yellow beam went towards Samuel, before the Ministry's outfit was replaced with Samuel's polo, trousers and trainers.

"Thanks! I was missing wearing these!" Samuel thanked Smiley, before Smiley nodded back at him.

"No problemo. It's pretty easy, actually. Well, I guess we'll just stay here for now," he said, before he walked out of the room to what looked like a library.

Samuel glanced at Florette, before remembering the weird hallucinations that he saw while first escaping. "I was injected with something when I arrived…and now I'm having these weird visions. Do you have any idea how to stop them?" he asked.

She tilted her head, before she searched through a bunch of potions and pulled out a small vial, with a silver liquid in it. "Since you seem to have only been affected by one of the steps of Perfection, Injector, it's easy to heal. You're lucky you didn't become more afflicted!" Florette said. She gave the vial to Samuel, who drank it down. Once he'd drank the concoction, his headache stopped.

Smiley walked back in the room, holding his phone in his hand. As he saw Samuel holding the vial that he knew was the cure from its label, he glanced at him sideways. On his phone, there was a message from Hypna. "Looks like we may have a candidate. Miss Pigtails seems to want me back, but the Big Boss's not letting her." Smiley smirked slightly while he showed his phone to the group. The text read:

"Hey Smiles, It's Hypna. Sorry about the whole body swap thing. I can't disobey an order from Eliza, you know? She's harsh at times. Look, if you want to, I can...persuade her to let you back in. It may take time, but I believe it could work."

Smiley took back his phone, and glanced at Florette and Void. "What do you say? You in?" he asked.

Florette and Samuel both showed concern and disapproval, while Void seemed to be all for the idea. "I can't make the decision for you, but having you with those guys gives us an advantage. We don't have to constantly spy on them to gain information on their plans. Plus, if we're caught doing anything, you would be able to bail us out. It's a win-win!" Void said.

The two of them stared at him, with both of them having the feeling that Smiley would most likely become bad if he was back at the Ministry.

Smiley beamed, before he focused on typing. He sat himself down, his twin coat tails levitating slightly to not get crumpled. The phone chimed and he read the response. "It looks like I'm meeting her at Cosmic Bites tomorrow, if everything goes smoothly," he said.

Void smiled, happy for his brother. "It's getting late. Maybe we could grab a meal someplace, since we have company."

Florette looked at the three boys, before Void had an idea. "Let's go to Stella's. After all, what's the problem with going to the same place twice?" He smirked, pointing to Smiley. He snapped his fingers, before teleporting everyone to the main plaza of the park.

CHAPTER 7:
MEETING THE MAGIC

The spires of the Cursed Palace glistened in the moonlight, as well as a tall, technological and futuristic looking statue standing in the middle of a bridge to the right of the group. There were orbs and glowing lights, lighting up and dimming in a rotating pattern. The group walked towards the bridge, which had glowing lights dotted around the railings, and boosters were stuck to the bottom of the teal bridge. A shimmering code pattern was ingrained inside the walkway, glowing in teals, greens and violets around the footsteps of the group. A large array of things was in front of them, like a thin, pale blue glowing track wrapping and weaving above the area, with teardrop shaped pods, tinted with a violet to teal gradient, sitting on top of them.

"This place is so futuristic! Cool!" Samuel smiled, taking in the view. The glowing lights were reflected onto the gems of Florette's dress and Smiley's badges, causing them to glimmer and shimmer, as if they were getting turned into computer data like in a Sci-Fi film.

"Hey, Samuel. Do you want a better view?" Smiley asked, and Samuel nodded enthusiastically.

"Okay, hold on tight!"

Samuel was covered with a yellow glow, before he was off the ground, and was grabbed in Smiley's arms. "Here we...go!" Smiley counted. He tapped his feet together, before the soles of his boots started glowing yellow, hovering slightly above the floor. He bent his knees slightly, before making them straight again. Both Smiley and Samuel were launched into the sky, a faint glowing trail following their ascent. Samuel gasped at the view, which sprawled out around him. The area was filled with bright, glimmering lights, with the patterns and colours being almost hypnotic. Machines and tech were abundant, with things like a floating pod racer, or a rocket flier, with the building of Cosmic Bites visible from where he was. It was a retro sci-fi themed diner, but with a twist. The food would appear to form in front of the guests in a glow of blue light. It was, of course, just an illusion, as where the food appeared was actually connected to tracks hidden in tunnels under the floor of the restaurant. But, it kept guests coming, so it stayed popular.

To the left, there was also a gigantic, glowing circular portal, with a track going through some twists and rolls, before dipping back into another portal and going back into a technical looking building which was painted with hues of silver, teal and lime. A path rolled down towards the main hub, ending with a big, geometric sign, a logo projected onto it in bright neon blue. The logo was a triangular shield with what looked like a pair of robotic wings, with 'Hyperspace' written in a sci-fi text.

"It's breathtaking, isn't it? I usually come here with some of my friends to race! I...rarely win," Smiley said, chuckling, before lowering them both down, and deactivating his hoverboots.

"Any second now..." Void spoke, checking an orange watch on his wrist.

"What's happening any second now?" Samuel asked.

"This," Florette replied, before a bright, aqua-blue aura, similar to a shooting star, streaked across the horizon, quickly dipping downwards towards the ground with a shimmering beam. After a moment, the aura faded, leaving a figure standing in front of them. The figure had a technically advanced suit, with a grey and purple colour scheme, with a star shape in the middle. Two wings were sticking out at the sides, before quickly retracting back behind it.

"Hey guys! Hey again, kid." The figure said in an excited tone before removing its helmet, to reveal a fair skinned woman, with shoulder length sky blue hair and stunning violet eyes.

"I met you at the entrance! Hi again!" He greeted the woman, who stuck out her hand to shake his.

"It's Stella, and I'm guessing you're this Samuel everyone's been talking about!" She smiled, before looking back to the spirits. "So, why are you guys here?"

Void walked forwards, greeting the girl with a handshake. "We decided to come over for something to eat, since this guy's here!"

Stella nodded, before pressing a button on her helmet and her flight suit armour being replaced with a casual violet shirt and some dark blue trousers. The shirt had constellations sewn in, made of silver fabric, and the trousers had two spacious pockets on the waist. Her shoes were a pair of silver pumps with teal highlights. "Let's go!" Stella smiled, before running across the futuristic area to the diner, with the others following after her.

They walked into the diner, which was still mostly as pristine as how it used to be. The spirits had added LEDs to the ceiling, which bathed the building in a comforting glow. They sat down at a booth, which had a light wrapped around the table, that displayed the colours of the light spectrum. "So, what do you guys want?" Stella said, before noticing someone behind the counter. "Hey, Techno!" Stella said, before a boy with a silver suit, lined with shades of purple, green, and blue, looked up at her.

His eyes lit up when he saw Stella, before hovering towards her, leaving a slight shimmer of lime green. The boy levitated over before doing a handshake, then deactivating the boots.

"Samuel, this is Levi. He's the spirit of the Pod Racers!" Stella introduced Levi, before the group greeted him, smiling. "He doesn't really leave much, as he's always busy making inventions, or keeping his ride up and running. I believe some of his technology actually is in the Ministry!" Stella explained, before pointing to Smiley's boots.

"Oh, these? Yeah, I got them from him! We did do some slight alterations, like a more responsive system, as well as making it be yellow, instead of blue or green." Smiley chatted, moving his hand as he explained.

Levi's dark blue hair was illuminated by the blue lights, making cyan shimmers glow in both the navy and the lime streak. He laughed a bit, before raising his arm up and pressing a button on his watch, before a holographic screen appeared in front of him. "Woah..." Samuel mouthed, before the spirit started speaking.

"What would you want for your meal today?" Levi enquired, tapping his chin slightly.

"I'm not that hungry right now, but a small bag of Cosmic Bites and a Zestie would be nice," Void replied, before all the rest of the spirits replied too.

"Okay! Some small Bites and a Zestie for Void...Salad and Diet Cola for Florette...Martian Burger, chips and lemonade for Smiley... Sausages, lattices and Fizz-e Cola for Stella, and..." Levi listed, before looking at Samuel.

"I'll have a chicken burger, wedges and some Mr Fizz please?" Samuel said, for Levi to nod slightly, and press a few holographic buttons with text appearing on the screen. Suddenly, Levi started hovering, and glided behind the counter with a green trail behind him. After a few minutes, a disc in the middle of the table glowed blue. The lighting swirled for a few moments, as the circle was surrounded by a wall that blocked the view of the disc. On the floor, a line lit up, as LEDs in the ground rushed forwards like a streak of energy. The lights stopped as rapidly as they had started and the barrier dropped to reveal the group's meal. The glasses magically filled with the person's chosen drink, before Levi appeared in the booth behind them all, sprawled onto one of the seats, eating a chocolate bar.

The group seemed to get started in a heartbeat, with Florette trying to keep the dressing on the salad, and Void casually picking on the nugget pieces at a leisurely pace. Once they were finished, they cleaned up after themselves in return for the service, and waved Levi goodbye to look around the area. The cold breeze hit them immediately, before they got used to the chill.

"That was... amazing!" The teen said, beaming.

Smiley looked down at him with a smile, just happy he was happy. "It was some transfiguration. Although, I'm guessing you've never seen magic, have you?" he said, before demonstrating with a pen, which he turned into a lollipop at the wave of a hand. "See? This is pretty easy, though it does require the ability to picture things in your mind," he explained, as he reverted the spell, before throwing the now reformed pen into the air and landing it in his hat.

"Well done. You're able to do simple magic. Try being able to literally displace your form. Now, that's impressive," Void said with a snarky tone, trying to jokingly upstage his brother.

Smiley rolled his eyes, and decided to ignore him.

"Smiley, can you get this to Florette, it's my home keycard. I thought we could have a sleepover. You know, with a guest here, and all that," Stella spoke, before passing a pair of silver keys, with blue tops towards him.

He grabbed them easily, and looked towards the tanned woman. "Hey Florette, catch!" he said, before throwing them to her. Out of thin air, a small black vortex with an orange rim appeared. The keys entered the vortex and vanished. "Where'd the keys go?" he said, looking around in confusion. Just as he started to worry, the jingle of keys rang from behind the group.

Void had them grasped in his hand, and was smiling sarcastically. "Who's got the keys now?" Void started running to the large, grey building that housed both Stella's apartment and Hyperspace.

"Wait! Come back!" Stella and Florette said, before rushing to keep up with the man, who had turned into a black, smoke-like cloud, and was flying towards the building.

CHAPTER 8:
SCOUTING FOR SMILES

The building towered over the group, while strips of lights glowed on the sides, and glowing beacons beamed from the roof. The group had caught up to Void, who was leaning against a pillar in the wall, swinging the keys in his hand. He handed the keys back to Stella, before he went back to a standing position.

"Florette, why can't you all leave, and why does it seem like anything that happens in here doesn't appear outside?" Samuel asked.

"The barrier stops most things from being seen or heard, but some things seep through. Outsiders may hear it as quiet melodies, or the slightest shimmer of light. Mostly though, we practically don't exist in the outside world. If we did leave, however, our bodies would disappear, and our souls would fade, as the outside world doesn't have enough magic for our forms to sustain ourselves. In a nutshell, they can't see us, and if we went to see them, we'd die," Florette said with a sigh.

"Okay! Follow me when I open the doors." Stella said, before placing a lime blue device that was connected to the keychain onto a scanner, with it flashing green, and unlocking the door.

In front of them was a futuristic room, with three corridors, one left, one front and one right. Stella walked into the front corridor, and strutted for a few seconds before coming to yet another door. She again opened this door and led everyone in. Inside there was a technological themed apartment, with a few rooms around them. "Okay. My bedroom is to the left and the guest bedroom is to the right. The bathroom is opposite my bedroom and my personal favourite, the entertainment lounge, is directly to the right of the guest room! Make yourself comfortable! If you need me, I'll be in my room," Stella gleefully explained, before walking into her room, the automatic doors closing with a slide.

The group looked around their room. It had six beds, which looked like giant tubes, with transparent plastic windows around where the person's face would be.

There were the same blue lines painted around, with futuristic-looking furniture, like white, blue and grey orbs, which were chairs with comfortable padding as well as enough space for even Void to sit in comfortably. There was also a sleek bookcase, a large flat screen TV, with hundreds of channels, and much more.

"This place is deluxe! How do you guys have this stuff?" Samuel asked, and Smiley replied calmly.

"Well, the owners of the park did kind of know of our existence, but they didn't know much. Just that we control the rides. They gave us places to stay, and kept the secret, in return for us to keep everything stable and working in the shadows." Smiley laughed, before yawning loudly. "I'm tired...are you guys too?"

The rest of the group nodded, before the spirits glowed slightly, and their clothing was replaced by nightclothes, like pyjamas.

Samuel realised that he didn't have any, since he didn't think he was going to stay. "I... don't have any pyjamas..." Samuel said, embarrassed.

"It's okay," Void said, acceptingly. "Watch this." Void glanced at Samuel for a moment, quickly charging a wisp of energy in his hand and throwing it at him, which caused Samuel to glow slightly. When the glowing stopped, everyone saw that Samuel's clothes had been replaced with blue pyjamas, with his normal clothes folded on the wardrobe.

"How'd you do that?" Samuel said, only for Void to smirk slightly.

"Oh, nothing much. Levitation, some creation, and teleportation...and I just realised that I rhymed," Void explained, before rolling his eyes slightly, as the other spirits laughed. He picked his hat off his head and placed it at the foot of the pod, before turning his head back towards the others.

"Well, I'm off to sleep, since I didn't get my normal schedule!" Void sneered with a joking tone, before sliding into the pod with a faded smile. "Well, goodnight everyone," Void said politely, before pulling closed the pod.

"Huh! He fell asleep quickly." Florette laughed, keeping quiet so Void could rest.

Smiley was sitting in one of the chairs, watching the scene. "You know how he is. He usually stays up late and sleeps it off until late morning. You could say he is nocturnal. All of this chaos must've burned him out!" he joked, still beaming.

"Well, let's just get to sleep," Florette said, with Smiley agreeing with her and going straight to sleep.

Samuel, however, took some time to think. "Why not just take me out of the park with magic? Surely they could at least push me over the edge before the magic fades," Samuel thought, with similar questions buzzing around his head like a hurricane.

Before he could sleep, a clicking noise came from Smiley's pod. Why was he out at this time of night? Samuel lay still, listening to the man's footsteps. Smiley got out, before shutting the pod with another click. As the footsteps faded, Samuel guessed that he had left the room. After a few minutes, the footsteps returned. He could hear him walking towards the pods, for an unknown reason. He stood at the pod which Florette was sleeping in, for a moment or two. Samuel froze, fearing that she was in danger. But nothing happened. "He's checking on us? But why?" he thought, forcing himself to stay quiet. For a strange reason, he seemed to hang around Void's pod for a long time. After a minute of looking at Void's pod he left the room, and Samuel could hear the echo of his footsteps leaving the building through the back exit. It was hard to hear, but he could tell that Smiley was talking to someone outside.

The conversation seemed calm, although he couldn't tell who he was talking to. All Samuel could guess was that they had a low voice and they were originally on the phone before the conversation began. Just as Samuel thought it was safe to think of leaving the pod, he looked through the pod window and saw the figure of Smiley enter the room. He lay back, keeping his eyes slightly open. There, right in front of him, was Smiley. He grinned with a shark-like smile, and walked away. As soon as he left the building a second time, Samuel could hear the sound of hoverboots being activated from outside. He left the pod, briefly noticing how Void was absent from his pod. However, he brushed it off as Void having something important to do. Focusing on the task at hand, he rushed over to Stella's room. "She's going to kill me for this," he groaned, before grabbing one of Stella's headsets and her flight suit's hoverboots, putting them both on, and running towards the exit, as well as Smiley. Something was going on, and Samuel was going to find out.

When Samuel reached the outside, there was no sign of Smiley, except for a yellow glow in the distance. "Got to catch up to him, fast!" Samuel thought in a rush, before taking off his scarlet trainers, and placing on the boots. They, as expected, were too big for him. "Of course. Too big. If only they were smaller." He sighed, before he felt the shoes getting tighter, until they fitted perfectly. "This world has magic, Samuel. What else is new?" He spoke to himself, before placing on the headset and microphone.

He pressed a blue button, before he felt more alert, and looked down, as a metallic suit and helmet came around him. "If I'm correct, this thing probably has voice or thought commands or something, if my science fiction movies are correct. Activate!" he thought, before the boots flared to life, hovering him slightly above the ground. "Cool!" he squealed with excitement, before breaking into a run, and leaping into the air. "Activate, and wings out!" he commanded, with courage in his voice.

The suit activated and before he knew it, Samuel was in the air. "Suit...Track Smiley?" he commanded, before a robotic voice spoke to him.

"Tracking Smiley," the voice replied, before he smiled to himself. "This IS like my Sci-Fi movies!" he thought. He kicked his legs out and went into a T position, boosting himself forwards. A blue, circular target was locked onto the yellow aura, telling him information. Most of it he didn't care about at that moment or couldn't understand, like altitude, or vital signs. "Faster!" Samuel said, before the boots, and the boosters on the wings and back was leaving behind a bright blue glow.

He was five metres behind Smiley, watching the bright yellow glow of his boots disappear into sparks. Suddenly, a voice came from the helmet's earpiece. "Astro to Samuel! Do you hear me?" The voice spoke before a second of silence, before a giggle came through. "Sorry, I used my codename! It's me, Stella. Why are you outside? Better yet, why are you using my flight suit?" Stella said, sternly.

"Oh, nothing! I'm just randomly following a certain smiling person at midnight," he answered, sarcastically.

"I see Void's rubbed off on you? Great. Well, you need to be careful as you're nearing the edge of the park. This is the time for serious manoeuvres! I'll help you, since I can see from my screen. Florette is here too." Stella explained, before the muffled voice of Florette said a quiet "Hi!", before letting Stella speak again. "Ok. Smiley's probably going to do some tricks. Be careful," she forewarned, before a beep came from Samuel's suit, with the words "Approaching boundary" in red, easy to read writing.

A howl of air rushed below Samuel, and when he looked down, he saw Smiley looking at him. "Hello, Samuel. I can see you're chasing me. Well, I can outsmart anyone in the park! Hmhmhmhm... Try and keep up!" Smiley said, daring Samuel before sharply soaring upwards, creating a cloud of Smile gas with his hands. He twisted into a roll and dived down almost vertically while putting his hands into a point, shooting through the air. Samuel quickly dodged the gas, diving down, before swiftly going straight again, catching up again with Smiley, who glanced back and jolted with surprise, hovering in the air. "You're still on my trail?... Usually most people would've lost balance by now!... I'm sorry, but I can't have anyone following me," Smiley explained, before raising his arm at Samuel, who was flying straight forwards towards Smiley. "Disruptus Mechanica!" Smiley exclaimed, tracing a circle in the air, pointed at Samuel.

Suddenly, the boosters locked up and started failing, before he lost his balance and fell to the ground.

"Samuel! Pull up!" Stella commanded into the earpiece, before manually putting the emergency boosters on, slowing Samuel down enough for the fall to not be fatal. The flight suit automatically shielded and protected Samuel for any impacts, as it sensed the danger. He fell and smashed down into a dark, brambled forest, the suit being scratched and dented by the trees and the fall, before Samuel realised what had happened, seeing the back of the tip of Sally's mansion. "Augh...My arm hurts, I think I cut it," he moaned, feeling the warm feeling of blood on his arm, before she replied through the helmet.

"You know you just fell from a height taller than even the Abyss!? You're lucky the suit wasn't damaged from the blast, otherwise you could've been a goner!" Stella yelled, annoyed.

"Okay okay, calm down. Are you able to heal me or something? I need to catch up to Smiley!" he argued, before the sound of

Stella's door opening, and someone yelling into the headset.

"Samuel? It's Void here! Are you okay? We heard Stella's meltdown from the next room over! Where's Smiles?" Void yelled, panicked.

"I'm okay, just a bit scratched, bruised and hurt," Samuel replied, with a slight groan.

"Okay. We have to teleport you back. Stay still," Stella said to Samuel, commandingly.

"But what about–" Samuel was cut short by Stella.

"Smiley's in The X-periment Facility by now. Also, you need healing," Stella replied, before Samuel saw one of Void's portals form under him.

He fell into it, seeing a glimpse of a dark, shadowed plane, before being pulled out, the lights blinding him for a few seconds. Samuel noticed that Florette had a green, shimmering orb in her hand, before she released it at him. He suddenly felt a warm feeling in his body, like the feeling when the sun shines on your skin, with the pain and aches being overwhelmed, and disappearing. Samuel felt where the cut was, to feel nothing there. "I'm healed!" Samuel said, rubbing his eyes.

"Yes you are. Now, take my flight suit off and go back to bed. It's 2AM!" Stella yelled at Samuel, before pressing a button on the helmet, making the armour transform back into the headset and boots, which he took off.

Samuel, Florette and Void went back to their room and fell asleep, with Stella being left alone. She felt like something was wrong, as she went and checked Smiley's location. She pressed a button, and, without Smiley knowing, watched what he was doing from a hidden camera in his spare bow tie. Smiley was entering the Secret Labs, before seeing Hypna, and talking to her.

"Hello again. I didn't know you were waiting for me..." Smiley whispered, quietly.

Hypna looked at him, smiled, then looked at his bow tie. Hypna's eyes were staring directly at Stella's. "Heehee... Before we chat, I believe someone is trying to spy on us." Hypna laughed. She pulled off the bow tie and took out the camera, using the magic from her necklace to keep the bow in place. She smiled from finding her discovery, before fixing anything that was damaged.

"To whoever is watching this, we know that you're watching. I recommend stopping. Bye." Hypna gripped the tiny camera, before putting it on the floor and breaking it with her foot.

Stella's screen turned to static, then switched back to CCTV, while she muttered things under her breath. She switched the futuristic computer off, and walked to the Entertainment room to calm herself down before going to bed.

"You're lucky I saw. We were nearly spied on. Now, where were we?" Hypna said, before laughing. "Oh yes! I know you need to get back to Technoland quickly, so I won't take long. But I have something to add to our agreement. Let's just say, I've found a better idea. But, if we do this, our lives will change... forever."

CHAPTER 9:
THE START OF THE INSANITY

S tella slowly awoke to pure, unbroken silence. She stretched up her arm and pressed a blue button with a lightbulb symbol printed on it. When she did, the lights inside the pod turned on, letting her eyes adjust to the light. While she waited, she allowed herself time to think. "What is even going on? Is Smiley a traitor? No!... No! He's Smiley! He'd never hurt us! It was probably an earlier version of that meetup between him and this Hypna girl that Florette told me about, right?..." Stella thought to herself, before opening the door and switching off the pod's lights. The room automatically lit up in a pale blue glow, allowing her to see. She stepped out of her pod, before putting her feet into a pair of comfortable, but well-fitting teal and mint slip-on shoes. She looked up at a clock on the wall, wanting to know the time. It was close to 6AM, so the others would be waking up soon. She walked across her room towards a sleek white writing desk with two drawers, with one containing paper, notepaper, and other similar materials, and the other holding pencils, pens and more stationery.

Stella opened the paper drawer and took out a notepad, before opening the stationery drawer and taking a grey pen out, and closing both drawers. She started writing a message onto the notepaper, the pen creating cyan lines where she moved it. She tore the page off and walked into the guest room, making sure to not make noise.

She walked carefully towards the pods, and glanced at each one. They were all fast asleep, with Void's eyes glowing slightly, as he normally did. Stella finally glanced at Smiley's pod, to the same answer. She silently opened the pod and placed the note where Smiley would see it, before shutting it and walking off. She had reached the door, when a loud click of a pod opening came from behind her, and a ball of crumpled paper hit the back of her head. Stella turned around, but no one was there; however, Smiley's pod door was open. She shrugged it off as him just getting a snack or going out for a stroll. "It's fine. Stop being irrational," Stella thought. But then, she unfolded and read the paper. While her message was there, something else had been quickly written down. "It's rude to spy on others. Maybe you should forget that." A chill flowed down her spine like a wave. She glanced back, and yet again, there was nobody there. At this point her heart was pounding out of her chest.

She remembered that the pods were somewhat soundproofed, so she could speak. "S-Smiley? If that's you, I-it's not funny!" Stella pleaded, fear making her stumble on her words. She crept backwards, before she bumped into someone tall. Before she could even turn around to react, a black sleeved arm came towards her. A gold gloved hand swiftly clasped roughly around her mouth, muffling her pain-filled, struggling cries while she saw a shimmer of metal fly down, and a sharp, stabbing pain shot through her neck in a blink.

She felt the world start spinning and turning, as a wave of both dizziness and stiffness washed over her...She tried to move, only to slip and fall towards the cold, blue floor, only to get caught by her attacker moments before colliding. Stella forced herself to open her eyes to see whoever had attacked her, but all she could see of her attacker was their face. A pale skinned man with golden hair with black tips, and vibrant yellow and black swirl eyes. She knew who it was immediately...It was Smiley.

His yellow, swirly eyes looked into hers, before they started to spin in a hypnotic pattern. "Don't fret, dear, it's me, Smiles! Give up to my sleeping serum, and rest. I don't want to hurt you," Smiley whispered, his voice echoing and repeating in Stella's head, but she couldn't do anything to get him off of her, or block out his mind control. She couldn't push him off or move whatsoever, as the serum was sapping her of her energy and awareness, as well as her movement. Stella also could see that Smiley was gripping her arms, and he was on his knees just above her legs, which still couldn't move due to the paralysing effect of the serum.

She couldn't even scream or cry for help because everyone else wouldn't hear, due to the soundproofed pods, and he would probably cover her mouth again. She tried to look away from his eyes, but they were too entrancing and her eyes would quickly look back at them, as if under control. She didn't have any time to do much either, as she was already falling into a hypnotic induced sleep. Stella used the last of her energy to try to speak, though only one, extremely weak word came out "Why..."

Smiley grinned slightly. "I just need to do a few things... that's all," he answered quietly, before Stella fell asleep from the hypnosis. "Sorry, Starlight, but this is for your own good." A thought streaked his mind, as he carefully picked up the now delicate body of Stella, who was breathing slightly.

He heard multiple clicks behind him, and glanced behind his back and saw the pod doors opening. He ran out of the building in a glow of golden light, without noticing that her spare earpiece had flown out of her pocket at the entrance of Hyperspace. He clicked his heels, changing their settings into making the boots silent. After a moment he flew off, with a sleeping Stella in his arms.

Meanwhile, Samuel, Void and Florette got out of their pods, and checked Smiley's, only to notice that he wasn't there. "Huh! Smiley vanished! Again...Void, check Stella's room!" Florette commanded Void, who flicked his hand at his forehead, in a salute-like style, before running to Stella's room.

"He couldn't have gone far!" Samuel exclaimed, trying to be positive.

"Guys! Stella's...Gone!" Void yelled from the other room, and everyone else rushed inside. Stella's pod was empty, unlocked, and with a note stuck in.

"There's a note!" Samuel pointed out, and Void quickly picked it up and read it, before gasping slightly.

"What does it say?" both Florette and Samuel enquired, to which Void replied, worriedly.

"It says...that we have a kidnapping on our hands!" Void declared, before rushing out of the room, with the note quickly flying to the floor.

He reached the entrance of the building, with the other spirits and Samuel following along. The cold wind whispered through the doors when Void opened them, with everyone racing out in a hurry, looking for their friends. Void was in a face of rage, his eyes glowing a bright, fire-like orange, while looking around for any sign of Smiley or Stella. "It was Smiley. It had to be! He kidnapped Stella!" Void yelled, in anger.

"Void! Acting like this will not get us anywhere!" she started, as Void begrudgingly calmed himself down. "We need to look for clues, like a fingerprint, or a note, or..." Florete explained, calmly, before Samuel finished her sentence, pointing at the entrance to the ride.

"Or her earpiece?" Samuel asked Florette.

She looked at him with hope, a smile on her face. "Yes. That would be good evidence! Do you see it?" Florette asked, to which Samuel replied with a nod and quickly walked to the entrance, before coming back with Stella's spare earpiece. It was slightly damaged, however still could be tracked. "Good! Now, we need to see the recordings," Florette said.

Void pulled out a device, which clipped onto the headset, and checked for what things it, or its linked earpiece, had recorded. "This looks promising…" Void spoke, trying his best to stay calm.

The group played back the video, and watched what had happened, from Stella placing a note on Smiley's pod, to her getting put to sleep with Smiley's hypnosis.

"It's worse than we thought. He purposefully both harmed and kidnapped Stella….who was the first one who knew of him flying away from Samuel… This isn't just for Stella…It's for revenge! We need to get to The X-periment Facility now!" Florette exclaimed, before looking at Void.

Without a moment to lose, Void and Florette both activated their speed rushes. Vibrant flowers bloomed in Florette's hair, while Void's legs were engulfed in mist. Samuel was given temporary roller skate shoes, and the trio rushed off in search of Stella and Smiley.

When the trio arrived at the gates of The X-periment Facility, a figure caught Void's eye. He tapped his square rimmed glasses, causing a zooming effect. The silhouette was illuminated by the dawn sunlight, revealing the figure of Smiley, who was flying slower than normal, to try and not risk dropping Stella.

"Boys and Girls…We got them," Void quietly cheered, before making his view normal. "We need to catch him off guard. Florette, hit him with a weak blast. Just enough to knock him down. I'll catch them. Okay?" Void commanded, for Florette to nervously nod. "3…2…1… Now!" Void called out, before a lime green blast whizzed towards Smiley, attracting his attention.

Smiley quickly turned toward the group and rolled to the side, all the while keeping a grip onto Stella. He looked down at the group, and deactivated his hoverboots, landing on the ground. Smiley spun his hand in a circle, mouthing a spell. "Time Snare." A golden glow flew towards and encased Stella in a time freeze, with the appearance of a yellow sphere, until Smiley broke the spell. Void and Florette both raised their arms at Smiley, readying two glowing spells.

"Smiley, Stop this now! Give Stella back, or we will be forced to attack!" Florette warned, sternly.

"Oh! I see you caught up with me? Ahaha... Why would I quit so easily? Don't worry yourself to the bone, Ivy. I'm not going to harm a little hair on her head! Well, unless she asks for it, that is," Smiley explained, before smirking slightly, as Florette walked towards him, the lime magical spell in her right hand glowing brighter, creating green reflections in Smiley's eyes, as well as dotting his golden hair which had a few misplaced spikes from the wind in the sky. "Ooh! You really think I'm scared of you? That's hilarious! Now, unless you want me to harm someone, maybe even our little sleeping beauty over there..." Smiley tilted his head towards Stella, who was frozen in sleep inside the bubble, like pressing the pause button on a TV.

"...You'll reabsorb those magic attacks. We don't want anyone getting hurt, do we?" Smiley finished, looking at his bright yellow nails while waiting for Florette and Void to respond.

Florette looked at Smiley's eyes, sternly. "Okay, but just this once, and only for Stella. If me, Void or anyone sees you doing anything suspicious again, we won't hesitate," Florette replied, harshly. She and Void both flicked away their attacks while Florette slowly walked backwards to Void. "Now. Free her," Florette ordered, calmly.

"Okay, as you wish," Smiley replied, before removing the bubble, catching Stella with his magic, and placing her in his arms. "Before I give her back, I just want to tell you something...I never play by the rules!" Smiley laughed, before clicking his fingers, and both he and Stella disappeared in a cloud of Smile Gas.

"Smiley!" Samuel yelled, before rushing to Void. "Void, remember when I was wearing a Ministry uniform?"

"Yes. You looked like a little version of Smiley!" Void answered, before looking at Samuel.

"I need that outfit, and an earpiece, or some way to communicate," Samuel listed, visibly rushing.

"Here." Void gave Samuel his Ministry disguise, and a black and orange headset, which blended in with his hair.

Samuel put both these things on, before spinning around once. "Do I look convincing?" Samuel quizzed, before Florette and Void nodded enthusiastically, both with a pair of headsets in.

"Go get her back! We'll come in if you get in trouble, okay?" Void cheered Samuel on, before they looked at each other and nodded, with Samuel running to the entrance to the Smile Facility.

CHAPTER 10:
MISSION INFILTRATE

S amuel reached the large, metal door which marked the true entrance to the real Facility, with the door being locked tight. He looked and saw the keypad on the side of the door. "The code must be Perfection again, I guess," Samuel thought, with a smirk. He typed the code in, before pulling open the door when the light turned green, and entering the facility. He pulled up his surgical mask which was inside the pocket of the lab coat, and walked into one of the hallways, which read 'Procedure Rooms and Chambers' on a bright yellow sign.

The atmosphere was as confusing as ever, with doctors, nurses and more whizzing around, with the same tests going on. Suddenly, a doctor walked up to Samuel, and smiled before asking him a question "Hey, Josh, can you tell me where Cell 2C is?" The doctor questioned Samuel, before he noticed a sign pointing to the opposite hallway, marked 'Cells 2A-3D'

"Sure! I-It's that way!" Samuel replied, trying his best to sound inconspicuous.

"Thanks, J! Stay Smiling!" The doctor smiled, before walking off.

Samuel looked through the crowd of doctors, before seeing two familiar sights, a pair of yellow-tipped, black ponytails, and a tall man, with a signature top hat.

It was Smiley and Hypna, who were bringing a hospital bed down the corridor. "Coming through! We've got a girl here who needs to be wiped!" He called for everyone to get out of the way of the two heads.

"Wiped? As in… mind wiped!" Samuel said in terror, with a nurse looking towards him.

"Of course! She must have seen us committing something, and has to have her memories altered. Do you want to see the procedure?" the nurse asked.

He quickly nodded, wanting to save his friend.

"Okay, they seem to be going to the Mental Alteration Ward. I'm sure they'll be perfectly fine with you peeking in!" the nurse replied, cheerfully, before patting him on the back, and waving as he ran after the two heads.

Smiley and Hypna placed the hospital bed to the side, before bringing the person off the hospital bed, Stella, into a room. Samuel rushed after them, before stopping and knocking on the door, trying his best to act like one of the doctors or nurses. Smiley opened the door, then looked at him with cheer. "Oh! Hey Josh! I thought you were on a break, something about having a rest?" Smiley chatted, seemingly not seeing Samuel's disguise.

"Well…boss, I just wanted to make sure the Ministry had more productivity!" he pretended, acting cheerful.

"You don't need to call me Boss, even though I'm the Head of Morale. Just call me Smiley, okay?"

The doctor smiled, before placing his hat down onto a tool table.

"Do you want to watch?" Smiley asked, politely.

"Sure! I'll just stay here?" He pointed to the side of the room, just behind the tool table which had Smiley's hat placed on it.

"Great! Now, come along now, our patient should wake up any moment now!" Smiley pointed Samuel to the spot where he had picked.

From there, he had a good view of both Smiley and Hypna, as well as Stella. His eye caught a shimmer from under the hat, where a small dark grey dagger was peeking out. He hesitated, then grabbed it. He looked at the dagger for a moment, looking at its ornate yellow grip and black highlights, before placing it in his pocket.

Stella's eyes fluttered open, with her frantically looking around once she noticed where she was. "Smiley! Where am I?" she questioned Smiley, who was in the corner, grabbing some items.

"Well, isn't it obvious, my dear? You're in the Smile Facility! Sorry I had to knock you out, it was the only option."

She tried to pull off the chair that she was placed on, but some shackle-like holders kept her in place. Samuel noticed that her earpiece was still in, and talked to Void and Florette back outside. "I'm in, and I've located Stella. They're trying to alter her memories or something, any ideas on how to reverse anything they do?" he said, before Void blurted out, his voice showing how frightened he was.

"Samuel. Get her out. Now! Once memories are wiped or altered like how Smiley does, they are permanent. The only way to undo the damage is to remove it. But, I believe that only Smiley can use mind magic and manipulation, and you can see how he's going," he commanded.

Samuel paused for a second, a plan in his mind. "I'm going to temporarily cut off Florette's link, so I can connect to Stella's. I think I have a plan," he said, before Florette cheered him on.

"You go, Sammy!" she said.

He pressed a button, before getting Stella's attention by talking normally. "So, Smiley, tell me who she is!" He pretended to be interested in Smiley's spiel while subtly pointing to his ear, getting her to link her earpiece to his hidden headset. "Okay. You're going to pretend like you're fine with going through this, but then I'll say if I could help. Then, I'll unlock you, and get us out of here," he said quietly.

"Sure. What about Smiley and Hypna?" she asked, worried, for him to reply.

"If they try to attack, I'll fight back. If push comes to shove, I can use their own weapons against them." He turned off Stella's link, reconnecting to Florette. "So, she's Stella, the Spirit of Hyperspace?" he said.

"Yes, precisely." Smiley nodded, before going to Stella.

"Wait! Before you do anything...can I help?" He acted like he had volunteered, before she looked at him, and sighed. "Well, it seems I'm stuck." Stella sighed, looking gloomy. "Just...make it quick." She feigned her submission, before Smiley smirked slightly.

He let Samuel in, with a wave of his arm. "Sure. You can make sure she doesn't fight back, Josh..." Smiley moved closer to him, before quickly gripping and ripping off the surgical mask, revealing Samuel's face. "Or, should I call you Samuel? Got you, kid!"

Hypna looked at Samuel with annoyance. "It's you!" Hypna said, before pulling out a sleeping rod, only for Smiley to stop her.

"Hypna. Remember..." Smiley whispered, mouthing something to the head of Kidnapping.

Samuel couldn't read his lips, and instead focused on releasing Stella. "There! Run!" Samuel yelled, causing Stella to fling up, and leave the room in a hurry.

"Hypna. Stay back, he's mine! Get Stella. Now!" Smiley commanded, before pulling out a syringe full of Smile serum from his hat, which he placed upon his head. "Samuel... you shouldn't have come here... It's a shame too.. For you, that is. After all, a new Co-Head would make things a lot easier!" Smiley explained, before running at Samuel. Samuel evaded the attack, landing on his feet. Smiley laughed before throwing his arm out and grabbing Samuel with his levitation. "Hehe...Got you. Now, stay still, we wouldn't want any accidents, would we?" Smiley warned, before bringing the syringe nearer to Samuel's neck.

He tried to move, but there seemed to be no way out. Samuel felt the syringe prick his skin, quickly using a strong kick to push Smiley away, which dropped the man to the floor. He climbed up, before going to practically stab the needle into Samuel, who grabbed the syringe away from him and threw it to the corner of the room, breaking it on impact. Smiley gasped with shock, before he laughed wildly as he noticed the dagger that Samuel had picked up. "Oh, isn't that unfair! Let me fix that!" Smiley burst out, before going to grab the dagger. "This is for Stella," Samuel threatened, under his breath, before throwing his arm forwards, the blade stabbing inside Smiley's waist, then getting pulled out.

Smiley recoiled in pain, clutching his side, before falling to the floor. "And that's why you don't mess with me," Samuel warned, before rubbing off any blood from his wound and putting a plaster on it, as well as wiping the hint of blood off the blade, taking it for himself.

Hypna rushed over to Smiley, checking his vitals. "Just get out of here. I need to heal Smiley," Hypna spat out, before tending to the wound Smiley had sustained.

Samuel rushed through the halls, his thoughts blurring. "Did I just stab Smiley? But, he attacked Stella! But he probably had a reason! But I had self defence!..." Samuel eventually stopped, seeing Stella surrounded by a group of scientists. Samuel ran towards them before grabbing one by the collar. "Leave her alone." Samuel then dropped the scientist on the floor.

Seeing this, the scientists started coming towards Samuel, only to be stopped by Stella. "Deflecto!" Stella yelled, before a sparkling blue beam came from Stella's hand, which knocked all the scientists down.

They turned around, quickly noticing how there were already people crowding around, and a familiar voice echoing through the halls. "He went that way, and he stabbed me! Get him!" The voice, which by this point was obviously Smiley, was full of bitterness and envy.

"Stella, come quickly!" Samuel rushed, before grabbing her arm and dashing up to the large, steel door. "I need to input a code," Samuel requested, and Stella figured out what he meant.

"Got you covered!" Stella replied, for her to put her arms in a x formation. "Protecto Deflectus!" Stella yelled, before a bright blue bubble formed around the two, gifting Samuel some time.

"Perfection," Samuel muttered, under his breath while inputting the code before he noticed that he had misspelled. "I misspelled it!" Samuel moaned, for Stella to start to get worried.

"Samuel... The shield is taking damage. You need to get this in now!" Stella warned, using her strength to keep the shield stable.

Suddenly, Smiley appeared with Hypna, eyes glowing like spotlights, and spinning like a hurricane, his lab coat and shirt stained with blood.

"Samuel. What did you do?" Stella glanced at Samuel, who muttered under his breath.

"I...kinda was forced to...stab him?...he-he..." Samuel mumbled, before a yell came from the doorway.

"Joy Beam!" Smiley yelled, before a golden beam blasted at the shield, getting stronger every moment and cracking the shield quickly. The shield shattered into sparks, with Stella using her deflecting spell again, knocking down some of the scientists while walking forwards. "Samuel, you need to put it in now! I don't think I have much magic energy left!" Stella warned Samuel, urgently.

"Done! Go!" Samuel yelled, as the steel door opened up. Samuel and Stella started to rush out of the Facility, before a gripping feeling pulled on their legs, dragging them to the floor.

Stella looked back to discover that there were a few scientists trying to pull them back in. Samuel went to press the headset, and yelled into the mic. "Help! Scientists are trying to drag us back in, with Smiley helping!" Samuel called for help, before the sound of a door being swung open came from the top of the stairs. Void and Florette stood at the top, illuminated by the sun, before charging two spells in their grasp.

"Nature's fury!" Florette yelled, launching a green, shimmering mist, while Void threw his voice down the stairwell.

"Midnight slash!" He threw his hand forward, unleashing a flurry of amber slices.

The two spirits blasted the spells rapidly until only Stella, Samuel and Smiley remained.

"Smiles. Stop!" Florette yelled, for Smiley to ignore her command, and continued towards Samuel, stepping over the collapsed scientists.

"What happened to you? You look like something stabbed you!" Void noticed Smiley's bloodstained clothing, before Smiley looked up to Void and sharply nodded.

"Yes. I got stabbed by a certain boy!" Smiley yelled, pointing at Samuel with rage.

"Self defence?" Void asked Samuel, for him to nod. "I see." Void finished speaking, before grabbing Samuel, with Florette grabbing Stella.

"Sorry Smiles. But, until you find some way to fix this, you're not welcome in my home," Stella threatened, with Void and Florette agreeing with theirs too.

Void, Florette, Samuel and Stella all left, before shutting the door behind them, and walked out of the Facility.

Smiley looked down at Hypna, who was trying to get off the floor, while being dusted with glimmering sparks. "Hypna, Let's do it. If they hate me now, then they'll scream when they see what will happen because of this!" Smiley laughed, before healing all the scientists and Hypna, helping them up.

The group of people sat down at the boundary, checking for any wounds on Stella or Samuel. They looked at the bandages on both Stella and Samuel, which were on the same side. "Samuel, did Smiley inject you with anything?" Void asked.

Samuel shook his head in response. "He got me with a needle, but I kicked him off me before he could press down on the plunger," Samuel explained, with a sarcastic face. "Still hurts, though." Samuel smiled a bit, before looking at Florette. "It's better than what Smiley got!" Samuel joked, for the group to laugh in response. Samuel took off the lab coat and put his trousers and trainers back on, rescuing them with his belt. He got himself up, helping Stella up with him.

"We'll have to get the others. Void, take Samuel and Stella to Fawnia's and stay there until I return; I'm rounding all the spirits up. They need to know," Florette commanded.

Void nodded sharply and got up. "I'll meet you two there!" Stella saluted slightly, before pressing her hoverboots, her armour forming onto her body before soaring into the cyan sky, and blasting off towards the large, gothic palace. Void flicked his hand, before Samuel gained wheels on his shoes, and Void's eyes started glowing.

"I'll go the slowest I can, so you can catch up." Void ran forwards, but it was more of a fast run then what Samuel had seen a day or so before. Samuel quickly caught up with the shadowy man, before Void looked at Samuel with a gleam in his eye. "Hey, Samuel. Did you get him for me?" Void asked mischievously.

"What do you..." Samuel started to ask, before getting what Void meant. "Oh!... Yeah, I got him good! He's probably embarrassed that he got knocked to the floor and stabbed by a 16 year old!" Samuel chuckled, before noticing that they were at the front of the palace, stopping in their tracks. The entrance was tall and intricate, with leaves and ivy patterned into the design.

The pillars were made of stone, with a shimmer of marble at the base, and flower pots with fake brambles hanging from the window ledges. "Where's Stella? She should be–" A blue beam cut him off, before Stella appeared with her eyes closed.

"See? Told you I'd...beat...you." Stella started to rub her supposed victory in, before noticing that Void and Samuel had beaten her to Fawnia's. She rolled her eyes, before standing beside the man.

"Okay, we're meeting the true ruler of Magic Land, not that fake Minister. Trust me, don't mess with Fawnia," Void forewarned Samuel, before walking towards the door and knocking on it.

"She's nice though. Just, don't mention…them." Void noticed that there was a slight mark on his shoulder pad. "Repairio," Void whispered under his breath, before the mark was fixed.

The door opened, revealing a woman draped in a long, grey cape. Her hair was dark, seemingly going on to her back. Her eyes were azure, and always seemed to show a blend of wisdom and kindness. She looked at Void, and smiled happily. "Greetings again, Void. I see you've brought guests!" The lady curtsied slightly, before Samuel awkwardly bowed. "I am Fawnia, the Queen of Magic Land! Don't listen to that lot's babbling about a Minister, I'm still the one that sits on the throne." With her hand gripped on her cloak, she spun on the spot and started to walk. As she did, however, her crown fell off her head and started to plummet down. Samuel rapidly caught it, just as Fawnia noticed its absence. She turned around to see Samuel holding it with relief on his face. "And why are you holding my crown? Were you planning to steal it!" she asked, before he stood up in shock.

"It slipped off your head, and I didn't want it to break, since it seems very valuable," he replied.

Fawnia picked it with her levitation and nestled it back in her hair. "Very well then. Let us continue." Fawnia sighed, before turning around and walking along, with the trio following the royal. While they walked, Void and Stella sternly stared at Samuel.

"Why did you do that, Samuel? She now probably thinks you're strange!"

"Her crown could've been damaged! What was I supposed to do, let it fall?!"

They stared at each other, both not backing down. Stella pushed herself between them, her sight on both.

"We're in the presence of a royal spirit here, and you start to argue? Seriously? Even Smiley has more control than that!"

"Stella, don't you even MENTION him at this moment! You of all people know what he did!" he yelled, alerting Fawnia.

"What are you three squabbling about?" she asked. All three stared at her with blank expressions, before quickly stopping their argument.

"Look, Florette is rounding up every spirit here for an emergency meeting. We have a rogue spirit," Void explained, causing Fawnia to gasp in shock.

"A rogue spirit? That sounds dangerous! Why did you bring them here?" the Queen asked.

"The kid's called Samuel, and he's just a kid, and Stella's been weakened," Void answered. He looked back towards the door, as he had noticed a faint twinkling sound outside, a sign of teleportation. "They're here," he said. He signalled Samuel, Stella and Fawnia to the great hall. The Queen rushed, holding up her cloak, before arriving in a grand, intricate room.

It had beautiful stained-glass windows, and smooth marble floors. In the centre of the ceiling, a large chandelier shone down, shimmering with crystals, which had colours that correlated to the colours of the most popular rides of the park. Yellow for The Perfector, Amber for Abyss, Lime for D3M0N, Rose for Curse, Violet for Hyperspace, and so on.

Fawnia flicked her hand, before multiple chairs, and three long benches appeared from thin air. "Take a seat on one of the bench seats." Fawnia spoke softly, for Samuel and Stella to listen, and sit down on two seats that were next to each other. They both looked to the left, as the sound of creaking and muttering rumbled through the hall.

CHAPTER 11:
EMERGENCY MEETING

T he doors opened as Florette, Void, Levi and about 20 other people walked into the hall, and in confusion, sat down.

"You are probably wondering why we have called you here today. Well, the reason is of a drastic nature. There... is a rogue spirit in this park," Florette announced, a lime orb levitating in front of her mouth and acting like a microphone. A gasp of confusion spread across the spirits like a fever, before one of the spirits put her hand up. She was a young girl, possibly 13, with a pair of curled pigtails that were split between a deep shade of orange, and a mix of yellow and black. She was wearing a dark grey dress, which was decorated with hints of both orange and yellow in parts like the skirt or the large bow tying it all together. Samuel noticed that the bow was glowing and dimming like a heartbeat, almost like it was her pulse itself.

"Mesmerith?" Florette asked.

Upon being called on, the girl stood up. "I have to ask, Who is this rogue spirit?" Mesmerith questioned Florette with her head tilted, as her eyes, which also matched the same duality pattern as her hair, spun in opposite directions.

Florette sighed, before commanding loudly through the voice enhancer spell. "Look around. Which spirit is not with us?" Florette asked, with a slight hint of sadness in her tone.

A worried murmur spread across the hall, until two spirits: Levi, and a girl with a silver, curly hairstyle, with a blue band around her neck, a futuristic target symbol floating just below it, stood up. "Florette..." The girl spoke quietly, in a nervous tone.

"Yes, Defendia, what is it?" Florette spoke for Levi to reply.

"Where's that yellow person that I served a few days ago?" Levi questioned, for Defendia to look at Levi, quickly adding on to his statement.

"Where's that Smiley person? I haven't seen him all day, and he usually comes around to grab something to eat from Cosmic Bites, or to make sure some technology is up to date with Levi..." Defendia asked.

Florette started to silently cry, the green orb fading away. Stella and Samuel looked at each other before nodding and rushing towards the front of the hall, where Void, Florette and Fawnia were sitting.

Samuel saw a microphone on the table, and picked it up, as well as Stella activating the voice amplifying spell.

"Vocalis Increase," Stella whispered before a blue haze rested in front of her mouth. "Look. We have a rogue spirit, and you just named him. Well done, you just made Florette cry!" Stella informed the spirits, causing everyone to be shocked.

"It's true. He kidnapped Stella, nearly erased her memories, and nearly got me too. Here's proof!" Samuel spoke into the microphone, before Stella got Void to bring out two things – the earpiece, and some CCTV footage that Florette gave to them, which Smiley didn't get the chance to tamper with before taking Stella, downloaded into a USB. Stella clicked her fingers, before a blue orb appeared and secured the earpiece and USB into itself, and flew up into the air. Fawnia dimmed the lights, and the video played, using a mix of CCTV footage, and Stella's view.

The video played, showing Stella entering the guest bedroom, before placing the note into Smiley's pod then locking the door and going to leave. The footage then changed angles, which showed Smiley reading the note in the pod and teleporting behind the corner, leaving the door open.

He threw the note with a flick of magic and went into hiding again. He then pulled out one of his syringes, and teleported behind the doorway, striking Stella when she walked into him and hypnotising her to sleep, leaving the note on Stella's pod, and rushing off with Stella in hand. The clip ended, with the lights turning on again, and the orb going dim, but still hovering, if Stella ever needed it again.

"You see? He's gone crazy!" Stella yelled.

Void stared at her with a disapproving look, before shaking his head. "Stella. He was always crazy! This is just him going off the rails...but this is probably tame...Just throwing it out there," Void pointed out, before sipping on a bottle of Zestie.

The room went silent for a minute, before a burst of laughter echoed around. "Hmmhmmhmm... I feel my ears burning... who's talking about me?"

Someone spoke, the voice being projected from every side of the hall. Suddenly before everyone's eyes, the orb turned yellow, and projected something no one wanted to see. The image of Smiley phased and fluttered, before setting still.

"Hello again. Was she talking about me? Or was it Samuel over here!" Smiley greeted everyone, before looking down at the coasters. "Oh my! Are you hosting a little meeting? You thought that me being me was too dangerous! How...exciting!" Smiley chuckled, before smiling creepily, staring at the spirits clustered together. "Well, I guess now I'm here, I have to say my own side of the story! Aha!" Smiley explained, his face lit up for a moment. "I have a better idea...why not tell you...face to face? Hahaha!" Smiley laughed, before the orb popped, and Stella quickly grabbed the USB and earpiece.

The entire hall was in a shocked silence, before there was a knock at the great hall door. Florette and Fawnia looked anxious, before casting a protection spell on the spirits and Samuel. "Protecto Deflectus," they both incanted, before the doors opened to reveal the single spirit that was not invited. Smiley. He had changed from his normal doctor's attire to something more formal. His hat had a small tweak, being that there was now a small bow made of ribbon on the back, as well as his normal tailed lab coat had been replaced with a black tailcoat, similar to Voids, with a pale yellow shirt underneath. He still had his signature bowtie and hover boots, but his trousers were instead plain black, and were tucked in. He also had his swirled goggles back, and was holding a cane, with an almost black base which was painted with grey crossed lines that looked like the tracks of The Perfector. For a grip, the cane had a yellow orb, an ink black swirl circled from top to bottom.

"Hello everyone. It appears there may have been a mistake? I wasn't invited to this little... gathering," Smiley exclaimed, walking though the aisle of people.

"What do you want from us, creep?" A spirit with long, grey and yellow streaked hair and orange eyes stared at Smiley with venom, his face in a scowl. He was wearing a dark grey hoodie, with the logo of his ride, Mindbreaker, or as The Ministry called it, Project 17. The logo was a white swirl, with hints of black, yellow and orange. He was also wearing a pair of night black pants and fire orange trainers.

"Oh. I thought you would be nicer to me, 17," Smiley spoke, flicking the spirit's chin.

"My name isn't 17! It's Twister!" Twister yelled, before being levitated towards Smiley's height, like pulling on a yo-yo.

"I don't care. You remember what would happen if you disrespected me, 17."

Twister looked at Smiley with a face full of fear.

Suddenly, Smiley's hand started to spark with golden magic, with two words mouthed: "Soul Taint." Smiley laughed slightly, as Twister started screaming in agony, a yellow glow going towards Twister's chest, where his soul would be.

"Smiley! STOP!" Fawnia yelled, with her long, elegant staff pointing at Smiley, charging up a blast. Smiley looked at the staff, which was made of gold, with a bright, glowing pink orb entrapped within a shimmering circle. "Drop him. NOW!" Fawnia commanded, before Smiley chuckled quietly, and followed her order, dropping Twister to the floor with a thud. Twister was whimpering in pain, a slight golden glow wisping from his eyes.

"Now. If no one will speak, I will tell MY side of the story." Smiley broke the silence and started slowly walking in front of the crowd of spirits.

He thrust his hand holding the cane into the air, before the orb glowed like a wand. A yellow glowing beam came out of the cane, before creating a yellow screen, onto which multiple things were projected: The flight between Samuel and Smiley, Samuel infiltrating the Smile Facility under the disguise of a scientist, and finally Smiley getting stabbed. "You see? These people have taken my privacy, spied on me, lied, used identities and assaulted me, then they say I'm the bad guy here for getting some karma? I wasn't even trying to hurt her. You can change anyone's memories surprisingly easily, even create fake ones, just by making someone believe or think something different! Yet I'm now the evil guy, and they're amazing superheroes!" Smiley ranted, before Void butted in.

"Smiles. Explain why you tried to corrupt his soul there!" Void exclaimed, for Smiley to calmly reply.

"I wasn't. I was only aiming to make him learn a lesson. Punishment. If you didn't see, I quickly removed any corruption when I dropped him." He looked at the gathered spirits, who were looking both at Void and Smiley in confusion. "Who do you believe? The people who tried to cover up stabbing someone, or the person who was stabbed?" Smiley asked, before everyone in the audience murmured for a minute.

Samuel walked up to Smiley, talking to him in a serious tone. "I know this is one of your schemes, Smiley. We all do. Have your fun, but whatever you're doing will be stopped." Samuel threatened.

Smiley collapsed in a fit of laughter, tiny tears falling down his cheeks. "Hahahah! Oh Sammy, you have got to be joking with me! Do you really believe that I'd say what I have planned? No! I'm not that stupid, kid. Anyways, the votes...are in." Smiley laughed, before taking off his hat, and multiple multi coloured orbs went into the air. "Let's see who won..." Smiley explained, before the orbs sorted themselves into the two colours: yellow and green. The spirits all gasped in shock. There were three more yellow then green orbs. "Hahaha! Looks like I won! I would just LOVE to stay and chat about things, but I have to go. Things to do, people to see! Bye." Smiley chuckled in victory, before tapping his cane to the floor and vanishing into thin air.

"We lost?!" Florette yelled, before noticing that there was a note on the floor where Smiley had disappeared. "Everyone, You are dismissed. Stay safe, alright?"

Fawnia dismissed all the spirits to their homes, including Twister, who was now okay, although he was clutching his chest. There, however, were multiple spirits who didn't leave.

Samuel noticed Sally, who spotted him too, and waved happily. "Samuel!" Sally cheered, for Samuel to smile back at her. "Samuel, these are the rest of the core group: Blaze, The Spirit of Wildfire, and Nebulus, The spirit of Andromeda." Fawnia said.

Blaze was a short man with dark brown skin and bright red, slitted eyes. He had sharp teeth, and spiked and untamed, flamelike hair. His clothing was wild, almost primal, with rips, tears and burn marks dotted around. There was also what looked like bracelets made of bark and wood wrapped on his arms. "Hey, dude. Nice to meet ya!" Blaze shook Samuel's hand, slightly scratching it with his sharp nails.

Nebulus, however, was the opposite. He wore a grey, technological patterned shirt, with black, hexagonal patterned pants. A green, scaled pattern was on his forehead, and his ears curved to a point. His eyes were a light shade of green, paired with a pale, almost cream yellow, making them look like an alien in disguise. "Greetings. I see you're the teen who entered our land? I am Nebulus." Nebulus calmly introduced himself, before stepping back.

"Hey guys. There's a note here…" Void spoke. He picked up the note, and read it aloud. "Hey there. If you're reading this, you probably know I'm planning something. Don't worry your heads. I'll start in a few hours. Just know that what is going on…will change things. Have fun." Void put the note into his pocket. "We have some time. Good. We need to prepare our defences, just in case. Florette, lock down the potions and spells in your Crypt; Fawnia, you secure yours. Stella, go with Nebulus and make sure that the areas are safe, except for The X-periment Facility. Blaze and I will go and help the rest of the spirits with their lockdowns and safety prep. Samuel… you have the most dangerous task of them all. Tell Stella to give you the stealth tech. We need to make sure that Smiley isn't doing anything dangerous. Don't get caught, and report back to us what has happened," Void commanded. Most of the spirits nodded, and ran off on their activities. Stella stayed, and gave Samuel a pair of greyish gloves, a pair of technological boots, and another headset. Samuel put them all on, and activated them. The suit was a stealth-based design, mainly dark grey and black, with a dark blue visor.

"Listen, Samuel. We won't be able to talk to you much on this mission, to avoid the risk of you getting caught. This suit is similar to Stella's flight suit, but it has a more lightweight design, at the cost of durability. Basically, it can take less damage. Also, you can muffle your footsteps and noises and go invisible. You can even climb on surfaces using those grips on the gloves. Your visor will display any details you need. Now, good luck out there!" Void explained, before the two people split up, rushing towards opposite directions of the park.

CHAPTER 12:
TURNING INTO TERROR

Samuel rushed along the paths like a blink, thanks to the technology of the suit. He slowed himself down, soon stopping in his tracks. As he planned, he was in front of the still intimidating fence. "I'm at The X-periment Facility. I need to make sure that Smiley doesn't do anything bad," he thought to himself, with data appearing on his visor. "Scan for life," Samuel commanded the suit's technology. A teal beam swept through the visor, and scanned the environment. His vision was then filled with pulsing, blue beams that revealed the figures of multiple people in the Smile Facility. He scanned through the groups of people, before seeing a figure hiding behind the pits of The Perfector. Samuel turned off the vision, before pressing a button on his headset, and feeling a warm feeling, like warm water, wash over him, turning rapidly into a cool, normal feeling.

He looked at his hands, but instead he saw the floor, which was concrete, with an orange streak running through. Samuel smiled, then looked around, before seeing an orange, glowing mass inside the pit of The Perfector. Samuel pressed a button, before the system was looking at the mass. "Computer, Information," Samuel commanded, for a voice to reply. "Name: Dr Smiley Miles.

THE SECRET OF THE SMILE

Age: 25." Samuel turned off the reply, and locked Smiley into the tracker. "Got you!" Samuel pumped himself up, before seeing the figure of Smiley get out of the pit, brushing his tailcoat for any dust, then walking into the Smile Facility. Samuel laughed, before running towards the Facility, and noticing that people could hear him. Samuel pressed another button, for a bright, cyan glow to cover his body, then dim away to shimmers, leaving nothing. Samuel walked through the doorway and rushed down the circular stairwell, with Smiley opening the code-locked steel door. Samuel flashed through, tumbling Smiley over, who jolted with surprise.

"Who was that? That hurt!" Smiley groaned. He climbed back up to his feet, and walked right past Samuel, barely an inch from brushing against him. Samuel followed Smiley, before he walked into the entrance of a crowded hallway. He quickly clicked his fingers and his hat disappeared into thin air. Smiley laughed, before walking into the crowd. The tracker beeped and started malfunctioning, unable to stay on him.

"Ugh. Suit, stop tracking and start magnetism!" Samuel spoke into the headset, before a tight feeling came on his palms and feet.

Samuel placed his hands onto the wall, before slowly climbing up, then placing his hands and feet on the ceiling, his body now in a crawling position. "Woah..." Samuel thought, before quickly crawling along the ceiling, turning off the magnetism after a few seconds. He fell to the floor and crouched on impact which cushioned his fall with little to no pain. He looked around, before seeing the figure of Hypna walk into a room. Samuel ran along the hallway, before stopping at the room. He crouched down, looking into the room through a window. There was a person in a dentist chair, secured with shackles. Hypna was looking puzzled, staring at a heart rate monitor-like device. The device instead was a joy rate monitor –there was a sign saying this on the side – as well as a bright yellow line on the display. The line was practically flatline. "She's not smiling!" Hypna talked to herself, before calling someone on her phone. "Hey, I need help at room

140. We got a code blue," Hypna messaged, before a male voice came through the phone, quickly ending the call.

After a minute or two, a black-cloaked figure walked through the hall and stopped at the door. A white-sleeved arm knocked at the door, before being let in, the door locking behind them. The figure pulled down the hood, revealing a familiar face. Smiley. He was talking to Hypna about what was going on, with a genuine-looking smile on his face. "So, this subject will not smile?" Smiley asked.

Hypna nodded cheerfully in reply. "Yes! I tried everything, but she did not even grin!"

Smiley looked at the subject, a lady with ginger hair and blue eyes, who stared back at him, with pleading sighs.

"W-why am I here?" The lady sobbed, making Smiley look at Hypna.

"What shall we do? We can't let her escape, of course, and we do need more resources..." Smiley asked, in thought.

"We'll have to discard her. After all, she won't smile, it seems," Hypna answered, for Smiley to look at her, then the subject, then down at his waist.

A yellow gun, with black highlights, and a grey barrel, which looked twistable, was in a holder. He looked at the woman, who begged for her captors to let her go, waves of tears running down her cheeks.

"Please! Let me go! I've done NOTHING wrong! I have a family, Mister!"

Smiley smirked, before tightly grabbing the grip. "Hehehe... Sorry, miss. It's just business." Smiley flicked a switch with his thumb, before the barrel sharply twisted right and locked in place with a click, with a small LED bulb on the gun's back shining red, with only him and anyone behind his back being able to see. He laughed darkly, before aiming the gun at the subject's head. "Red. Care to guess what it symbolises?" Smiley asked, rhetorically.

The subject started going pale at the sight of the gun aimed towards her. "Please don't be–" The woman didn't even have time to finish her sentence before the gun's trigger was pulled.

A loud popping sound, similar to the sound of a firework, bombarded Samuel's ears. His ears were ringing, muffling what he could hear. When Samuel opened his eyes, he was panged with horror at the sight. The subject's body was sprawled and limp on the chair, the subject's face frozen, eyes misted, and a large, crimson wound straight in between, with more of the crimson blood splashed around the area.

"Red means bullets. You lost!" Smiley mocked, before placing the gun back into its holder.

Samuel stumbled back and gasped, not noticing that the invisibility was off. "Smiley... I gotta get out of here quickly!" Samuel stopped the recording and rushed out, alerting the scientists to his presence.

"A spy! Get them!" a nurse yelled, the yell rumbling around the hallways. A swarm of scientists chased after him, trying to incapacitate him. Samuel quickly ran into a closet, hearing the footsteps thunder by, like a stampede of animals. After a minute the rush stopped, and Samuel left the closet, dashing for where he thought the exit was.

Suddenly, a familiar face ran in from another corridor and bumped into him. It was Smiley, but his white lab coat which was usually unbuttoned, allowing people to see his yellow t-shirt underneath, had been cleaned and buttoned up. "Samuel! You need to get out of here! Hypna's lost her marbles...again...and is trying to hurt you!" Smiley warned, his voice full of supposed fear and anxiety.

"Why should I believe you, Smiles? I know what you did back there. You're just as bad as her!" Samuel yelled, for Smiley's face to twist into bitter annoyance for a second, only for him to take a deep breath and look Samuel dead in the eyes.

"Samuel. I'm not lying. Would I lie?" Smiley asked, in a flat tone, for Samuel to stare back.

"Yes. Yes, you would," Samuel replied honestly, before the sound of frantic footsteps clicked from the hallway Samuel had just come from, with Hypna skidding to the end of the hall with her yellow sleep rod in hand.

"I'm not being stopped now!" Hypna yelled and started sprinting towards Samuel, throwing him against the wall, raising her arm to strike.

"Aghh!" Samuel yelled, before Smiley, whose eyes were glowing and spinning, quickly pulled Hypna off him and threw her to the other side. Smiley rushed up to Hypna, before grabbing her by the arm, throwing the stun rod to the end of the hallway. Smiley was then suddenly thrown to the side, tumbling to the floor, struggling to get up.

Smiley stood back up, to see Hypna grabbing Samuel, trying to push him to the floor, with Samuel doing the same to her. Hypna threw Samuel to the floor, also falling down herself, leaving Smiley standing up in front of them. Hypna and Samuel both started to get up, before Smiley looked at both of them, and made his choice. Smiley walked over to Hypna and helped her up, then pulled out his gun, leaving Samuel on the floor.

"Smiley. I know what you did, I saw it. You...killed that woman. This won't be the end!" Samuel threatened, before Smiley flicked the gun into 'Syringe' mode, with Samuel finally seeing why Smiley had buttoned up his lab coat. The subject's blood had stained his clothing from the killing blow, and with his almost constant smiling, he looked like a deranged maniac.

"I'm sorry, Samuel. You should've left when I said. Looks like I'm going to have to force you," Smiley explained, loading the gun with a syringe with the same transparent liquid that Samuel was first injected with, turning the red light into a yellow hue.

Samuel regained his thoughts, then realised what to do. "I'm sorry too," Samuel spoke, for Smiley to look confused for a moment.

"What do you mean?" Smiley and Hypna asked.

Samuel laughed, putting a hand to his headset. "You guys just lost a victim," Samuel mocked them, before activating the suit's repair, healing, speed and invisibility modes all at once, before speeding away from the two people. Samuel ran behind a corner, before panting for breath. He was exhausted, but forced himself to climb up onto a surrounding building, slumping down to the floor shortly after shutting off all devices except repairing, healing and invisibility. Samuel allowed himself to relax and rest, the sun shining warmly on his skin. After a minute, he remembered why he was sent there. Samuel sat up, before creating a screen and a keyboard out of holograms. He tapped and scrolled on a few buttons before 'Void. Watch this and get back to Fawnia's. Now!' appeared on screen, and he sent him the recording of what had happened. After a few moments, the message was sent, and Samuel lay back against a vent, allowing himself and the suit to heal.

Meanwhile, Void and Blaze had finished helping the spirits, who were all safely inside their homes, with technology, from magic proofing to lock systems, in place. The two spirits were about to rendezvous back at Fawnia's Palace, before a dark, echoed 'bing!' came from Void's black and orange phone. He picked it up and checked what the sound was notifying, only to see a video and a text. He checked what they were, for Blaze to stare, inquisitively. "What's up, Shadows?" Blaze asked Void, who replied calmly.

"One, stop calling me Shadows. Two, it's a text from Samuel via the stealth suit." Void stared at what the text contained, then spotted the video.

"Huh, a recording. Let's watch it!" Blaze chipped in, for Void to nod.

The two men saw a small bench nearby, and both sat on it and watched the video on the phone. After the video, both spirits were in total shock.

"Oh my god. Smiley killed someone. He MURDERED someone!" Blaze gasped, before looking at Void, who was as pale as a ghost.

"This is just the start. He said something big is going to happen in a few hours on the note. We need to alert the others. We have a murderous, rogue spirit in the park," Void stuttered, in shock, before shaking his head and running full speed towards Fawnia's Palace, with Blaze flying alongside Void, a slight smoke trailing behind both spirits. They reached the palace and rushed in, spooking Fawnia.

"Ah! Why are you two in such a hurry? I just finished locking down the potions and spells! What is wrong?"

Void rushed around, looking for the rest of the spirits. "Where are they?" Void yelled, for Fawnia to move her hand in a swaying movement, which Void knew meant to calm down. Void took a deep breath, before wiping the beads of sweat from his brow. "It's gotten worse. Smiley...killed someone. He shot them in the head! He's gone too far!" Void explained, for Fawnia to go stiff.

"I had a vision that something even worse is going to happen. I feel like there is going to be more death...and that Smiley is now too untrustworthy. Go and warn Samuel!" Fawnia forewarned, before looking worried and rushing away.

Void typed a text to the rest of the group using his phone. "Guys, Fawnia believes that there are going to be more deaths. Keep safe, and come back ASAP." A slight bing sound played as Void pressed the send button, before the text was sent to everyone.

CHAPTER 13:
MURDER AND MINISTERS

Samuel woke up and opened his eyes, only to remember why he was here. "Silly me, I fell asleep!" Samuel sat himself up and checked the time. "Two hours? Seriously!" Samuel then noticed that there was an unread message on his suit. "Computer, open message," Samuel commanded, before the message opened, with Samuel reading it quickly after. "More death and an untrustworthy Smiley? Thanks, V." Samuel thought for a moment, before glancing down and spotting Hypna walking out of the Smile Facility with a familiar figure, their cloak hanging on their shoulders and draping down.

Samuel activated the invisibility, silencing and defence abilities, before jumping off the building and quickly landing on his feet, luckily only sustaining a minor ache for a moment. Samuel rushed towards the group, but still kept a distance, just enough to be able to hear them.

"It's a great day isn't it, Your Joyness?" Hypna asked, happily.

"It is quite a lovely day, dear, though you can call me Eliza at the moment. We're having a break, remember?" Eliza smiled before unclipping a clip on her cloak and taking it off and placing it on the floor, shortly before lying down on it, relaxing in the sunshine. The duo lay down and sunbathed, while watching the clouds for a few minutes, before a buzz came from the Minister's watch, causing her to see what the buzz was notifying. "Great. Gary wants another meeting about the lack of a Head of Morale," the Minister complained, before sitting up and clipping her cloak back on. "We should do this more often, Hypna!"

Hypna nodded, before stopping the Minister from walking off. "I just wanted to say that it has been amazing. Goodbye," Hypna spoke, quietly.

"What do you mean, Hypna. We're both going to the meeting, right?" the Minister asked, shaken slightly. A loud thud came from behind the two girls, the Minister flinching slightly in shock. Just as her robotic hand switched to a laser blaster, a sharpened dagger was plunged directly into her chest. The Minister screamed in agony, her face frozen in pure pain and fear.

After a few moments, the bloodstained dagger was then ripped out from her chest, scarlet splashes flying out and staining both the killer and Hypna's clothing, with the knife glistening with shades of red from the blood. The Minister's face went blank as she fell to the floor, shades of crimson and scarlet flowing out from the wound, and dripping from the dagger. It was done.

"Hehehe...That was great." The killer laughed, with a robotic voice coming from a mask they were wearing, then looking at Hypna, who was already starting to clean up the blood.

"Why did you choose the most...messy...option? This is going to take forever to clean!" Hypna complained, for the murderer to wave their hand, before the blood was cleaned up and combined into a pulsating, shaking, hovering blood red orb.

"Luckily for me, that fool Tom made lunch again. His fingerprints are on the knife!" The cloaked figure laughed psychotically, with the dead Minister being levitated away with yellow shimmers.

The body was dumped under one of the tracks, before a broken cart was placed over the body, and the orb splashed around the area, replacing the blood, with splashes of blood on both Hypna and the killer's clothes joining with the rest, cleaning the clothing. Samuel had an idea who this killer was, but was determined to find out either way. He walked slightly closer and sighed, knowing his noises were silenced by the suit. "Computer. Identify the cloaked figure," Samuel commanded, which confirmed his fears. Smiley. The computer locked its sights onto the cloaked figure, who was hacking into the CCTV cameras.

"Got it. Now, let's go. We've got a title to claim. Hehehe!" The figure chuckled, before taking Hypna by the hand and disappearing into glowing yellow shimmers. The knife was placed on the floor, as if it had been discarded. Samuel allowed himself to become visible again, before going to check the pulse of the Minister, discovering that she had been dead for ten minutes.

Samuel kept in his rage and shock, quickly taking a picture with the suit's camera and rushing off, hearing frantic footsteps thundering from the entrance of The Facility. Again everything blurred around him, and his heart pounded out of his chest. He started to panic, before he realised that he was in front of Fawnia's Palace.

He fell to the floor in a state of panic and confusion for what he could think was a minute, before feeling a hand on his shoulder. Stella and Void were looking at him, worried. "What's wrong with him... Samuel! Can you hear us? You just fell onto the floor, and started breaking down," Void said in panic, with Stella trying to sit the boy up.

"I saw someone get stabbed in the chest..." he stuttered, shivering like he was cold.

"This is insane! Who was stabbed?" Stella asked, helping the boy to his feet.

"Eliza...The Minister," he responded, before going quiet. Stella helped Samuel inside the palace, while Void went to gather the other spirits.

The rest of the spirits sat down with the direction of their friend, while Samuel was lying on the table to regain his thoughts. The galactic girl recounted what had happened, while Void occasionally butted in with a correction. "The Minister's dead? Finally I can get my power back!"

Fawnia became excited, but calmed down after noticing how the attention was on her.

"Yes, but Smiley, our most likely culprit, was closest to Eliza in rank. Just a few steps down. Void, you know about the Ministry from experience. How's this stuff work?" Stella asked, before Void looked up from his watch.

"I was around during the control of the previous Minister, so I experienced the transition between him and Eliza. When a minister steps down or dies, an election begins. Each of the heads will propose their plans to the drones down below. Whoever is the most popular wins. Your run-of-the-mill election, if it was fair. Most of the time there was a lot of...corruption. People would fake votes, or slander the other contestants. Since Smiley—who we know is highly revered in both the Ministry and the Heads of Insanity themselves—is also in the running, this could be some cause for concern," he said. A silence rang around the room, showing the lack of understanding of everyone else.

"Since nobody seems to understand, I'll explain it myself. It's worrying because of their behaviour. Smiley is most likely going to use his influence over Perfection to rig the system in his favour. That, along with Hypna's talent to lie and twist narratives, means that this would be a hole-in-one for him. In fact, if we apply logic to this predicament, it could mean that we just uncovered an assassination," he speculated, his face blank and cold.

Fawnia and Florette nodded at each other, and the others followed suit. They needed to stop Smiley, whether he gets the role or not.

"Do you have anything that could help our problem?" Florette asked, looking across the table towards Fawnia, who was flicking through a book. She landed on a page, tracing her finger along the words.

"There are a few options. Old-fashioned fighting is one, but I'm sure nobody wants to rush straight into people who know literal brainwashing. We could use enchantments, but draining enchantments will sap the energy of all magic and magic users around it, which would harm us as much as them. Multiplying sounds good, until you realise that if the item is lost or snatched, the battle could quickly turn into our downfall." The queen's face slowly turned sour.

"There is one spell we can use, but it is a...last resort," Florette said, thinking of how to phrase what she was about to say.

"There is a powerful curse called the Curse of Atonement. It reverts any magical entity's power back to how it should always be, and returns any stolen power, enchantments or anything else of the like away from the target. There is a downside, from which it gets its name...the target is trapped in a magical prison where they cannot escape from. While in this prison, the entity can either stay in the purgatory like soul realm, or watch the world go by, unable to speak, talk or move. It is a very demanding spell, so we would only have one shot. That's why it has rarely been used. It is a fate worse than death."

Void glared down to the floor. "No. We are not putting anyone through that torture again! Nobody sees the reason he's doing this, do you?!"

"It would be the only way to stop Smiley!" She was going to continue, but she was stopped mid sentence by Void harshly standing up, with his eyes glowing brightly.

"He's doing this because of you! When the killings happened, nobody tried to see his side of the story or see him as anything less than guilty. He may have even kept that in his mind until he died! Yeah sure, he's back, but don't you think there could be some underlying motive? I'm not going to put my brother through a decade of torture again!" Void screamed his heart out. He twisted around to look at Fawnia, his eyes piercing like daggers. "We cannot use that spell! Get some enhancers and weakeners or something, but not that spell!" Void commanded, quickly walking to the door of the dining room.

He glared venomously at Florette one more time, before walking out of the room, slamming the door behind him.

"Wow. You made Void snap. Congratulations!" Nebulus and Blaze pointed out, before going on their phones.

Florette sighed, putting her head on the table. She looked like she was about to cry, but she withdrew it, and instead just sat in silence.

"Great. Another argument. Trust me, Samuel, if we had five pounds for every time those two argued, we'd be rich!" Sally chuckled, before being silenced by Fawnia.

"Samuel, go and see what's wrong with Void. He might need someone...unbiased to talk to right now. Venting, you know?"

Samuel nodded, before he calmly exited the room, following Void's footsteps.

Samuel wandered for what felt like hours, before he saw multiple empty corridors, and what seemed to be a bricked-up entrance of some sort. "This place used to be a drop ride, didn't it?" Samuel remembered, thinking of the old ride, Curse. He looked towards the wall, noticing a row of intricate paintings with plaques below them. The first painting was a landscape painting of a scene: a group of furious townspeople, holding torches in the air. In front of the crowd was a bonfire, with a woman tied to a stake in it. "This is a Witch Trial. How old is this painting?" Samuel wondered, his view drawn to the metal plate below the artwork.

"This painting is of the Oakwood Palace's most famous Witch Trial, and the basis of the legend of the Oakwood Curse. The accused was a peasant girl. Upon her execution, she screamed a curse upon the Palace and the area around it. The curse made it so the land was doomed to misery and bad luck. However, a worse fate was not uncovered until later. Those who looked upon the full moon from inside the palace grounds would become entranced to climb to the top of the tallest spires, and jump down to their deaths in the same courtyard where the witch's pyre once burned," Samuel read out. He then walked forward towards the next set. This painting depicted a scene of the old Duke of the Palace commanding his servants to seal the door to the tallest tower, to combat the curse. The silver plaque read thus:

"Fearing that the curse would take his and his family's lives, the Duke commanded the tallest towers to be sealed away. The seal remained in place for millennia, with some saying that the Duke himself would keep the wall stable, even centuries after his death. Without anyone to maintain it, the palace fell to ruin, and was left to rot. But one day, that changed."

He wandered forwards for a final time, being faced with two sets. The third painting of the group was clearly more modern, as the paint was more bright and vivid. It showed a scene of two construction workers, injured from their time working on the palace, handing over the deed to the palace over to a woman in a suit. The bronze plaque read:

"When construction work began on the ruins to restore the palace to how it once stood, it is believed that the curse awoke from its centuries-long dormancy, determined to push the supposed intruders out of its domain, whether by leaving, or by death. The blood-chilling screams of the woman would thunder through the halls at night, the courtyard would fill with smoke and the smell of burnt wood, and people swore they saw her charred figure in the corner of their eye. After the haunting progressed into attacks on the workers, they all quit, giving the rights to Enchanted Attractions for their project."

The final painting in the group was of the entrance to the palace, with a purple, swirling storm overhead, pierced only by the spire. "Today, many say that the curse is still lurking, and waits for the most fearless of people to face its power. Will you live to tell the tale of your breathtaking time, or will you become another victim of Curse: The Fear Fall?"

Samuel arrived at the entrance of the tallest and fastest spire, and saw Void's hat laid to the side. "Void! Where are you?" Samuel yelled up the tower, before a small orange shimmer glided to the floor, alerting Samuel to Void's presence. "He's at the top. Great!" Samuel groaned in his head before starting to climb up to the top of the frames of the tower.

"Samuel...just go. I don't want to talk to anyone at the moment." Void spoke to Samuel, his void cold and annoyed at the same time. Samuel continued climbing up the metal structure, nearly losing his grip twice. "I said...Go!" Void yelled, causing a glowing orange ring to fly down the tower.

Samuel flattened himself against the frame, feeling the heat of the ring fly just an inch away from him. "Void? Why'd you do that!"

Void walked to the edge of the tower and looked down at him. "Just go! You don't need to know!" Void yelled.

Samuel continued to climb up, when an orange blast flew directly at him. He lost his grip, falling down the tower. Luckily, he was able to grab back onto the bars and climb back up again, even gaining a bit extra height. He now had climbed halfway to the top of the tower, and could see Void stood frozen at the top. As he stood, his hands became swallowed by a dark haze.

"Shadowed Nightmare," Void said, causing the haze to collect into the shape of a clawed hand. The spell launched towards Samuel at full force, with darkness and shadows breaking off. It slammed into him, and trapped him in its effect.

When he opened his eyes, he was standing in a section of the Joy Facility. He looked around, noticing how the door to the Abyss Project area was no longer boarded up, and slightly ajar. "Wasn't that closed?" he said, confused. He peeked through the slim gap, to see a scientist busily typing on the computer. However, she seemed to be unaware of Samuel's presence at all. Swallowing his fear, he walked into the room, and waited for a reaction. After a minute or two passed, he realised that the girl didn't even react, like she was on loop. "So this is like a nightmare flashback. Alright. What do you have for me, nightmare?" he thought, looking through a large, glass window. The window was looking into a large room. The walls were grey, and protected by a silver plating that was scratched and scorched in some areas. Steel-coated pipes ran across the walls, but Samuel couldn't tell if they were for decoration or for some unknown purpose.

The room itself contained a simple desk set, a bookcase, and a TV stand. However, the thing Samuel was focused on was a tall, metallic pod, similar to what Stella had in her home. It was faint, but there was a figure inside the pod. Suddenly, the girl stopped using the computer, and walked towards the window. Samuel thought she was surely going to see him, but she just walked right by him. The woman pressed a button on a small console near the windowpane, causing the pod door to unlatch and lift open.

"Subject 4B-725, you can wake up now!" The scientist spoke into a microphone, her tone just as sweet as the one he recalled from the info channel when he first woke up in the Facility. However, Samuel was snapped out of his thoughts by the sighting of a familiar face.

The person in the pod stepped out, revealing his identity. He looked different from what he looked like in the present, but Samuel could recognise him from a glance. He wasn't wearing his normal attire, which was replaced with some clothes that The Ministry gave its subjects, and his hair and appearance was drastically more unkempt, but there could be no denying that they were the same. "I've told you a thousand times, Lottie, I like to be called Void!" he said, stretching his shoulders to not feel stiff.

"Yes, I know. But, I still have to call you by your codename for official documents until you finish your testing," she explained, before pulling out a microphone from a headset she was wearing. "Hey, Tiffany, bring in the Code Blue, will ya?" she said into the mic, with a voice coming back from it. Soon after, the cell door swung open. A blond-haired man was pushed into the cell, the door shutting behind him. He tried to open the door, but it was locked shut. On the other side of the room, one of the pipes opened, revealing a metal flask.

"This is the Empathy Test. We know you're against hurting others, you have...empathy. However, you can't be picky when you're in danger. Will you take the easy way and drink from the flask, or drain this man? The choice is yours," she explained with a faint smile.

Samuel looked at the test, and was puzzled as to why Void had to choose between a person and a bottle. Suddenly, he heard a yell. The collar around Void's neck had pierced into it and started to make a humming sound. When he managed to get himself back on his feet, Samuel noticed that his irises were now a very pale orange colour. Void looked at the man on the floor, who was looking at him back, fear in his eyes. He shook his head, and went to grab the flask. But as he gripped the flask, Lottie pressed a button on a small remote in her hand.

He screamed in pain, as the collar on his neck shot an electric current through his body. In his pain, he dropped the bottle on the floor, which fell with a clatter. When he tried to pick it up again, she continued the shocks. Samuel went to grab the remote out of Lottie's hand, only to phase through her, like a ghost. "I can't help! I can't even touch her," he realised, looking back towards what was happening in the cell. Void had collapsed to his knees, since he was unable to withstand the voltage. He got back up to his feet, and again looked towards the captive that was huddled into the corner. But this time, there was no remorse in his eyes. Samuel felt his stomach drop, as he swiftly turned away from the window. The sound of the blood-curdling screams of the subject gave him goosebumps, before the room was plunged into deathly silence.

Lottie smirked, pleased with the outcome. She trotted towards the laptop on the desk, and started to document the results with a chilling indifference. He looked back towards the window, noticing how Void was standing silently, looking at the man on the floor. Samuel took a step back from the window, with the room still in view. He was about to turn away, when he noticed how Void had moved.

He was now staring directly at the window with a blank expression, his collar and cuffs littering the ground. "That's not good!" he said, diving down to the ground. Before she could react, a black shockwave of magic tore through the room, shattering the window effortlessly. Samuel protected his face, hearing the alarms in the area scream and yell. He looked up, and saw a scene that made his breath pause. Lottie was lying limp on the ground, presumably dead. Another scientist, possibly Tiffany, was being held up in the air by Void. He heard a snap, and the heavy thump of another body falling to the floor. He hid his eyes, praying that this was a dream. But, when he opened them again, he saw that Void was staring at him. He was looking directly at the boy's eyes, and smiling like he was playing a game. "Got you," he said. He morphed into the shadows and rushed towards Samuel, with his eyes showing more of his intent than words. Just as Void went to grab his collar, he snapped awake from his nightmare.

It soon dawned on him that he was now lying flat on top of the tower that he was once climbing, and saw the Void he knew standing nervously to his right. He could have sworn he saw a slightly wet, crimson-red tint on Void's mouth, but he brushed it off as a trick of the light.

"Void! But you were...There was screaming...they were killed," Samuel stuttered, breathing rapidly. He took a deep breath to calm down, and sat himself up.

"It was just a dream, kid. The curse puts you in a nightmare. I don't know what yours was about, but I can assume it must not have been pleasant. Usually they go away after one minute...but you were out for about ten!" Void said, his regret for his actions making his voice slip and waver.

"You were the one who gave me that nightmare? I could've gotten killed back there!" Samuel yelled, staring at the spirit.

"I did catch you, though. I'm guessing Fawnia or someone sent you to talk to me. The truth is…I don't want to hurt Smiley, because I feel guilty about his death, like it was my fault. He was on top of Abyss, trying to talk to me. I tried to tell him how dangerous it was to be up there, but he wouldn't listen. Then, he slipped. I couldn't catch him on time. I tried to call for help. I tried to do anything to help him…but I was too late. All I could do was stand there while he died. She doesn't understand how much it… tore me apart! Even if we had our disagreements over petty things, he was still my brother!" Void's voice wavered, before breaking. He took off his glasses, as tears filled his eyes. He looked at Samuel's direction, only able to see misted colours, both due to his crying and his damaged eyesight. Samuel saw Void's eyes clearly, and gasped in shock. There were two, deep looking scars across them both. "I never got over his death, even when he returned. All that got me was a fight. He attacked me, and now I'm blind. Yet another thing which backfired on me," he said. With a small amount of flair he placed his glasses back on, before noticing how Samuel was looking a bit dazed.

"Eugh…why do I feel weird…" Samuel asked.

His head was thudding with a migraine, yet he also felt dizzy and lightheaded. His arms were sore, and were so weak that they could barely keep him sitting upright. A cold, icy chill was wrapped around his body, and he was visibly pale. A warm, wet feeling was on his neck, which made the cold worse.

Void looked at him and carefully helped him up on his feet. "You seem sick. It seems like you've caught something. You should be alright with a mix of an Energy and Healing Potion. Oh, and a well-deserved rest. As long as you do that, you'll be alright by tomorrow," Void said, clicking his fingers. An orange rimmed portal materialised at the bottom of the drop tower, its reflection glowing slightly in Void's glasses.

"Now, I need you to trust me here," Void asked, before holding his hand out to Samuel. He tiredly accepted, just wanting to get down the tower. When Samuel blinked, Void was holding him in his arms. "Hold on, we're going to go for a spin!" Void said. He jumped down the tower, holding both Samuel and his hat at the same time. The duo then both flew down into the orange rimmed portal, seeing the same dark abyss-like place that Samuel had seen for a brief moment when he was teleported back into Stella's home. Samuel tiredly blinked, then saw that they were inside Fawnia's Palace. Void landed on the marble floor, with the portal fizzing away with a finger click. At this point, Samuel could feel himself drifting to sleep, but pushed through his tiredness to know the full story. Void turned the corner, making sure he didn't drop the boy in his arms.

The spirits were clustered at the end of the hallway, worried about Samuel's safety.

Florette looked towards her left, to be greeted by the sight of Void. She rushed forward, her shoes clicking against the marble. "Void! We thought something went wrong. We didn't mean to send him to potential danger! Is he okay? Is he hurt?" She asked. She breathed for a moment, to stop her mind from racing.

Stella stepped forwards to help her friend calm down, so she didn't panic. As her eyes wandered, she ended up looking into Void's. They had become brighter, more lively, and were now tangerine coloured. A faint smile appeared on her face, now knowing what had happened. "Everyone makes mistakes. Luckily, he seems alright," she said to him, despite not looking his way. When she placed her hand down on the boy's neck, she felt what she expected: A cold chill. "Yeah, you chilled him out. Nothing dangerous though. A good night's sleep should make him better in no time," she said with a smile.

Even though she was talking out loud mostly to keep the others calm, it was also to keep herself focused. When she was sure he was alright, she carefully pulled her hand away. Her eyes, however, were pulled towards the familiar red stain on her fingertips. She had dealt with blood before from accidents while flying, so it didn't bother her. Keeping her hand out of sight, she rubbed her fingers to remove the stain. With a sigh of relief that both her friends were safe, she looked to Fawnia. The Queen was standing there awkwardly, with a confused glance. "Well, now that's sorted, what do we do? If we leave, a certain someone could strike, but we all need rest. Especially Samuel," Florette said.

"Okay. He can rest for tonight in the guest bedroom, the one to the right. Florette, when we leave, you need to start up an Energy regeneration and healing potion blend, alright? We've had this happen before, we know what to do," Fawnia commanded. She waltzed towards Void with a regal flair and looked at Samuel, who was struggling to stay awake. "Samuel dear, we're taking you to the guest bedroom so you can sleep it off. You just get your rest, alright?" she said calmly.

The boy managed to nod, before shutting his eyes. The trio of spirits took Samuel up to the room, making sure they did not wake him up. Void placed the teen down on the bed, with Stella using her powers to change Samuel into the pyjamas he'd borrowed from her, and Fawnia waving her arms and tucking him in. As the three of them left the room, the lights automatically dimmed.

"Why did you do that? You have bottles for a reason!" Fawnia asked him. Despite speaking normally, her tone seemed judgemental.

"I was annoyed at being pushed around. I guess I just lost it for a moment. I know I have bottles, but it isn't the same!" he said, turning his head away from the woman and focusing on walking down the stairs. He sat down next to Blaze, who was making rings of fire in his hands.

"Hey Stella, stay behind and talk to him, alright? You two are pretty close, so I think you need some time to talk," Florette asked the space spirit, who thought for a moment, then nodded in agreement.

"Well, now that he's resting, what do we do? It's late, anyways." With a flick of his finger, Void tipped his hat over to the right.

"I guess we just stay indoors for the night. Make sure to stay alert for Smiley, and take it easy," Florette answered honestly. With a smile, she disappeared in a burst of green, shimmering dust.

Most of the other spirits left one by one to their own homes, leaving Fawnia, Stella and Void in the hall.

"So...are you going to stay, or not? Company is always appreciated!" Fawnia asked.

"I don't really know, if I can be honest. I'll probably return to the Abyss, but I might stay a while, if that's alright with you," he responded with a shrug.

Fawnia heard his response, before smiling politely. "Alright then, I'll see you in the morning," she said, as she walked up the stairs.

When the Queen was out of earshot, Stella stood up. "So, I'm assuming you lost yourself for a moment?"

Void turned towards her, a smile on his face. "What do you think, dearie? Kid's drained, literally!" he joked with her.

Stella laughed at Void's attempt at a joke, before calming down for a moment. "I am kind of annoyed you didn't ask. We have the message system for a reason! All you need to do is mention red and I'll be waiting for you. Just don't go asking at 3AM without giving me time to wake up!" she said, as she raised her voice slightly. Her arms were crossed loosely, and her gaze was looking at his.

He stood himself up, and stepped towards her. "I know. I'm sorry about forgetting, I just got busy. I promise I'll message the next time. Besides, it feels kind of weird to constantly have you on dial without anything in return. I could...buy you something? Like flowers or chocolate or whatever you like. If you'd be alright with that, of course." Void started muttering, his hands wrapped around each other.

"It's alright. Everyone messes up and forgets things. Just don't forget to put yourself above your work, or you'll burn yourself out! Aside from that, I love that idea! Lilies are my favourite, so maybe you could find some? If Florette doesn't turn them into another dress decoration, of course," Stella mentioned with a smile, before giving Void a hug. "See you, V." She let go of him, before teleporting away with a rippling beam.

Void sighed with a genuine smile appearing on his face, which was most rare. His expression soon faded when he looked down at his phone, focusing on a recently abandoned number. "Hope it still counts. I'm not risking this for nothing." His voice didn't show any care, as if he'd shut off his feelings at the first thought. He slipped his phone away, before glancing down at his watch and fading into the darkness of a nearby corner.

CHAPTER 14:
SPILT BLOOD AND TRUTH

hree weeks passed with little to no avail, as Samuel got better after the incident with Void. Despite trying to put the fear he felt in the nightmare behind him, he still kept it and Void's story in his mind. "Why would Smiley attack Void? Guess it's yet another mystery that I'll have to solve," Samuel sighed with a sarcastic tone, as he meandered aimlessly around The Crypt, hoping for something, anything, to catch his eye.

As his legs had started to get tired, he sat himself down on a nearby wooden bench and pulled out his phone to pass the time. Luckily, the spirits over in Technoland had made sure to maintain their own internet signals, but it was quite hit-or-miss as to whether it worked, at least in Samuel's eyes. He would occasionally try to call, text, or even alert his family or friends to the fact that he wasn't dead or hurt somewhere. Whenever he did though, they either didn't answer, or the signal would not allow him to even speak before the phone cut off. So instead, he had put all the spirits' phone numbers onto the phone, allowing him to stay in touch. At this moment, Samuel was boredly looking around the internet, trying to see if anyone else had had a similar experience, or knew of spirits.

There were no traces. With dwindling hope, he looked up The Perfector and was stunned at the result. There were tens, maybe even hundreds of articles of people who had met a tragic fate; they had all either gone missing, been found dead, or things of that same grim calibre. Despite the different locations and stories of the different victims, everyone had a single thing in common: a person with yellow and black hair, and an unnerving smile had been spotted.

Samuel couldn't believe his eyes – the Ministry were kidnapping, and even killing, people on the outside of the park! Then, he clicked on the final article, which had a blurry, but still recognisable picture of the culprit. A tall, skinny man with a top hat and the signature yellow and black hair, and eyes that were looking to the right of the camera, a small girl lying limp in his arms.

"That can't be…he can't leave the park! Florette told me… wait a second." Samuel noticed that the figure in the image, which was recognisably Smiley, was wearing a bunch of dark, metal bands. Two being on each hand, and one around his neck, like a necklace.

They all had a yellow circle in the middle, and were seemingly glowing, along with Smiley's eyes. "Maybe those bands supplied him with magic or something." Samuel shrugged it off, more worried about the fact that everyone in The Ministry, including Smiley, was seemingly linked to tens of hundreds of crimes. Samuel switched off the smartphone, before putting it away in his pocket. He decided to take a stroll, and ended up at the path that trailed towards the X-Periment Facility. He was about to move on, but noticed that the portal hole in Abyss was glowing and swirling, almost as if it was real. He sneaked into the Facility, trying to avoid confrontation with any members, but was startled by a familiar voice behind him.

"Kid, I don't recommend going into that portal, if that's what you're here for. That's the portal to my domain, you know!" He twirled around, to see Void looking down at him. He was smirking slightly, but still kept his calm demeanour. "If you went in there without any special technology or trinkets, you'd be dead in five minutes flat," he warned, before hovering slightly, going into a casual sitting position.

"There's nothing really there either. Just darkness, shadows, a few lost souls, you get the idea." He shrugged, moving his glasses slightly. Samuel noticed how Void's eyes were dimmer than when they'd first met, and extremely less bright than when Void attacked him by accident. "Yeah, I can see you're looking at my eyes. They're like a mood ring. Brighter when happy, and dimmer when I'm calm. Anyways, stay away from the portal." Void smirked, before walking past him, placing something into the teen's pocket, and standing by the hole of the portal.

Samuel looked at the item, which was a black face mask with a geometric orange design printed on the front. He put it on, before a full, black mask came around the bottom of his face, with a glow enwrapping his whole body. Samuel rushed up to Void, realising that he was waiting for him.

"So, you didn't listen, huh? Heh...you're cool, kid." Void patted Samuel slightly on the back, before teleporting them both to the top of the drop of Abyss, using a cloud of his black smoke. "You know what to do now?" Void asked, decisively.

Samuel nodded back, with Void turning around at the edge of the track, turning his hat into shimmers that disappeared into thin air, and securing his glasses. "Good, it would take ages to explain. Just trust me and that mask, that little trinket can protect you from the Abyss's coldness, its powers, and the lack of air!" Void rambled, before inching nearer to the edge, the breeze slightly shaking his hair. "Just remember...embrace your fears!" Void quoted his ride's catchphrase, before he jumped backwards into a backflip and plummeted straight down, quickly turning from a backwards position to feet-first, seconds before he dived straight into the portal.

Samuel glanced down, seeing the long fall, fear smacking him in the face. "O...okay, Samuel...remember what Void said... embrace your fears," Samuel whispered to himself, before gulping down as much air as he could and dived straight down, with the wind rushing down like a slap to his face; he shut his eyes as he fell into the portal.

He felt a strange sensation, like going from a pool to a hot tub, quickly turning bitterly cold, like being submerged in icy water. He opened his eyes, and like Void's words, there was only darkness and coldness, with shadows and mist everywhere.

"Told you! You can breathe and speak normally, Samuel, just don't take the mask off fully. It even allows you to drink through it," Void reminded Samuel, who was currently bobbing up and down, then started to swim his way over to the shadowy spirit, who saw the sight and laughed. "Just calm yourself down, and think of moving. The abyss is made 100% of magic energy, you know," Void pointed out, before Samuel followed his instructions, and he was indeed hovering around, though he still liked occasionally propelling himself with his arms.

"This is cool! Pretty cold, though," Samuel told Void his thoughts, before feeling goosebumps on his skin.

"Here." Void used his magic, and shrunk down his tailcoat, putting it on Samuel.

Void, under his tail-coat, was wearing a bright orange T-shirt, with black streaks along the side.

"Thanks, Shadows!" Samuel accepted with a smile, with Void chuckling under his breath in response. He sighed with an eye roll, before fading into the darkness and appearing beside Samuel. "You got that from Blaze, didn't you? I know he's my friend, but I don't really like being called just Shadows." Void started ranting, but calmed himself down shortly after and clicked his fingers, making an entire apartment style home appear from nothing. Void clicked his fingers again, before the home became lit, shining in a warm orange glow, as if it was made of flames. Void put his top hat and coat on a futuristic looking hat holder, before gesturing for Samuel to sit down on the black and orange sofa, which he did.

Void suddenly appeared at the fridge, looking through its contents. "Hey, Samuel, do you want a drink? I've got Fizzy, Spepper, and Zestie, though I can bring anything up, since I control the Abyss." Void leaned on the countertop.

Samuel thought for a moment, slowly coming to a decision. "Hmm...I'll have some Zestie, please."

Void grabbed a can of Zestie from the fridge for the boy, and an unmarked bottle that was filled with a maroon liquid for himself.

"What's that?" Samuel asked, looking at the bottle.

"It's just some juice I like. Don't worry!" Void answered, with a nonchalant attitude. He clicked open the resealable top, and took a drink.

Samuel took a drink of the pop, feeling the fizz of the bubbles. He abruptly jolted, as he smelt a sickly metallic scent coming from Void's drink. He stared at the man sitting comfortably on the sofa, who took a moment to breathe after taking a drink of the bottle's unknown content. Samuel took another sip, while squinting at Void. When he looked closely, he could see a pair of sharp teeth in his mouth, which weren't there before.

As a possible revelation struck, he unintentionally breathed with liquid still in his mouth. As he started to cough, he dropped the can on the ground.

"Woah! Calm down. Don't die in my apartment! Stella wouldn't forgive me," Void said in a panic. He patted the boy's back carefully, so he didn't use too much of his strength.

Samuel managed to regain his breath, but his focus was still on the red stain that was on Void's mouth. "You look like you have blood on your lips." Samuel said. He took another breath, while a chill rushed down his back.

Void looked down upon him, wondering if he should say anything, before making up his mind with a sigh. "Look, I was the first creation made by the Ministry, as you probably already know. Last time I checked, they don't even have me on record, besides my...tasks. Anyways, during my creation, I was accidentally infused with a dangerous substance, a previously unknown magic source which kills all living things around it...they called it Abyss Essence. My soul had shattered, but the magic miraculously kept it stable. Because of this, I became a being of the Abyss. Its energy keeps me alive, in a way. But, it comes at a cost. I have to take the life force of others to sustain my own. Their energy, for mine," Void started to explain, his view focused on the crimson fluid inside the bottle.

"I now have sharpened teeth, something you might call fangs, amongst other oddities. I can hear people's pulse and see in the dark, things like that. The reason I have these abilities is both to get life energy, and as a side effect of being infused with the Abyss Essence. Life Force, for humans like you and even spirits, is contained in one thing. Blood. So to survive, I need to drink blood to get the life force inside it. If not, I'll slowly get weaker before dying." Void's attention pulled away from the bottle towards the boy that was sitting beside him.

Samuel was frozen on the spot, his gaze falling to the floor. "When I was sick on that tower, when I had to sleep at Fawnia's because I had no energy left – that was from you drinking my blood, wasn't it? Are you some kind of vampire?" Samuel uttered nervously, placing his hand on where he was wounded, in the hope of protecting it.

Samuel put on a brave face, but Void could hear his heart racing. He looked back at him, and nodded with a faded smile. "Yes, you could say that. I'd rather be called Vampire than a stroke of luck. I know I should've told you as soon as I could, but I didn't want you to feel like I was a threat." Void finished speaking, as his expression became cold. Just as he tensed himself again, he flinched as he realised that Samuel had his hand on his shoulder.

"It's alright. Nothing bad really happened, and that's what matters," Samuel forgave him, making Void smile at him, though his smile looked more forced.

He gently pushed the boy's hand off him and helped him up, then the pair both finished their drinks. However, Void kept a small amount in the bottle, possibly for later. He tapped his hand onto the counter, as the bottle and the now empty can appeared onto the counter, and everything but Void and Samuel disappeared back into the thick mist. Void gripped Samuel's hand, and clicked his top hat and tailcoat back on, before reopening the portal back to the Facility. They both hovered into the portal, and arrived back in the park, where Samuel took a deep breath of air. Void levitated them both out of the portal hole with a wave of his hand.

When they landed on solid ground, Void turned to the gaping hole of the portal. "Watch this. Alternis Deactivate!" Void cast a spell with a shake of his hand. His hand was resonating with a grey aura, which morphed and moved, as if it was made of water. Suddenly, the lights on the large portal rim dimmed, as the swirling dark shades of the portal dissolved into thin air, allowing the track to reconnect and turning the portal off. Samuel removed the mask, the glow returning to the source, before Void slipped it into his pocket.

"So, yes, that bottle was blood. It's not fresh though, so it doesn't taste as good as it would be if it was taken directly from someone. Anyways, we should go see Florette. She's probably having a meltdown!" Void smiled, his mood visibly improved.

The two gained their specific speed boost, and rushed along to The Crypt.

Samuel
Matthews

Hypna
Swirls

Eliza Woods

Void
Shadows

Stella
Galactic

Queen
Faunia
Reigh

CHAPTER 15:
VOIDED FRIENDSHIP

When the duo arrived, Florette was skimming through a shelf of potions, all with a variety of colours, amounts of fizz, and more. She was also joined by Stella, Blaze, and a multitude of other spirits. Void and Samuel walked in, greeting the other spirits with a wave. Samuel sat among the group, while Void quickly turned and leaned against the wall, his hat tipped downwards. He looked at the green girl with a piercing focus, before shaking his head in disbelief. His mood had been dampened again, although he feigned a smile.

Florette finally picked out a blue potion, then turned around, her dress glittering slightly. "Guys...I think I have created a solution to our Smiley problem. This potion is a power weakener which, if ingested or injected, renders most powers either painfully weak or useless. We can even put it in a device which keeps the wearer's powers to a minimum," Florette explained, a spark of genius in her eyes.

"So, what do we use this for?" Blaze expressed with confusion, as he wasn't paying much attention.

"If we are able to, we could put this on a dart, and some unenchanted devices, like those old and tapped out power bracelets and the collar of stealth!" Florette clarified, looking like a teacher or a strict mother at times.

"Yeah, what does this have to do with what we're doing here?" Sally mumbled, her expression lacking any enthusiasm, annoyed.

"We can try and restrain a certain spirit, if you catch my drift." Florette winked, before watching as the people in the room all realised what she meant. While most of the spirits were happy about Florette's discovery, Void was silent.

"Oh! That's a great plan!" Samuel exclaimed, praising Florette's idea.

Void, under the security of his hat, started silently mumbling things under his breath. "*Oh yeah, great plan!* It's even more *amazing* that you go against the one thing that I said to you all." Void was then stared at for a moment, before Florette continued her lecture-like explanation. "So...we could find Smiley, or maybe even bait him out, then, when he doesn't see us, we shoot him with one of the weakening darts! We then put the power restrainers on him, then boom! He won't be able to lay one magical finger on any of us!"

Samuel stayed silent, though he did give her a short round of applause.

Void, however, didn't clap. "So, when do we do this?" he asked with a thin veil of calmness, clearly struggling to keep himself from snapping at the nature spirit. Fawnia noticed this immediately, and tried to make him breathe and calm down with a swish of her hand. Instead, he glared at the ex-Queen in annoyance.

Florette did not notice his feelings, and instead focused on the potion plan. "Tonight, if I can finish these quickly. Void, could you grab the empty power bracelets and collar please, and Stella, can you get me the darts and dart gun, okay?"

Both spirits seemed to agree, and walked off to search.

Samuel had switched on his phone and started to play a cute little tapping game. After a minute, Void's voice resonated from a corridor to the right, asking for Florette. She obliged and walked down towards him. Samuel silently followed along, so if they needed help he could quickly bring one of the other spirits along to them. He stepped to the side, keeping himself out of sight. Florette walked to the centre of the room and saw Void looking around, and waved to him kindly.

"Hey Florette. I've found the collar, but I am still trying to find the bracelets. Can you please come and help me?" He questioned, for her to smile and nod in reply.

She started looking around, but stopped when she felt that something was wrong. She felt a strange feeling, like a dark, hateful force was crushing her. Then, without warning, she was flung off her feet and pinned roughly against the bookcase. When the shock of what had happened faded, she could see Void walking towards her, his eyes glowing. "Hey Void...this isn't a fun joke. You can let me go now..." Her voice was wavering with fear.

Void looked at her, his fangs showing. "I'm going to say one thing, and you need to listen. Don't even think of harming my brother. You don't realise that going through with this plan will break that important promise you made in return for my obedience to your little rules and morality codes. You're putting yourself and the others into deep trouble, and I'm sure you wouldn't want me to return the favour." He growled, his eyes showing a rage that chilled both Samuel and Florette.

"I know that breaking the promise is a dumb idea, I get that. But he's gone too far! He tried to brainwash Stella, Void! Isn't our safety, isn't protecting her more important that some stupid promise? He needs some sort of retribution for his crimes!" Florette said.

Void calmed down and stared right into her eyes. Suddenly, his eyes were covered by a bright, red flash, and his iris changed into a crimson colour.

"Florette. Listen to me. You will not break the promise. You will not hurt him, or you will regret it," Void said. However, his lips were not moving an inch. He was talking in her mind.

She tried to push him away, or block his stare, but she couldn't move. She was frozen in place, and she could feel her strength fading. She then realised what he was doing. He knew she was refusing to listen to him, and now he was making her listen through mesmerisation. If she didn't do something soon, she wouldn't be able to fight off the magic, and would most likely fall for the spell. Meanwhile, Samuel was watching the situation from the background, unable to hear what Void was saying or doing. To him, the two of them were just staring at each other. He debated whether to stay behind and wait, or step in to split the two apart, but decided to stay hidden.

Gathering up enough energy, she blocked out as much influence as she could, and braced herself for whatever happened next. "Quit with your mind games. I won't just quit doing what's best for everyone, Void!" she screamed in her head, breaking his connection. As soon as the link snapped, she could feel her strength returning in waves. The red glow of his eyes flickered, returning to amber.

He stepped back, unable to understand what had happened. "How...that usually works," he said, his surprise showing. His magical grip on her vanished, and she fell to the floor with a loud thud. She used the bookcase as a grip to pull herself up, though her heels made it harder to get herself to her feet.

"You won't control me, Void. I won't stay quiet!" she said with bravery. She pivoted herself around, and galloped away.

Void went to run for her, but Samuel sprung out from the corner, catching him off guard. "You got busted! Now you're going to have some explaining to do!" Samuel said. He stumbled around, trying to regain his balance.

"You should've stayed out of this!" Void said, before moving his hands in a swift movement. As his hands cut through the air, a dark glow swirled from his palms. "Apologies. But, you shouldn't have been so curious. Dreamless Sleep!" he said, before he threw his hands forwards towards Samuel. The energy rapidly entwined him, like a thick fog. He tried to combat the effect, but soon struggled to even keep on his feet. "My advice would be to give into the curse, or you'll hurt yourself trying to fight it," Void said, his tone distant and unapologetic.

The teen dropped to the ground, with Void catching him before he collided. He lifted his hand, as Samuel seemed to float in the air. Void looked at the boy that was defencelessly hovering in front of him, with his left hand gripped to summon his blade. "Not now. Too easy, and too suspicious. Won't be fair without a fight," he murmured, before unclenching his hand. He breathed in, hearing the faint heartbeat of Florette in the corridor, and letting his senses lead the way.

In the library, Blaze got himself up, his nerves on alert. "She wouldn't be this long! Am I the only one to have heard all that commotion from down there?" he said, for Sally to shrug and roll her eyes.

"Calm yourself down! They'll be alright. Didn't know you were a worrier," she said, as Blaze sunk back into his chair.

Meanwhile, Florette was lost in her crypt's own catacombs. She glanced back, hearing the muffled footsteps of Void coming closer. She turned left, then right in the seemingly endless tunnels, until she realised that she had run into where she started. Her eyes caught the sight of Samuel, suspended in the air. She looked sad, but regained her thoughts and continued to run. She dived around a corner, and tried to get the attention of the other spirits. "Can I get a little help here? We've got a code red!" she yelled. However, just as she finished calling for help, she was again thrown into the air. The spirits, hearing her call, sprung into action and quickly gathered a plan.

She struggled against the dark aura pinning her to the wall, but its power still kept her trapped. She was tired from running, but was still determined to escape. The aura contorted while still keeping its pressure on her, forming Void. She glanced into the spirit's eyes, which were now pale. "This isn't good. I have to get out of here!" she thought, while struggling to move free from the vampiric spirit's grasp.

"You're stuck, and I don't recommend wasting your energy. I tried to warn you that there would be consequences to breaking the promise, but you still refused and fought against me. So now you've proven that you don't care about the promises you've made, and now I'm thirsty from running for half an hour to find you. Stella was forced by you to become my 'target', as you put it, in order to protect yourself and the rest from having to go through the same pain. Maybe if you knew how it felt, you would care a bit more." He spoke in Florette's mind, shifting between disappointment and anger.

"Don't move. It will make things...worse." He spoke in reality, his deep voice commanding and intimidating. The black gloves that would always be on his hands were flung off, and flickered away like a broken light. He used his left hand to lift up Florette's head, revealing her neck. On Fawnia's command, Stella and Blaze ran out the room, planning to corner Void.

While they searched the sprawling maze for Florette, Fawnia and Nebulus rushed down to the storage room, where they bumped into the cursed Samuel. Nebulus tried to shake him awake, only to be repelled by the freezing cold temperature on the boy's skin. Fawnia noticed the amber mist clinging to Samuel, and recognised it immediately as one of Void's curses. "Enchantium Destructo!" Fawnia said, creating a rose pink light from her staff. She fought the curse, and eventually overcame its power. Her magic overtook the amber and freed Samuel from the curse.

Samuel woke up with a gasp, landing on the ground. "Thanks for the save. Now, let's go stop him!" Samuel said.

The two spirits beside him nodded in agreement, and all three rushed out of the room. They met up with Stella and Blaze, who greeted them with a brief smile. The group picked up the pace, fearing that time was against them.

Meanwhile, Void was inching closer to Florette's neck, his eyes at this point showing nothing but pure anticipation. Florette was barely able to move, while her skin grew frost cold from Void's touch, making her neck go numb. She whimpered slightly, feeling a dull pinching feeling from the sharp fangs that were piercing her skin. Her eyes welled up with tears.

The feeling of a warm liquid grew, along with the lump in her throat. She glanced down in fear, to see whatever sight awaited her. Void had pierced her neck, and was drinking the blood that flowed from the wound. He stopped for a moment and looked into her eyes, which were dilated from fear. His eyes brightened from the white shade to their normal amber colour, as he smiled. "That wasn't so bad, was it? I guess you're feeling tired. That's normal. Blood loss, and all that. Don't be scared, I've had my fill," he said. Florette tried to grab him, but he used his reflexes to stop her. "Now, now. That's not how you treat a friend! You of all people should know that!" he said, before his hand became engulfed in darkness. "You need a rest. Sweet dreams," he whispered to her. Florette tried to move away from his hand, but she couldn't even shake. She cried out again, before falling asleep from the spell.

Just as Void started to laugh, a sound he didn't expect to hear for a while rang out. "Void! Why'd you do that? Also, I thought you said your eyes were a mood ring!" Samuel said.

Void turned around, while Florette was still suspended in the air. His mouth was dripping with blood, and his eyes were glowing from the dim lighting. "I got...peckish. She'll be alright. Just needs a potion and a rest, like you. And, if you want to know, the mood ring thing was a lie. I didn't want to tell you the truth then. My eyes actually show how thirsty I am. The brighter they are, the less thirsty I am. Brushing that little explanation aside, how in the name of Fawnia are you awake? My curses are...notoriously hard to break," Void said, as Samuel stared back at him. Void's eyes darted around, noticing all the other Spirits were armed with their weapons and blocking the exits.

Blaze was wielding a wave bladed sword that burst alight in flames, while Stella was wielding a pair of silver and blue pistols. She snapped them together, creating one large firearm that was ready to fire a violet beam. Despite aiming a gun at him, she looked more disappointed than outraged. Void growled while dropping Florette onto the ground yet again. He started directly at the spirits, quickly licking whatever was left of the blood off, glaring at them with an annoyed stare. "I'll come back, you know I always come back. But remember one thing. Don't hurt my brother, or things will be much worse than what happened a decade ago," Void warned, before disappearing into a black mist.

Florette was lying on the ground with her body limp, but shakily breathing. A trail of crimson ran down her neck like a trickle of water in a fountain. Stella checked her pulse, and she was fine, though her heart was beating slower due to her being asleep. They were lucky they had caught Void in time, but they had worse things to worry about than the recent past, specifically the fact their friend was on the floor bleeding. "Ivy, are you okay?!" Stella said. She picked up Florette from the floor and placed her gently in a chair close to an intricate, green and silver hearth. Her eyes gently fluttered open while Stella placed a blanket over her shoulders. Blaze clicked his fingers, and a warm flame appeared in his hand. He used the flame to ignite the fuel and start the fire in the hearth, heating up the room to a comfortable level.

"What happened?...Where's Void!" Florette asked.

"It's a long story. Let's just say, we now have a brother duo with us on their hitlists," Samuel explained, before pulling out a cotton ball and placing it on Florette's wound. When the blood clotted, he stuck a plaster on the wound. After a moment of silence, Sally came off her phone and looked up.

"Guys...what happened? I've been on my phone, so..." Sally asked.

Stella stared at her with annoyance. "Well, long story short. Void got moody, tried to force Florette to not hurt Smiley in some way and tried to attack her and curse Samuel, but we stopped him, and now he's...who knows where!" Stella summed up the past 20 minutes, for Sally to groan in annoyance.

"Great. We have now got a crazy dude and the vampire chasing us." Sally chuckled, before putting her phone down.

"I also stopped him from doing anything major. Good thing we caught him in time," Samuel added.

Stella mumbled in agreement, before giving Florette a cup, containing some of the energy potion.

While she drank the potion, Sally looked at her. "Is she okay? She looks like some dude ruined her birthday party."

Florette glanced at her. "You know that I could've been extremely hurt, or worse, before?" she snapped.

Sally shrugged, before going to the corridor where the attack had happened, noticing that there was something on the floor. "Guys. Is Void a flower fan?" she asked.

Fawnia waltzed over, before looking down. "Strange...a rose? Maybe Florette knows about this..." Fawnia picked up the flower and walked with Sally to where Florette was sitting down in the chair, sipping on a cup of tea to wash down the potion. "Florette, we found this where Void was standing. Do you know anything about them?" She handed her the rose.

"Well, it appears to be a black rose. Black roses are commonly seen as a symbol of death. There are also drops of blood on it, most likely my own, and... That's peculiar, the centre is orange. A black rose, mixed with orange. A Shadow rose, if you may. I didn't even know he could do this!" she responded, with a gasp.

"So, this dude is leaving flowers, like some weird Easter Egg hunt? Great," Sally grumbled.

But Samuel shook his head. "No. Void placed this Shadow Rose where he bit Florette... Wait a moment, this reminds me of something I saw this morning!" Samuel gasped, for Stella to look at him, pleased that there was more mystery.

"I looked up the Perfector on my phone, and got all these stories about people being found dead, injured, or going missing. The ones who were found, both dead or alive, had these scars on their mouths. The survivors had no memory of the attack, and the scars were barely healing. The last one lasted for nearly a decade before finally showing signs of recovery." Samuel explained, showing the articles on his phone.

"Hmm...I guess this must've been The Ministry's doing. So, what does this have to do with our flower fiend?" Blaze asked.

"It's simple. The scars were a symbol, kind of like putting your signature on a document. It's basically saying that the crime was committed by one specific person, team, or organisation. The Ministry seems to be a scarred mouth and Void...seems to be these flowers," Samuel finished, before a realisation dawned on the group.

"He probably teleported outside. Where he could go after more people...We just put everyone in danger!" Florette gasped, realising their mistake.

"Hey Samuel, can I see the bracelets, the collar and the potion?" Fawnia asked, as Samuel nodded and gave her all the items she had asked for. Fawnia walked over to a table which had magical looking symbols and runes on. She placed all the items down, dropped a few droplets of the potion inside the bracelets and collar by small holes, which Samuel recognised as the glowing circles that were on the bands that Smiley was wearing in the photo. The holes were sealed, before she waved her hand, and each item started to glow in an azure hue, with some darts tipped with the liquid too.

"There. This should do for the Smiley plot." She smiled. Florette looked even better, as she had cheered up. She tried to stand up, but Stella looked worried.

"You need to heal!" She said.

Florette smirked, before she used a healing spell on herself. "I'm healed," she said with a wink.

Samuel smiled, handing her the dart gun.

"How are we going to get Smiley to be in range?" Nebulus asked, with a flat voice.

Samuel gave it some thought, then came up with an idea.

"Do we have any protective clothing? Because, if my body's protected from getting attacked, I could get Smiley's attention by being in the camera footage. He'll see it, and immediately come straight out. Smiley wouldn't dare miss an opportunity to get revenge, after all!" Samuel plotted, with Stella giving Samuel a pair of boots and an earpiece, except they were an icy blue, instead of the azure colour that Stella usually wore. Samuel put them on gently, and pressed the middle button on the headset, which formed the armour, only to reveal that it was made specifically for him, with a similar design to his normal polo, except made of the same magically enhanced tech as Stella's. "Neat! Now, let's get this plan started!" Samuel grinned, before he, Florette, Stella and Blaze left for the plan, leaving Sally, Nebulus and Fawnia inside The Crypt.

CHAPTER 16:
A ROSE HAS ITS THORNS

The group were hidden behind a corner, overlooked by the dominating electric fence perimeter of The X-periment Facility, with the same signs, warnings and CCTV camera dotted around. The police tape, however, had been completely ripped off the bars. Samuel breathed out, before Florette looked at him, confused.

"So, where do we go?" Florette asked.

"I know from an experience of hiding from Smiley and his sidekick Hypna that the tops of the buildings are not videoed, or I would not be here today. Stella, how's your aim with this?" Samuel said.

Stella laughed and pressed a button on her headset. A blue, glowing visor covered her eyes, with multiple symbols and shapes dotted around it. "This is my visor. I have an aim mode downloaded onto it. It locks onto the target, and helps my aim. There's practically no way I can miss a shot!" Stella smiled, overjoyed.

"Blaze, you're the fastest spirit in the park! Florette, you can control and summon plants, correct?" he said.

Blaze winked, before his flame-like eyes glowed bright crimson with emberlike sparks wisping out, that faded away as he dashed around the building in a blink, leaving behind a trail of bright flames which quickly extinguished. Florette breathed in and out, slowly levitating in the air, with her hair hovering upwards with a few streaks of pine green pulsing through.

She opened her eyes, before her eyeshadow and pupils were painted with lime green tones. Suddenly, six green rings twirled around, and long vines flew out, before floating in front of Samuel.

"Ta-da! I can also create thorns, and other plants. It's how I create my potions!" Florette smiled slightly, her voice slightly echoed, before one of the vines playfully flicked Samuel's chin, and they all shrank back into the rings, with Florette's eyes and eyeshadow turning back to normal.

"Okay. So, Stella, you go to the grey building to the left of The Perfector, and bring the dart gun and darts.

"Florette, you need to distract Smiley using your powers, but stay out of his attack range, and finally Blaze, you will put the bracelets and collar on Smiley. Do whatever you deem necessary, and I will get Smiley to come out." Samuel revealed his plan, to which the spirits accepted. Samuel secured his neck, while still keeping his face visible through the helmet visor, before all the spirits teleported to their specific positions. Samuel wandered out of hiding, entering the main pathway inside the facility, before looking for any true CCTV cameras.

He smiled, before clicking his fingers, causing the CCTV cameras to be able to see him. Suddenly, he saw that multiple cameras were locked onto him, and were focusing. "Hey, Smiley! I'm right here, with no spirits at all, same with weapons. So, why don't you come out? Unless you're scared you're going to be stabbed by a 16 year old again! If you don't, then you're..." Samuel started, before a dark, yet singsong voice spoke behind him.

"A smiling freak? I thought you would be more...original!"

Samuel turned around, to see the shadowed figure of Smiley looking directly down at him. "Smiley. You know something? I'm not scared of you anymore. I have friends that can help me,"

Samuel threatened.

Smiley simply started to laugh, his sharp teeth showing. "You just said they were not here. I can tell of some other people's presence, but I feel...curious. What did you do to my dear sibling?" Smiley asked, stalking around the boy, smiling throughout. "He appeared with his teleportation, then started trudging towards his ride building, slamming the door behind him. Weird thing is, his fangs were showing, and he looked mad. You know, whatever you did, I think he's got a grudge now..." Smiley explained, before looking at Samuel with a face of glee. "It's good you didn't bring the others! Then I would've needed to have a party! Unless that is, I don't need to wait!"

Smiley grinned, before firing a beam at Stella, who blindly shot a dart trying not to get blasted away. Samuel quickly jumped to the side as the dart flew right past him, bouncing on the ground. Florette gasped, seeing that Samuel nearly got hit, and used her vines as attacks. Smiley chuckled, as they flew towards him, all three getting cut with a single slice of his dagger.

Smiley launched a static like orb at Florette's hiding spot, trying to lure her out. Florette ran to the side and summoned a barricade of glowing thorns to protect herself. The thorns radiated with light, and shot out a barrage of splinter-shaped projectiles towards Smiley. With their energy depleted, the thorns then vanished into a gust of petal-like sparks. Smiley laughed, as his fingertips burst alight, tracing his hand movements in the air.

"Protecto Aegis!" Smiley cast, before a wall shield appeared from the sketch. He threw his arms forwards, ricocheting the shield towards the sparks like an attack. Florette rolled back to the side, while she watched the wall collide and shatter the beams. Blaze looked from the unprotected Florette to Smiley and dashed towards him at breakneck speed, trying to temporarily distract him. He swung at him with his sword, slitting the man's waist and searing it with the flames. Smiley screamed, his eyes spinning faster. He tumbled to the floor, using his magic to mostly heal the wound. He rolled to the left and stood himself up, before grinning with both his eyes and hands glowing. "Deflecto Surroundia!" Smiley cast, before a flickering, golden ring flew away from him and knocked down all the spirits around him.

Not missing a beat, he grabbed his gun out of its holster and aimed it at the spirit's head, clicking it to its bullet-firing mode with his thumb. Florette stood up, knowing that what she needed to do would come with consequences, but she needed to step in. With a deep breath, she launched out a vine. It tore through the air and slammed into Smiley at full force. He was left barely conscious on impact, tumbling to the floor. Blaze attached the enchanted bands on Smiley's hands and neck, stepping away just in case. The group had started to leave, with Florette crossing her fingers for a peaceful compromise. Just as they had crossed the perimeter of the X-Periment Facility, the ring of the Abyss portal started to whirr, as flashing lights sparked and flickered from it, signifying its activation. She sighed, bracing herself for what was coming.

Samuel panicked and started to sprint out of the zone, only for a weak gold aura to collide with his legs and make him trip and fall onto the path. Smiley hesitantly stood up, as all attention was on the portal. From the curling depths of the portal, a black, misted cloud flew out like a wave. The portal then deactivated itself as its purpose had been achieved. The mist collected into one spot, forming into Void, whose furious stare showed more than words. Stella flew down to the ground behind Florette, hoping to negotiate.

"I told you one thing to not do...one thing! I'd be fine with hating me, even calling me a monster...But you just had to hurt him, didn't you? But me doing the same is wrong. You promised, you hypocrite!" He said, pointing his finger at the green woman.

"Look, Void. She didn't mean to break the promise, she just wanted to stop Smiley from threatening us. He tried to brainwash me and Samuel! The vine thing was only to save Blaze!" Stella said, in an attempt to de-escalate the situation. Instead, it only resulted in an angry stare.

"That doesn't change the point that she knew what she was doing! She could have stopped him without violence, or simply explained her situation to him. But she jumped straight to a plan which fundamentally depends on deceiving, attacking, and incapacitating Smiley. You're probably the only one here who didn't break the promise, Stella. I don't have anything against you, it's the rest that have broken their side. You can still go!" he said, trying to get her to leave.

After a brief moment of consideration, Stella folded her wings, signifying that she would stay.

"Suit yourself! I won't say it wasn't worth a shot. Well, if you're all so willing to break your promises, I should reconsider what promises I've made too," Void said, before he summoned one of his duel blades.

"There's one promise I made to you all that I swore to keep, to protect everyone here. But, it seems that we're being liars, aren't we? The promise? To ignore my true nature, and give up my life's purpose. To not be what you see as evil," Void threatened.

Stella sadly realised what was happening, and looked back at Samuel. "Samuel, listen to me...quickly! You need to run. He only made that promise on the clause that we'd not break our side. Looks like Florette broke our side of the deal. I don't want to frighten you, but if you stay he'll probably...No, definitely...try to kill you. Run!" she yelled.

Samuel responded with a thumbs up and sprinted away as fast as he could, stumbling for a moment after narrowly dodging a golden projectile which flew towards him like the wind.

"Ignis Dash!" Blaze yelled, before a crackling lash of flame grew on his hand. He threw the lash forwards like a whip, which wrapped around and hexed the teen. Suddenly, his speed practically doubled, with a streak of light blue flames flickering momentarily at his feet. He rapidly blinked away, leaving the spirits behind. In a broad motion, Smiley threw the collar off, with the bracelets deactivating without the collar nearby. He laughed at their attempt at containing him, before he walked towards his brother with a vial of an unknown red liquid in his hand.

"Well, I see you made your decision…You'll regret this." Void laughed, before gripping the vial in his hand.

"No! Don't drink it! You could lose control of yourself and your powers!" Florette yelled, worried for herself and her friends.

Void's eyes had the same red glow as before, but this time, they weren't showing his telepathy. His fangs were showing again, and he was staring dead in the eyes of the spirits, practically shooting ice at them. "What if that's the plan? I'm so in control of myself that I'd never allow myself to go…over the edge. The only times anything truly bad has happened, I wasn't in control. What if that wasn't the case? If this works, I recommend that you run." Void warned, before drinking the entire liquid, the vial falling to the floor and shattering into shards of glass, to the right of Void.

Suddenly, he fell to his knees as his skin went from his normal peach shade to a snowy pale tone, and his eyes were tinted into crimson. He threw his glasses far to the left, with them crashing into the ground. The lenses were shattered and his scars were now highlighted against his pale skin. He stood up shakily, while grinning. "I'm guessing you know that when Void drinks someone's blood, he acts a bit like that person, until he personally ends the effect. Well, we had an idea. In that vial was a sample of my own blood. Now, with hints of my own personality, he's unleashed his true nature…a cruel, emotionless monster!" he explained, holding his dagger. "Thanks for that. Now, let's have some fun," Void spoke, his voice more dark and menacing. He tilted his right foot back slightly, before bolting straight towards the other spirits, slashing his blades. The spirits dove to safety, some just barely missing his blades.

Blaze stood up and growled deeply, a fire-like glow coming from around him. He started hovering above the ground, surrounded by a bright red aura as his sharp nails became claws, and two flaming wings made of wood came from his back. His pupils became sharper, and his skin turned from brown to grey. The demon flew into the air, and threw flames down onto the brothers. Stella activated her armour and summoned her dual laser guns, tossing the useless dart gun to the side. She flew into the air as a cyan glow trailed behind her, quickly gliding in a disc shape over the two siblings and firing her pistols down, raining neon teal beams onto the ground that made cracks and burn marks where they impacted. Smiley rolled away from the blast, while Void spun his blades above him, shielding himself from the beams.

Florette made a large flower bud in her hands before tossing it at Smiley. The bud exploded, knocking him backwards. Luckily, he managed to twist into a dodge roll. She then created a swirl of petals around her, teleporting herself out of direct sight. Void jumped, aiming to slash at one of Stella's metallic wings, quickly getting grabbed by Blaze, who tried to kick Void down to the ground. Void looked at the demon, before going to grab his shoulder, with Blaze using his claws to scratch at Void's arm, quickly switching and instead using a fireball on him. It hit Void's chest, making him fall down, toppling Blaze over too, both of them falling down to the ground.

Void, however, was able to catch himself, with Smiley quickly charging a healing spell and casting it on his brother. Blaze wasn't so lucky, and hit the ground face first, snapping him from his demon form, while knocking him out. Stella swung around, before hovering in the air for a moment, shortly noticing that Void was running towards the unconscious Blaze, his two blades out, ready to strike. She gasped, before sighing slightly. "Computer, activate attack mode, now!" Stella commanded, before blue, opaque spikes came out of the bottom of the wings, looking similar to feathers on a bird, as well as her guns transforming into shimmers, the sparks going into her armour, and becoming a blaster on her right hand. She swung herself up slightly, the new wings swishing backwards. "Wing beams!" Stella commanded. The spikes on her suit's wings suddenly lit up, firing out multiple cyan beams that were flying towards Void, who transformed into a cloud of mist, and disappeared. The blasts flew towards Blaze, which Stella dove down and quickly deflected.

She pressed a button, causing a cyan-themed bubble to appear around Blaze. Both the bubble and Blaze vanished with a snap of her fingers. She then grabbed his sword, which she had kept from teleporting, and placed it in a holder. "He'll be safe." She sighed, before focusing her mind once again and then turning on her heel.

Florette had sealed herself within a giant flower bud, which was being targeted by Smiley and Void. She only had one idea left, but it was extremely risky.

She decided to go through with the idea, before pressing a button on her headset. When the button was pressed, both her attack form and helmet were removed. This gave her more movement speed, at the cost of revealing her weak points. "Hey, stop hurting my friend!" she yelled.

Her yells caught the attention of Smiley and Void, who turned to look at her.

"Ooh... bad choice. You just revealed your weak spots!" Smiley mocked.

She pulled out her pistols and created her larger blaster, bracing herself for the weapon's stronger recoil. She fired a large, teal laser beam at the two spirits, hitting Smiley, but not Void. Smiley screamed, before skidding to a halt, struggling to get up.

Void stared at Stella, with a rage like nothing else she'd seen. He stood there for a moment, before his eyes turned black as ink. He moved methodically, like a machine, inching towards her until he was only a few metres away. "Wrong move," he said with a flat tone. A ball of black mist formed in his hand, flowing and contorting in its confined state. He shot her a sneer, before throwing the ball on the ground. As soon as it touched the concrete floor, it seemed to explode in a tidal wave of black engulfing mist. As quick as he had thrown it, the area was taken over by the wall of shadow, making sight beyond your own hands and anything just in front of you impossible.

"Now this is interesting. Can't see a thing, dearie? Who knows…maybe I can help with that one day. But, I know what you want. So, here's the hard part. How can you save Florette if you can barely see five metres in front of you!" He mocked her.

Stella used Blaze's sword to slash where the spirit's voice came from, only to just be cutting smoke.

She looked down, before flicking on the flames on the blade, giving her at least a larger amount of vision. She shouted for Florette, only to hear nothing but the sound of distant laughter and movement. Just as she went to take another step, a golden streak flashed past her. If she had continued to move, she would have been hit. She looked around in panic, realising that she could be attacked from any corner. Just as the pressure began to set in, she saw a lone portal nearby. From its colour, she could tell it was from Void. But, when she looked through it, she recognised the location: Technoland. For a moment she considered stepping through it, but she knew that her doing so would mean danger, or worse, for Florette. While they did have issues in the past, she wasn't going to abandon her. Pushing through her fear, she cut through the portal with a blade, which caused it to shatter and dispel.

As the portal light faded, she saw the glow of Void's striking eyes in the darkness. He shook his head in what could have been disapproval, before they were tinted red. She followed him, wanting to confront him on why he was acting this way, to be greeted at a sight which made her blood freeze. Florette was lying limp on the floor, with Void stood over her, wiping blood from his mouth.

"No!" Stella yelled, as her friend vanished with a burst of light. After a moment, all that remained was a small glowing orb in place of her friend. Void stared coldly at the soul, then broke it into shards. She gasped in shock, and fell onto the floor, heartbroken. "No. She…can't be," Stella cried, with her hands over her mouth, before she saw Smiley walk towards her, a knife in his hand. He laughed slowly, while Stella shuffled backwards, begging for the person who was once her friend to not kill her. Smiley inched closer, with Void by his side. Just as the two of them were only a few steps away from her, she noticed that there was something wrong with them. They were dimly lighting up the space around them, and were shining with an amber glow.

"Wait a second...they're an illusion!" She spoke, before slashing the illusions in their chests, causing them to turn back into smoke and magic charge.

"Well done, dearie. You saw through the Illusion. Can you find your friend, however?" Void spoke, his voice echoing from every direction. She wandered inside the smoke, trying to find her friend and still making no progress. As soon as she had stopped for a moment, however, she felt a chill run up her back, and her heart started racing. She turned around, her focus locking on to the familiar pair of red eyes that seemed to, with every heartbeat, inch closer. In a panic, she snapped back around to start to run, only to be met by a normal-eyed Void.

He smiled at her, while holding her arm by the wrist. Without his gloves, Void's cold touch chilled her hand down in moments. While this feeling would usually be a sign of comfort, as they both were more open and honest to each other than to the rest of the spirits, in the moment it was bitter and frightening.

"Well, hello sweetheart. My, your heart is nearly beating out of your chest. For someone like me, that is irresistible! After all, what is simply a sound of life for you is a sign of blood for me, and you know how I am. But, I've used up so much energy that I'm struggling to stay nice. And I'm sure that you don't want me to snap to...him. So, why don't we take some time off? Maybe we could spend some time together someplace where it'll be just you and me. Maybe...The Abyss! But, I know what you're going to say. You need to save Florette, so you can't come right now! However, maybe she can be alright for a few minutes. I've told Smiley to not harm her, and he knows to listen to me."

Stella still refused, determined to help her friend. He stood there in shock before his eyes shifted again to red, as he stared deeply into hers. "I'm sorry, dearie, but you don't have much of a choice," he said softly, in an almost deceptively kind tone. Just as Void said the last word, Stella's arms and legs got grabbed by some tendrils, which pulled her off her feet.

Florette flinched, as she heard her scream through the darkness. She dispelled her flower, hoping Smiley did not follow her. She ran through the smoke-like haze in the vague direction of the noise, with a light spell ready in her right hand. She calmed herself down by breathing slowly, lowering her pulse to be less noticeable by Void. "Stella?! Can you hear me? If you can, scream or yell as loud as you can!" she prompted, for a loud, familiar scream to ring behind her. She ran as fast as she could through the darkness and arrived at Abyss. Void was standing to the side, while Stella was being pulled towards the portal by black, ink-like tendrils that were wrapped around her arms and legs. She was trying to use the energy from her hover boots to get herself free, but the tendrils would not budge.

Florette tried to cut through the tendrils using a sharp, dagger-like leaf. However as soon as she had done minimal damage to one of the tendrils, she heard Smiley laughing behind her back. Void and Smiley were standing behind them, their weapons out.

"Why are you doing this, Void? Why're you hurting my friends! I've always been there for you, and that's how you repay me?" Florette pleaded for him to reconsider his actions.

Void stared blankly for a moment, before he shut his eyes. When his eyes opened, they were back to their normal amber colour for a moment. However, he shook his head with a sharp growl, as his eyes shifted back into red.

"...You really think I buy that? You've always been suspicious of me. You always called the rest of the group your friends instead of our friends when you were talking to me. I had been part of this friend group for years, and you had never once talked to me like a member. I bet the only reason you've tolerated my presence is because you didn't want to lose Stella.

"I saw the way you would stare at me and Smiley from the corner of your eye while denouncing the Ministry and their evil acts, and how you would wear silver jewellery whenever you knew I would be in a meeting, since you knew that it burns people like me. You assumed I would attack you without reasoning or provocation for no reason other than I was a Vampire. You even pressured everyone to fear and distrust me! You always told the others that we were wrong for our actions, for our manipulation of others, for our mind control. But you always seemed to neglect your hypocrisy. Do you remember how you would get information out of Ministry spies and scientists? Sure, there were the cases of them telling you, or us just telling it to you. But you never bring up what happened when they wouldn't slip. Does the name Psychosis-Ignoring Mind Reader ring a bell? It was a device that Nebulus and the Technoland spirits were demanded to make, under your supervision. You said it would help the fight against the Ministry, by allowing you into their minds. You saw from the prototypes that you could, and you never thought for a moment if you should."

Florette glared at him with undisguised rage. Yet he ignored her anger.

"You used that device to force Ministry members to tell you all their latest plans, but you never seemed to care what happened after! Do you wonder why me and Smiley don't just drill into people's minds and take what we want out? Not only does it require a lot of energy, it can leave them mentally damaged, comatose or even brain dead! That little nightmare machine was a mental drill that took people's lives and minds away, but it was ignored and brushed aside, in favour of more slander against us! Going into people's minds is literally what me and Smiley do. Yet it's corrupt and sinful for us, and an act for the greater good for you. Even if we put that to the side, I know that you've never trusted me! You knew what you were doing would put yourself at risk, and that you were dragging your friends down with you, yet you continued. And now you go and break the deal that you yourself pushed Stella to make with me, knowing that she was uncomfortable with the fact that she would have to become my donor. This plan is all just some thinly veiled attack at me, isn't it?" Void yelled.

Florette looked at him, understanding what he meant, yet not wanting to show it. "Yes, fine, I've made my fair share of mistakes. But I wasn't wrong to distrust you both! All I have done was to help everyone, even if some people were left worse off. If you're trying to prove yourself as some innocent saint, then why are you hurting my friends? Trying to project your flaws onto me won't help, and I am not going to take any more hate!" she snapped. Her eyes flared to life in a green glow, and her hair floated into the air like she was underwater. Aethereal, shimmering green rings appeared at her hands as thick, green vines entrapped the two men and brought them into the air. The vine containing Void, however, was covered with glowing, rune-like symbols that blocked his power. The red eyes flickered and faded, as the runes disrupted the effect.

The mist cloud faded away, and Stella launched herself away from the portal using her rocket shoes. Despite being saved from being trapped in the Abyss, she still looked at the scene unfolding in front of her in shock and dismay. She stood frozen, not knowing who to stand for; the one whom she swore to help, or the one whom she'd called friend. "I'll not let you both go until you admit the truth! You're the bad guys here, the ones plotting to destroy us from the inside. I'm only going through this plan to prove a point!" But her expression dropped as she realised what she'd let slip.

"What plan? The plan was to incapacitate Smiley, not some forced confession!" Stella asked. She turned towards the nature spirit, confused at what she meant. The two were staring at each other, with Florette's empty, shining glare making Stella feel unnerved.

"The Smiley plan was only the bait! I knew that there was something up with these two, so I got Fawnia to send an invitation to you all, except Smiley. Since it was breaking the promise, I knew it would get Void's attention. All I needed to do was wait for Void to come, and then capture them both. After that, it would be a waiting game before one of them cracks and tells us the truth—them being the real villains—and I'm proven right!" she said, clapping her hands in excitement.

The two girls started an argument over the morality of lying to them all, before Void interjected. "Dearie, you can stop arguing now. It's not a good look. The problem is between me and her. You don't need to hang around, you're free to leave. Maybe…I could check in later, when I'm not tied up by people wanting me to admit to crimes I've not committed?"

Stella stayed yet again, despite his warnings. He looked down at her with a hint of what could have been sadness, before his expression died. Smiley matched his brother's stare, and gave him a short nod. "Hmm. Well, we do have something on our minds, but we won't say unless you let us down," Smiley said, his eyes slightly spinning, though he wasn't trying to hypnotise anyone.

Their captor shrugged, not believing what he was saying. Void caught on to what his adopted sibling was doing, and joined in. "Perhaps you want more detail? There's currently a device that is connected to my magic essence somewhere in the park. As long as it can sense my magic, it'll remain dormant and safe. That is, if you hadn't just tied me in an energy blocker," he said, his face expressionless.

"What will happen if the device loses your energy?" Stella said, believing him.

The vampire chuckled, his head tilted forwards. "Heard of a shockwave? Now imagine a shockwave that has the power to disrupt the magic, including enchantments and long-lasting spells, of anything it touches. What do you think will happen when it touches the barrier? I'm sure you don't want to feel disintegration."

Stella stepped backwards, her eyes wide and her mouth agape. Florette focused on her, and then at the two suspended men, and sank her eyes. "Fine. But you'll regret it if this is a trap," she said, as she whispered a spell under her breath. Her long hair floated back down to her back and her eyes returned to their normal state. The vines freed the two men and vanished.

He flicked his hand in a circle, seemingly disabling the device. He patted her on the shoulder, then tilted her head up. "Nice plan of yours, anyways. If you try, you could become a detective or something."

Stella looked away for a moment, not recognising a red flash go over his eyes. After the brothers were a couple of metres away, she tried to tell Florette to leave the area. However, she didn't move, and didn't even notice Stella tugging on her arm.

Terrified, she looked around for any signs of what was happening, before she noticed something that made her heart sink. Florette's eyes were covered by a deep red glow, a symptom of completely falling into one of Void's trances. It was, indeed, a trap. When he saw her panicking, Void went back over to the women, with Smiley following suit. "I can see that you've noticed what has happened. I didn't want to control her, she forced my hand. Nobody polite would accuse someone of being a traitor, then keep them captive! You get it, right? Well, she's currently entranced. She's under my puppet strings, as you could put it." Void spoke, before mouthing something.

"See? If I want it, she does it! I'm Florette, and I don't trust people!" Florette spoke robotically while under the powerful trance. Stella was shocked, stumbling back, trying to get away from the three spirits.

"Oh! I've just thought of an idea that might fit this situation..." he said. He shut his eyes for a brief moment, as the glowing light in Florette's eyes disappeared, breaking her out from the trance.

She blinked for a moment in a daze then gasped, her eyes and head darting around frantically, looking for a way to escape.

"Stella, help! I'll tell everyone the truth—I'll reveal the plan and how I had lied to everyone—if you just give me a hand here!" Florette begged, as her eyes showed something Stella had never seen from her friend: pure fear.

Just as she had grabbed her friend's hand, Void had charged his Dreamless Sleep Spell in his fingers. The two looked at each other in fear, as the spirit placed a fingertip on the woman's forehead, guiding her head down as she went limp in his grasp. Stella tried to pull her away from him, but a chill crept down her arm every moment she held Florette's hand, almost freezing her to the bone. She instinctively pulled her hand away, as her mind thought her hand was in danger. Just as she loosened her grip, Florette was lifted into the air like a marionette, a puppet on a string.

"What are you doing, don't hurt her!" she cried.

Both Smiley and Void turned around, their stares aimed directly at her. "Don't worry yourself, dearie. I won't hurt her. After all, she can't feel anything right now. Besides, I can do whatever I want. If she can make everyone fear me and my brother here, I can mess with her a bit. Remember, you chose to stay!" He responded to her command in a sarcastic, yet sweet tone. His demeanour shifted, as he bent downwards, submerging her in his shadow. His gaze was focused on her chest, where her soul would appear to him. But, she could feel that something wasn't right. His expression was cruel, almost animalistic in nature, and his eyes displayed a sort of sick, twisted freedom that turned her stomach in knots.

"At times, you could see a good person in her. She wouldn't have trapped me if she was good, though it's not like I need to worry about anything, really. How could somebody, say, kill the undead? It always cracks me up to see people in horror films trying to kill the monster, instead of simply running away...Especially when the monster was someone they had wronged all along. Such a shame too that our friend didn't decide to drop her plan. I wouldn't have drank that blood sample. There's a silver lining, though! I can think clearly, but it's more like euphoria than clarity. Can't really tell right from wrong right now as well, honestly." He started to ramble, clearly acting more like his sibling, who was nodding along in a strange understanding.

"If I hadn't touched it, this situation would likely be ending differently, you know. I wouldn't want to hurt you guys. It's tragic she wasn't as kind as you, dear. Maybe I would have given her something to...help her with her research into how mental damage affects the soul. My help could have been so useful. After all, mental stress from potentially traumatic incidents is basically second nature to someone with the same affliction as me. Maybe she would have liked eternal youth. Pity," he said with a grin, as his fangs jutted out.

"No!" she screamed. She tried to split the two apart, but got restrained by Smiley, who had phased behind her while his brother was talking, anticipating an attack. "Let me go, Miles! You know this isn't right," she yelled.

He growled, his sharp teeth gritting together. "I prefer his plan. One more thing...never call me Miles!" he snapped back, before he threw her down to the ground with a thud, twisting her leg in the process.

"Agh!" She screamed in pain, holding her leg. It wasn't broken, but she certainly wasn't going to be running until she had the time to heal it. She looked towards Void when her face quickly twisted to horror. In front of her, Void had once again bitten into Florette's neck and was drinking the crimson blood that was flowing from it.

This time, however, he continued drinking with no restraint or mercy. Florette was limply hovering in front of the vampire spirit, her skin was paler, and she was crying slightly, despite the sleeping enchantment Void had placed onto her. The crimson stains of her own blood were flowing down her neck and dripping to the floor, leaving maroon spots on the concrete. Stella struggled to stand up, as her leg pulsed with pain. "Stop, you monster!" Stella yelled at the top of her lungs, starting to cry. Void unlatched, staring Stella dead in the eye, bearing his fangs.

"Oh. I'm just a monster, now? Adorable! Funny how you always say the opposite. Did you forget that, or is it only when you know you're safe? No matter. I tried to get you to leave, yet you persist. Do you have any reason to stay, or do you just have a death wish? I find it hilarious how people time and time again forget the simplest things. Like what, you ask? Maybe the fact that trying to go against me is never a good idea. It never ends well! Still, people try. Like our friend here. It was a stupid plan, all things considered. Did she honestly think that someone she thought was a liar and traitor would...tell the truth? You really see the irony in her plan when you realise she wasn't a saint either. And yet, she thought it was smart! I hope you don't make the same decision, Stella. You wouldn't be able to bear fighting with me, anyways." Void smirked, with Florette's blood still wet on his fangs.

"After all, you've tried to attack me, to defend from my strength...but you couldn't even save your friend. How sad."

Stella gasped, before noticing that Void's grasp on Florette had faded, making her start to fall to the floor, limply. Stella threw her arms forwards, catching the falling woman with her magic in time. "Florette! Ivy! Please...don't die!" Stella cried, her eyes filled with tears, which were rolling down her face and splashing onto the ground. The now limp form of Florette erupted in a wave of limelight, breaking away into glittering light and fading away.

Nothing remained but Stella kneeling on the ground in front of a large, jade and silver orb floating in the air, with a mystical glow coming from it. "Oh...her soul? Why don't I just..." Void went to snatch the soul orb, only for Stella to grab his wrist roughly, making him unable to even lay a finger on it.

"...Do you really think I'm going to let you kill my friend, and walk off calmly? In your dreams...you vampiric creep." Stella growled, before throwing Void to the floor instead, the spirit rubbing his left wrist in pain. "Florette, if you can hear me like this...let's teach these monsters a lesson!" Stella called out, for the orb to glow brightly, as if agreeing to the plan.

Stella embraced the orb, absorbing it into her chest, her eyes turning into a bright, lime glow, and she levitated off the ground and into the air, a green and cyan orb forming and flying around her. Stella's headset fell off, to be caught by Smiley, who looked at the device with joyous glee. Void looked on with a look of both annoyance and amazement, watching the teal orb hover down, before revealing the result. In front of the two men stood a tall, pale brown skinned woman with two different coloured eyes. Her left eye was brown, and her right was violet. The lady's hair was chocolate brown with green streaks, and went from brown to teal the further down the hair you looked. It was kept in a long plait that ran down her shoulder.

She wore a multicoloured dress, with the top being green and the skirt being blue. In between the two parts there was a rose which functioned as a sash, parting the two. The top was patterned with a flower pattern hemmed in, while the bottom was covered in glitter that made it look like a starry sky. She was also wearing a pair of purple sandals, and a futuristic headset. "The magic power, grace and intelligence of Florette, and the strength and durability of Stella…I am Galaxy Rose!" she said.

Smiley laughed hysterically. "Ahahaha! Galaxy Rose? Of course you would give yourself a complicated name!" He mocked her with a smile.

She growled, before looking from Smiley to Void. "You've been doing this for too long, Vampire." She looked determined. She summoned her weapon, an elegant forest green and teal fan.

"A fan? Oh no. Please save me from this horrific fan!" Void spoke sarcastically, provoking her to attack.

"It's horrific, alright!" Galaxy repeated, as she shook open the fan. With elegant swipes, she sent glowing slashes towards the two. However, they narrowly dodged them.

"Ahah! Your aiming seems to have gotten worse, Stella!" Smiley laughed, before noticing that Galaxy wasn't in front of them, with only a glimmer of sparks in her place.

"Oh! That's wrong, but thanks for trying." Galaxy mocked, before Smiley was thrown to the sky, with Galaxy jumping up to meet him. "Don't mess with my friends!" she warned, before knocking Smiley out of the sky with a blast from her fan.

He plummeted to the floor, hitting the ground with a thud, with his healing abilities kicking in seconds before impact and stopping him from dying, but instead knocking him out cold. Galaxy gracefully floated down, a small smile on her face, then gently folded her fan up and walked away. "I hope this is a lesson learned."

Void looked even more enraged. "You don't get it, do you? I'm still in control of The Blight. I can do much more than normal." Void growled, throwing one of his blades at Galaxy, for her to use the fan as a shield.

"It seems magic won't do..." Galaxy sighed, before touching the blade with a single finger, turning it blue. "I can use other spirits' powers against them, especially weapons." She smiled, swapping her fan for Void's blade. "You want to duel, well, let's duel!" Galaxy exclaimed, using Void's blade as her own.

"Hmm...clever. I can summon another, however, to make this a fair fight." Void smirked, before another blade appeared in his hand. Void rushed towards Galaxy, only for her to swirl to the left and not get hit.

He tried again, only to have the same result, just right instead of left. Void laughed with a sneer, as he jumped forwards to finally hit her. In a last ditch attempt, Galaxy swung back with Void's own blade. Both spirits were flung back, and fell to the floor, coughing. Both Void and Galaxy looked down to see that they were both stabbed and wounded by each other's blow.

One more direct attack, and the recipient would most likely die. Galaxy struggled to keep her form, but failed and turned back into Stella and Florette's soul. She looked at the orb, before making her magic rush to her hands. "Encapsulate Transportia..." Stella cast. The soul was entrapped in a blue bubble, then vanished with a flash. She turned around and looked up to see Void dominating above her, holding his sword which he must have grabbed back along the way. He had healed the stab wound, leaving only a black stain on his clothes. For a moment, he seemed to hesitate with his own actions. But the shock soon dulled down to a blank stare, like his own emotions were switched off.

"Nice try! But you've got no more tricks now. Maybe you'll wake up as someone...different. I think you'd be captivating, if you just lost the heartbeat," he said without his normal tone. He braced himself, before swinging down to strike the vulnerable and injured Stella. Just as his sword was inches away from her, a familiar voice called out from the entrance.

"Spirit Shards!" Fawnia yelled.

A cluster of purple crystal shards formed around her staff and flew forwards, stabbing through Void and launching him backwards. He collided with the cold, concrete wall, and was knocked unconscious. Smiley woke up and saw Void on the floor. He stood himself up and ran to him like his life depended on it. With no time to spare, he removed the shards and used up most, if not all, of his magic energy healing the multiple wounds on Void's body. He shrunk down in exhaustion, his arms and hands splattered with black blood. Stella looked to her right, and saw Fawnia rush towards her. She had taken off her grey cloak, revealing the pale red dress that was once tucked underneath it. The midday sun that managed to breach the clouds reflected off the countless red rubies and pink spinels that were sewn into the fabric, making her almost dazzle in the light.

In her hand, she was holding onto the grip of her golden staff, which was recharging from the powerful attack. She started to run towards Stella, since she could run faster without her high heels. She took a breath, after reaching her friend's side. "After waking up, Blaze told me to come quickly. Whatever happened here is serious," Fawnia explained, with Blaze in tow.

Nebulus came towards the two, carefully picking Stella up off the ground. "Queeney, we've got something else to worry about. Stella's wounded!"

Stella flinched slightly as he placed her down as gently as he could on a nearby table, then checked the wound. "It's a stab wound, clearly from a more curved blade. So, it was Void's sword. Either he did this or someone took his blade," he explained, as he fished a potion out from his pocket.

She took the potion and drank it down eagerly. The wound began to close, and with the help from Fawnia's magic, healed up completely. She sighed in relief, before sitting herself up, a grateful smile on her face. "Thanks guys! Now, let's see what our twins of terror have to say." She slid down from the table and walked towards the two brothers, with the rest of the spirits by her side.

Smiley flinched, seeing the group come closer towards his brother. He stood himself up, quickly blocking their progression. "Stay back! He's still hurt, and I know you all are mad at him, and I, as both his adoptive sibling and a doctor, forbid you from coming closer unless you can prove to me you mean him no harm!" Smiley yelled out, defending Void, who was laid against the wall, stable but unconscious for the moment.

"Smiley Miles. Please, we'll not hurt him. We just want the truth," Nebulus explained, with a calm voice, looking at Smiley, who was obviously trying not to snap at the alien, after he said his full name.

"Fine. He should be awake and normal soon. Luckily for you, the blood sample he drank should have faded away by now..." Smiley accepted, before walking to the side and sitting on a railing, wishing Samuel was here to see what was about to happen.

Void's eyes opened, and while they were at first a bright crimson, they shifted back into his normal amber shade, along with his skin colour, and his fangs fully retracted back, as if they were never there. "What in the world happened?..." Void moaned, with a shaky voice. He carefully stood himself up, as if returning to his normal state drained him.

157

"What did you do!" Nebulus snapped.

The alien looked enraged, a taser like device in his hand. "What do you mean? All I can remember is drinking that liquid... and waking up here."

"You know very well what you're guilty of. Do you remember what you did to me?" Stella asked, pointing at a mark on her wrist, from the tendrils.

"Yeah! What about it." Void blurted out, before realising his mistake.

"Finally slipped? You've always been lying, haven't you? You lied about not knowing about stabbing me, or nearly killing Blaze, and the worst of all. You have specks of blood on your mouth that you forgot to remove. I bet you know whose blood that is, don't you...you murderer." Stella revealed to the group, who gasped with shock.

"What?! *Murderer?* I would *never* do anything like that!" Void replied to her accusation, his voice cold and tipped with sarcasm.

"Who...how...why?" Fawnia said. Her navy eyes were flowing with tears, which were rolling down her cheeks.

"Florette. He killed her right in front of me! She couldn't even fight back, as he controlled her or something...he took it all. Her life, her blood..." Stella explained, her voice shaking.

"You...you're not good, are you? I knew that you and your smiling sibling over there felt off from the start. We trusted you...She trusted you. We thought that you could overcome your vampiric nature, but we were wrong from the looks of it! What else have you been lying to us about? Let me guess! Did you cause us all to be trapped here in the first place? Was our friendship a lie?" Blaze yelled.

Void looked at the scene, before his face and mannerisms changed completely. His shocked frown twisted into a dark grin, and he lay back against the wall, slowly clapping his hands. "Wow. Congratulations! You caught me red handed, after so long. I killed her, in front of little Miss Stella here!" Void smirked, before turning into his black mist form, then disappearing into thin air.

The spirits looked around, before a shadow figure appeared behind them, for Fawnia to spot it and point it out. "To be fair, I should've got Smiley to do a memory wipe... it wouldn't have been spoiled. Also, it isn't my fault that she got in the way." The figure continued maliciously, for Blaze to throw a fireball at it to make it switch back to Void. He started staring at the demon, who looked back in triumph.

He sat himself down onto a nearby bench, his legs crossed casually. "You know what...I might as well be honest. When I was affected by the blood sample, I wasn't crazy. I just didn't care if I hurt people. Actually, that's how I would act if I stopped trying to control my darker thoughts. One more thing. Stella dear, do you wonder why I was smiling after committing the crime?"

Stella shook her head, confused.

"Ah, of course you don't. I'll tell you then. Drinking blood feels like what normal people would call...adrenaline. It feels amazing!" Void yelled.

"You're just as bad as Smiley, aren't you?!" said Blaze, remembering what Samuel told and showed him and his friends about the spirit.

"Smiley, to my knowledge, has only had to end the lives of about 12 people to this date, correct?" Void asked Smiley.

He nodded, looking towards the group of gathered spirits.

"I've had to end 40. There were nine from when I was still in testing, 16 from my role in the Ministry, six from people falling into the abyss...and never returning, and the other nine? Can you guess?" Void asked. Despite reciting the frightening amount of lost lives, he still kept his calm demeanour, with an amused look on his face.

"There's only been one time in my knowledge where seven people were killed in the park, which was...wait, you couldn't have!" Fawnia deduced. Her blood ran cold, as a dark thought spread across the group.

THE SECRET OF THE SMILE

"Mhm? What is it?" Smiley spoke. Void was now near his brother's side, leaning against the wall.

"The Perfector Incident. But, nobody was caught! All that was identified was a staff member!" Blaze said.

The demon's hair seemed to spark, like fire itself.

"Hmm...A staff member? Need I remind you that all of us here can change forms? It doesn't have to be a human. If we entertain the idea of it being a human, most humans don't think it's morally or legally right to kill. If there was someone who did, it would be relatively easy to fake being a staff member, the harder part would be not getting caught on camera. The problem is, those that want to kill aren't dumb. They wouldn't walk around in plain view of security cameras without hiding their face or identifying features. On top of that, human life is short. A killer that is smart enough to not get caught for a decade, and practically disappear from record besides some messed up tape footage would know that it isn't worth it if they'd be imprisoned for life if they inevitably get caught.

"About the Smiley theory, there's also two sides to it. While his mental state is more unstable than the rest of us due to The Ministry, and he is prone to taking things too far, he also would never have sacrificed his fame unless he was forced. Nobody fits exactly." Void smirked. He stood there for a moment, debating what to do, but he finally made a decision. "That is...unless we've had a traitor in the group all along," he added.

Stella looked confused at the mention of a traitor, and started to think. "A traitor? Nobody here would betray us. Unless they were lying about that too. Fawnia, you're the one who keeps all the knowledge. Any idea what he's talking about?"

The Queen spun her staff, causing a book to appear in front of her. "This was an account that me and Florette wrote about the murders, and Smiley's subsequent death. I wrote the facts, she wrote theories and ideas. I can assume that there will be something to help in its pages," she explained, flicking through the pages.

Blaze, who had sat himself down on a solid cloud of smoke that he made, rolled his eyes in boredom. "It'll take forever to find anything, there was so much information that we could be here forever! Plus, it's obvious that he's being misleading," Blaze said, staring at Void from the corner of his eyes.

The towering man laughed at their struggle, before stepping forwards. "I'll save you the time. Smiley's death is chapter 12. No idea why you'd want to check there, she didn't write anything. For some reason, she left her section blank," Void stated, making the book fly towards the chapter with a wave of his hand. He stood, waiting for a thank you, but was ignored. On the page, there was an account about Smiley's mysterious death.

The spirits could tell Fawnia wrote it at a glance, due to the cursive handwriting. It went into detail about the day when Smiley was found dead, and how his death was most likely a slip from the Abyss, or a magic failure. Just like Void said; however, the part where Florette would have given a theory or wrote her notes was blank beside a short message saying how there was no evidence of a possible murder.

"Nothing? There's nothing here!" Stella said.

Void smirked, thinking he'd been proved right. However, she soon had an idea. She put her hands together, and summoned Florette's soul to her. "I've got a dumb idea, but it might work," she said with a mischievous smile. She popped the bubble containing the soul, and focused its glow on the large gap of space underneath the short message.

Where the light touched Florette's section, it uncovered some hidden writing. The message seemed to have been written in a hurry due to its rushed handwriting, using some invisible ink that reacts with magic. It was quick and to the point, with a simple message: Don't trust Void. The message started to ramble, a side effect of Florette's problem with keeping on track. But the command was clear. The group nodded to each other, agreeing to the plan. Since nobody read it out loud, neither Void or Smiley knew the contents.

Stella quickly wrote down the message on a piece of paper she tore from a notepad in her pocket. When she was done, the soul was again entrapped in a bubble like aura, and vanished in a warp like effect. The book also vanished, its purpose achieved. She looked back at the vampire, catching his gaze. His expression was warm and caring, making her internally want to back down and let him go. After all, would he still care for her if she let him be labelled a monster? She kept her mouth shut, knowing that she would try and brush things off if she allowed herself to speak. Just as Stella was about to crack from his seemingly caring gaze, Blaze walked up from behind her and put his hand on her shoulder in support. When he smiled at her to remind her of the task at hand, he saw the man's expression change back into indifference as he turned away from her.

"Hey Void, can you tell us your view of how Smiley died? Just keep it brief," Blaze asked, standing in for her.

Void seemed to accept this, although he didn't look towards them both. "Alright, I'll try to remember. Well, me and Smiley were always rivals, but there was no harm done. That was until the fame went to his head. He neglected me, took all the attention, even went so far as to call me a mistake. Then, the killings happened. He came crawling back and begged me to believe he didn't kill the guests. I didn't, and went to stand on the Abyss to calm down. The feeling of the wind allows me to allow myself to let go a bit and calm down If I feel overwhelmed.

"Anyways, I went up to get my mind straight, but realised that Smiley had teleported in front of me to speak face-to-face. I didn't want to talk at that moment, but warned him that being up on the track is dangerous. He underestimated the breeze's strength, and got knocked into the pit before I could catch him. I called you all to try and help, but by the time you all came, he had already died. That's the whole of it," he said, recalling the events of Smiley's death.

Stella, having got her mind back together, worked the events out in her head. "Hey Smiley, do you remember anyone else being there at the time? You were the victim, so you'd know if anyone was there." She was acting as inconspicuous as she could.

He pondered for a moment, and nodded. "Yeah. There were a bunch of people. Camera crews, law enforcement, you get the gist. There was someone else though. Poor girl had a mauled hand. I'm surprised she even managed to survive with it! She became the Minister, and...well, you know the rest. Why?" He answered with a cheerful voice. Void, however, took a sharp sideways glance down at him, as if to tell him to stop.

"So, you were killed when Eliza was rushed to hospital? Here's the problem with that. She could see us spirits, and magic in general. Wasn't she caught on camera pointing up? Yes, it was above Abyss, but if she saw you at the tracks, she'd be pointing at them. It doesn't make sense," she said, pointing out a flaw.

Void breathed deeply, his eyes set on her. "Well, there's a hole in your argument. We only have proof of attuned behaviour from after her kidnapping by The Ministry. They could have easily given her a treatment that allowed her to see us, or brought her up to speed. If I got kidnapped by people with hypnotic eyes that looked like the roller coaster my family died at, and they somehow had technology decades ahead of the rest of humanity, magic would be easy to believe. There is little to no documentation that we can get our hands on that says anything that pointed to her being Gifted instead of being a sign of creativity or vivid daydreaming. Now, if she were to be a sworn believer in fantasy and magic, I'd be backing you. But, there's nothing to say she was different to any other average girl who read Fantasy books as a hobby. Plus, there is a normal phenomenon that explains the weird actions. She was found with, as Smiley put it, a mauled hand. She had clearly lost a lot of blood, and seemingly survived due to pure luck. People who lose blood tend to act strange, as the areas that affect the senses cannot get blood flow. Their ears ring, their vision blurs, that sort of thing. Who's to say she didn't misconstrue a ride cart or some other object as a figure? Eliza was also dosed on painkillers that were safely administered to help the doctors secure the arm and keep the pain at a minimum until they could get her to hospital. Drugs do a lot to you, like hallucinations. This could simply be a case of a girl on pain medicine due to severe blood loss and life-threatening injuries misinterpreting a normal object as a figure." He said his rebuttal, a small frown on his face.

Stella froze in panic, not wanting both herself and the now late Florette to be seen as victim blamers if he was telling the truth. She pulled out the version of the note she quickly copied down, and read through it again.

Fawnia saw her struggling, and put her foot down. "Alright, listen here! I'm not allowing Stella to struggle alone in this little debate. I've figured something out, and there's no way you can debunk this! You said Smiley went up the Abyss tracks to talk to you, and even teleported in front of you, which must've been the edge of the track. Here's the nail in the coffin, no joke intended, for that theory. Smiley had, and always has had, Acrophobia. I'm guessing you understand that it means the fear of heights.

"Stella once even told me that he purposefully sabotages his chances to win at her flying races by staying low to the ground. If he has to fly high, he focuses himself on what he is doing, and not the surroundings. So, why would he purposely go up a height that would be deadly if he fell, and near the edge as well? There's no way he would purposefully go up that high, unless he didn't have a choice. Like, being pulled up into the air by you, perhaps?" she snapped.

Void paused, showing no expression. "If you really think I'm wrong, then I implore you to tell us all your idea of a logical, and supposedly true story of how it happened." He challenged her without care.

"Fine then. You could say I'm giving my idea of a testimony," she said, feeling proud. She brought out her staff, and used it to create a magical projection that followed her story.

"Alright, so both Void and Smiley were brought up to be competitive. This meant that they both wanted to be the better of the two, so they'd do anything to impress. I'm not a psychologist, but teaching people who don't know right from wrong yet that their worth is dependent on who is the best will lead them to be jealous of each other.

"Fast forward to when Smiley got famous, making him the better person. Of course, Void is right about the whole power going to his head thing, as we do know that Smiley was a bit dismissive of Void at the time. However, the same can be said of when Void was the dominant ride. He said that he was not affected by Smiley's dismissal and disrespect of him, but I think many of us remember the times where he would start complaining about how he never got attention besides from the occasional rude remark from guests.

"Void then jumped to the killings, which is up for debate of who was the killer. Anyways, Smiley said he wasn't the killer and begged for forgiveness, according to the witness's story of events. We know Smiley was most likely innocent from the fact that he would never sacrifice his stardom, and the fact he wound up dead anyways. Void refused his apology. This is where the story gets...interesting. Smiley himself would have been a witness of the killing, since he was the spirit of the ride, so he would have been alerted to an unknown intruder. So whoever was the killer would want him gone. And what happened next? Smiley died. Or should I say, he was murdered!"

The others looked surprised, due to the severity of the accusation.

"Yes, he was killed. As we know, Eliza saw someone in the air, most likely a spirit or two. And who is one of the few spirits we know that can float? So, Void. Was this really a tragic accident of someone falling to their death, or a murder to finally silence the person who had evidence against you!" Fawnia finished and turned towards where Void would be standing, only to be faced with a black, morphing shadow. She stepped back in fear, making sure her dress would not be damaged by the floor.

The darkness contorted and shifted, before gathering back into a humanoid form. But it didn't look like Void. It was a somewhat tall man, with deep green eyes and brown hair that was both professional and intimidating. The thing which caused the group to feel paler than a haunting of ghosts was the immaculate Perfector staff uniform he was wearing. He laughed, like something you would expect in a horror film. "Did you get what you were looking for? Find out the things you felt you needed to know? Well, congratulations! You know the truth. It was me all along. Not just the murder of Smiley, if you get what I mean," he said, his tone rough and unhinged.

"You were the Perfector murderer. But why?" Blaze asked, his claw-like nails posed for attack in case Void became violent.

The man shifted his form back to normal and stared down at the demon, and then returned his gaze to Stella. "Because I was abandoned. I was raised by people that saw me as a mistake, who broke me and made me into the killing machine they wanted. My emotions, my empathy...they were all torn away in order to complete my training. I've only ever felt when I met you," he said, pausing to try and keep his thoughts in check. Stella stepped forwards from behind Blaze, thinking she knew what he meant. "Everyone actually helped, but...Stella was the one that broke through to me. But, in a way, it made things worse. I realised what I was made to do before I met you all, how I killed...I realised it was wrong. I finally recognised my...darker side. I call it The Blight. It's my dark thoughts, made sentient by Vampirism. He is a reflection of myself, and tries to push me to commit actions for my own self benefit, even to the detriment of others. Under his dictation, I wouldn't care about anything but myself, and my own... crueller desires. If I let him gain control, I would drain most of you here of your blood without a second thought. I had to keep myself in check, restrain my own feelings, in order to live a relatively normal life. However, everyone's support kept me stable.

"But that all changed when Smiley came around. As soon as his ride opened its gates, people seemed to be entranced. They flocked to him like worthless moths to a flame. My brother sat on the throne, and was praised like a God. But nobody seemed to notice how to make way for him, I had to be tossed to the wolves," he explained, before being interrupted by Nebulus.

"But, we weren't affected much by Smiley. Yeah, ten or 20 guests may have left us, but we still were fairly visited," he interjected, his arms crossed in distrust.

"Emphasis on the 'we.' As in, you guys. Stella was still swarmed, and Blaze's plaza was bustling. But, well, I was void. Empty. I was grateful to get a few teenagers who came because The Perfector's queues were too long!" he yelled, his fangs out. He reigned himself in, as his fangs retracted again. "Sorry about that. Well, I kept myself together with the hope that Smiley still cared for me, and that my ride was still standing, and that I at least still had the spotlight. You can guess this didn't last long. You gave so much attention to your performances at shows that you never even noticed how I appeared less and less, and eventually was removed entirely. Smiley was the park's new icon. He got the lead roles, he got the glory, he was even paired with Stella as anything from her friend to her love interest! That was my role! But I was delegated to the villain, the sidekick, the third wheel. But that's not the best part. You know that plan where if a ride wasn't reaching a certain limit of guests in a month, it would be put on the list for removal unless it's rating increased?

"Well, guess what! I decided to have a look through the list, to see if I was in the clear. Abyss was at the top. They had even filed for permission to use the land for another ride, more linked to The Perfector. The company had stolen the title I had worked for and gave it to some modern day gimmick with no future because he had loops, and then planned to throw me in the scrapheap for another mindless drone! If I didn't do anything, I would have lost the coaster. And I don't think the Ministry would waste their resources keeping a false spirit with Vampirism alive. They didn't even know if my broken soul would allow me to make it out the other side! But you guys sat idly by with your fans and your attention, while I was most likely facing my own death. None of you tried to reach out!" He ranted, his eyes empty and cold.

The spirits went silent, knowing that it would be better to let him finish. Stella, however, seemed to appear regretful.

"I tried to plead for help, or more time to prove myself. The wave of rejections proved to me that I could not trust anyone to help me. I used everything in my power to make myself more popular, but nothing worked! As the deadline for what could be my fate loomed closer and closer...I became more desperate. And as I fell more and more into my own hatred of my brother and those that ignored my pleas for help...The Blight became more powerful and convincing, until one more thing would break me. Then, I heard Smiley laughing at me behind my back, calling me a failure and a mistake. He only stopped when he saw me, but didn't bother to say sorry. That's when I heard the Blight again. Saying he shouldn't be allowed to throw me aside to rot, that I needed to get payback in the way which would hurt. And what better way to hurt someone with fame is to accuse them of something that would take their fame away? I remembered my tactics, my way of shutting him out. But I was done being ignored and overshadowed.

"I didn't just listen...I let him take control. The last thing I remember after regaining control is the staff room, splattered with blood and decorated with fresh bodies. The knife was in my hand, and for a moment I felt what I hadn't felt for years. Power. Eliza was on the floor, unconscious. I could've easily killed her right there. But I didn't, because I knew it was worthless to waste the time. So I wiped the memory of her seeing me by going into her head and breaking the memory from there. But that took time, so shortly after I shadow-walked out of the room and returned to my apartment. I cleaned myself up and got rid of any blood that may have gotten myself caught. I'm a very logical person, you know! Then I just needed to shift the blame to Smiley. I may have suggested the possibility of a complete mental breakdown to the higher ups, so they would think of getting rid of him and that eyesore. He found out the next day, and yelled that he knew I did it, pointing out how the paramedics, police and news anchors had arrived at the scene. He wouldn't stop his tirade, until he again said that I was a mistake, and that I should never have been created.

"I snapped. I flew into the air with my mist abilities, taking him with me. He didn't finish his sentence before I let him go. The idiot didn't die on impact, so I had to finish him off. Either way, I later called you all with some fake tears, and kept up the lie. If I had known an idiotic girl pointing would work against me, I wouldn't have thought twice about ending her. I don't care if you call me immoral. But if you do, say it to my face. After all, I'd be dead by now if I did nothing." He had spoken his truth, looking emotionless.

"What about your eyes? How did you get the scars?" Blaze asked.

He looked down at him, deciding to follow his request. He leaned back against the wall behind him, keeping himself focused. "You should know, you were there. But, I'll recall it anyway. Well, when Smiley returned, he seemed calm and serene. He greeted everyone with a smile, and appeared normal. That was, until me and Stella came in. He went psychotic, throwing you and Nebulus to the side when he burst out from your restraint. He grabbed a nearby glass and smashed it into a razor sharp shard, lunging at me and her in pure madness. I saw him race towards Stella, and moved without thinking. I shoved her to the side, saving her from the attack. But, I wasn't so lucky. He stabbed me in the eyes with the shard, and left deep wounds across my face, only stopping when he had to be pulled off. But, by that point I had already blacked out. I still kind of feel...unhappy that she had to see that. Florette and Fawnia managed to heal the wounds and restore some eyesight, but I would never see without glasses again." Void glanced towards Smiley, who looked away, showing a sign of regret.

"I knew inside that Florette had known something, she always was so hostile towards me after his death. Now I know why. Whatever she did, she found out. Maybe she overheard me? It's of no matter now, since she's dead. I'll admit, I never liked her anyways, but had to pretend so nobody disliked me. So, I'll just say it here. I've been planning to get rid of her for years," Void explained flatly, causing all the spirits to look at him with pain, fear and rage.

"You were our friend! You're just insane, aren't you? No wonder you didn't want us to use the punishment curse on Smiley! Because we could use it on you after. Am I right?!" Blaze burst back, making Void look at him and laugh.

"You know, I'm not denying your...accusations, but I am not insane. It's the Blight that makes me kill. I just follow along. If that's what you think is a choice, then I'm scared of your idea of manipulation," he explained, with some humour slipped in at the end.

Stella looked at him with rage. "If I'd known you were just faking pain for attention, I wouldn't even have cared. I thought you were struggling, that you were grieving! You betrayed me, Shadows! You betrayed all of us. Don't expect me to give anything up for you now, you twisted creature!" Stella yelled. She moved in his face, shoving him away and running from the scene with tears in her eyes.

Fawnia spun around with her sight on Stella, chasing after her with no regard for herself, or her dress. With the two girls gone, only Blaze and Nebulus remained, staring daggers at the two brothers.

"Let's get out of here. They don't deserve our focus," Nebulus said in an icy tone. He held onto Blaze's arm to try and bring him along, but the demon would not move, like he was rooted in place.

"You can go. I have something to do," he said.

Nebulus accepted this with a sigh, and left in a brisk walk.

Smiley looked at his brother, who was standing silently, staring at the ground. "I'll go back to the Facility. You can stay here for a bit, if you want to..." Smiley said. He put his hand on Void's back, before flickering away like the static on a screen.

Blaze stood for a moment, thinking of what to do, before he reached down into his pocket and pulled out a photograph. The photo was of the group all smiling happily, like nothing had ever happened.

Blaze looked at the photo and snapped his fingers, pressing down on the section of the photo that contained the shadow spirit. In his grip, a small flame started then died down. Blaze crumpled the damaged photo up into a ball of paper and dropped it onto the ground, staring into his old friend's eyes. "Goodbye," Blaze muttered, through gritted teeth, quickly turning back and walking with the group.

The sun had long been covered by dark, heavy clouds with the low growl of thunder rumbling through the shock of an occasional blinding flash of lightning. Rain began to pelt down like tears, drenching anything it could touch. Void stepped forwards, puddles forming near his feet. He picked up the crumpled picture, before smoothing it out again. The picture was soaked with rain, with creases everywhere. The worst damage was how the piece where he had once stood had been burnt off, with nothing remaining except a small piece of his top hat's brim. He turned the photo around, to see that the message was altered from the soaked ink and the flames. Where there was once a kind message of friendship, a cold message now was in its place. It now read: "It was always your fault". Void sighed, a bitter sadness appearing on his face.

"They've done it. I never thought they'd just abandon me... but apparently times have changed. I finally decide to be honest and tell the whole truth, and I get thrown away and left to die. They're hypocrites! Florette harmed and manipulated them all with little to no positive change, and she's revered as a hero. But I'm the monster for not wanting to literally die without a fight! Well...if it's a villain they all want, why should I deny?" He burst into laughter, before the photo became completely covered in a black, morphing shade. The darkness shifted into a more complex shape, before forming into a Shadow Rose. He cloned it into six with a flick of his hand, and placed five of them on the floor. With the rain beating down on him, he tread across the concrete paths, his face cold and focused. Despite the air being cold and bitter, he seemed to not even notice the chill, or the thick, torrential rain. He stopped at the entrance to the crypt, accidentally stepping into a forming puddle. He placed down a few items, knowing how the others would spot them: the final rose, a quick note made to be waterproof and the small tiara which Florette was fond of wearing. He took the hat off and stalked into the trees, fading into the shadows. To get a vantage point, he climbed up the tree and sat on a thick branch, dangling his leg off the side. As he got used to his position, he heard the sound of footsteps coming from the path he had previously walked down. With an adjustment of his newly fixed glasses, he recognised the group as the other spirits.

Stella was looking down, when a silvery glimmer of light hit her eyes, ensnaring her attention. "Wait a second...that's Florette's tiara...she was wearing this today, wasn't she?" Stella said, holding gently onto the silver tiara like it was a precious artefact.

"There's a note, too, and...a Shadow rose. Turns out you were correct Samuel! Wait a moment...Where's Samuel?" Nebulus was hit with realisation, his voice going from dark and heartbroken, to panicked and worried. "Florette told him to run to where Void would never go. We need to search for him!" he finished, his face full of gloom. He was holding onto Fawnia's hand to comfort the grieving queen.

"What does the note say?" Fawnia whispered out; her normally extravagant tone had been replaced with a low whisper, her heart broken from the loss of the person closest to her. Her dark brown hair was soaked and dripping from the heavy rain, which was flying down to the ground like an attack.

"The note says... 'Hey again, it's me. Well, I wanted to give you our late friend's little tiara, as a memento of sorts. You can keep it, I don't really have a need for it, and neither does Smiley. The rose's just a marker to me. Also, I recall that our human friend ran away when I appeared...I recommend you figure out where he is and get him to safety quickly, as Smiley would love to get some revenge after getting stabbed five weeks ago. Also, it would be much easier to create another vampire from someone who can't use magic against me!... I would hope you come quick or the fun'll start without you! Void.' Samuel... he's in trouble. If either of them get to him, they would kill him. Stella, does your suit still have charge? I have an idea," Nebulus said, his green and yellow eyes switching from the parchment to the spirit of Hyperspace.

"Hmm...I don't know. Let me check my headset... Wait, it's missing! That pest! I can't access my suit, or its energy, without it!... GREAT!" Stella burst out in rage. Stella blasted a glowing orb directly at the forested area, which exploded on impact, creating a bright flash to illuminate the area. The spirits all jolted in shock, seeing Void's figure in the trees.

He gasped in shock, before he jumped out of the trees, narrowly missing the explosion. He flew through the air, before tumbling in the grass to the side of the path, leaving himself lying face first in the small fielded area. He coughed a few times, before trying to get up. "Eugh... well that was a close call. Not my version of a greeting, but I'll take it," Void muttered, moments before seeing

Fawnia rush directly up to him, making them stare face to face with each other.

"Are you just here to torment us?!" Fawnia cried out, pointing her staff at him, which started to charge, petal like embers floating away from the magic-filled centre.

"Oh...do you know something called a personal bubble, dear, or do you just like how I look?" Void smirked, making Fawnia step back in confusion.

"W-what? No! Why are you here?!" Fawnia asked, with Void chuckling slightly, clearing his glasses of dirt.

"I just wanted to see your reactions. Of course, I could've just left at any time, but where is the fun in that? Also, I felt like it would be fair to give you all a chance at finding Samuel; I'm not a cheater, you know." Void glanced up, before he started to wander away from the group with a confident stride. "Here. I got it from Smiley. Come quick." Void grinned slightly, throwing Stella's headset to the past queen, soon before vanishing into mist with a spin.

"We gotta be quick, before they get to Samuel!" Fawnia rushed, before giving the headset to Stella, who looked at it, then got Nebulus's idea.

"I got it," Stella answered, pressing two buttons on the controls, releasing a blue glow onto her right hand. The glow was absorbed into it, creating a teal light emanating from her palm. "I can give the last of the headset's energy to Blaze, as a speed increase spell, which would make him even faster and slightly more powerful with magic! That was a good plan, Nebulus!" Stella revealed, making the spirits nod their heads enthusiastically. "Momentium Increase!" Stella cast as a teal orb building up in her hand, then firing out straight at Blaze.

"Okay now, go get our friend from Smiley and Void!" Nebulus cheered, before Blaze nodded, rushing off with a teal tinted trail of flames coming from behind him.

CHAPTER 17:
CATS AND MICE

Blaze sprinted at his fastest speed through the perimeter of the park, a few metres away from the barrier, which stops the spirits from fading, that was sparkling and swimming with the colours of the rainbow, like a large, magical bubble that's visible only to the spirits, as well as those on its insides. "Okay. Florette told Samuel to go to the last place that Void would go. Since I know him, I know he absolutely loathes all things cute, pink, and girly. So, maybe Samuel's in the Candyland area? If that place isn't pink, then Void isn't a vampire!" The flame spirit chuckled happily, before stopping for a moment and heading into the pathway between Technoland and the Cursed Palace, spotting a pale pink path, with gold, sparkly sides, trailing towards an archway, made to look like two large candy-canes, with a chocolate sign being held there by fake marshmallows.

The name Candyland was written in a swirling, decorative design, looking like pink, glittery frosting. Blaze slowed himself down, and searched around the area. There were trees made with rock candy logs and sugar paper leaves, chocolate frogs in a lemonade lake, and many more sweet treats. He looked around, before spotting one of the attractions, which was a wild mouse-style roller coaster, with a bright colour scheme.

He flinched, hearing the voices of two people echo out of the loading station, which was themed to be a giant liquorice box. Blaze peeked through a small broken window before seeing two familiar figures.

"So, have you found him yet? The chase is fun!" The taller figure, which Blaze identified as Void, was leaning against one of the carts, his amber eyes standing out the most. Nearby, a shorter figure was sitting on the railing of the queue line, swinging his legs back and forwards. The figure's shorter height and cheerful demeanour clearly revealed that it was Smiley.

"Nope! Do you think one of the spirits of this place is protecting him? They're sweet and caring," he complained. His yellow, hypnotic swirl eyes were spinning and illuminating the area in a dim yellow flood.

"Well, we better find him quickly, this place is practically giving me a headache. Too much...pink," Void complained slightly, with his hand becoming enveloped in a dark, black glow. He laughed, before placing his hand on the carts, before the carts and some of the track was corrupted by the spell, becoming a shade of black. Blaze turned around, to see a red, braided haired girl yell in pain, before falling to the floor.

He rushed over to her, spotting the person who she was hiding. The boy, who was wearing a pale red and blue coat and a red hood and mask, glanced at Blaze, before his cyan eyes lit up, going to hug the flame demon.

"Blaze! It's me." The boy pulled down his face mask, revealing the face of Samuel, who looked down at the girl, worried. "That's Lucy, Lucy Rish. She's the spirit of the ride Liquorice looper!" Samuel explained, before Blaze noticed how her colour in her hair and eyes were fading into monochrome hues.

"Lucy! Are you okay?" Blaze asked, his expression showing his confusion.

"That...Abyss spirit...threw me out of the building...I think he's corrupting my ride," Lucy whispered, struggling to get up, with Samuel helping her to her feet. Her pale red hair now had a dark grey streak, which had taken over half of her braid.

Her eyes were a pale pink colour, with shimmering irises. She was wearing a small, simple red dress, which had a sherbet-like shimmer, and a rainbow liquorice as a little belt. She also used a small piece of black liquorice to tie her braids back. She looked quite young too, possibly only 14.

"Here, for the pain. Void and Smiley will eventually leave, and your attraction should return to normal tomorrow," Blaze listed, before pulling out a health potion, quickly transforming the liquid into a gumball, and giving it to Lucy, who eagerly took it and immediately put it in her mouth.

"Thanks, mister! I'll go tell Lemmy and Shelly that it should be safe to leave soon!" Lucy smiled, before skipping off, the health potion gumball healing her.

Samuel pushed off his hood, his face and hair fully visible. "Well, I'm glad she's okay. I think Void and Smiley didn't spot us." Samuel smirked, shortly before noticing that Blaze was backing away, looking worried. Samuel turned around to see nothing but his own shadow. He laughed it off, and went to speak to Blaze. Samuel turned around to see that Blaze was being held by a shadowed figure, who stepped out of the dark to reveal Smiley.

"Look down," Smiley said.

Samuel glanced down, noticing that his shadow couldn't be casted by the sun as it would have to be near sunset to get even close to its position. "Void. You can stop faking being my shadow," Samuel commanded, the shadow slumped then shrank away into Void's normal form.

The spirit was smirking, while hovering slightly in the air. "*Aww...* but it was *fun,*" Void sighed, with a hint of sarcasm in his tone.

Blaze fought his way out of Smiley's grip, quickly rushing to Samuel's side.

"Oh hello, fireworks. You seem to be protecting this kid. New hobby?" Void mocked, his fangs showing.

"Shadows. Don't even touch him," Blaze threatened, pulling out his sword.

"Look. I don't want to be here as much as you do, flames. I hate pink, and this place is covered with it! So, why don't you leave us be, so we can both leave quickly." Void spoke, landing back on the ground.

Blaze put his arm to the side, to protect Samuel. "You're not going to go and kill or turn Samuel! If you're trying to, I'm afraid you will have to go through me first." Blaze challenged Void and Smiley, who both brought out their weapons with a flick, bringing them to their side in an attacking stance.

"...So be it," Void threatened, before going to strike Blaze with his blades. Blaze clashed Void's blades with his sword, making him stumble backwards. Smiley went to stab Blaze in the side, for the demon to grab Smiley's arm and blast the spirit with a fireball from the other, which hit him dead centre and flung him backwards.

Blaze's eyes glowed red, as Samuel looked at Blaze frantically. "Kid! Get to the crypt! I'll follow behind you!" Blaze shouted, Samuel nodded, before activating his visor and rushing away from the candy-coated zone.

Void tracked the boy's movements, seeing his pale blue glow flash off into the distance. He started to run towards the glow before Blaze focused his magic towards the ground. The entrance of the land was blocked by fire, which pushed towards Void, knocking him to the floor with a skid, now being next to Smiley. Blaze stood in front of them, his sword out and ready to strike.

"Okay. so...don't destroy us?" Smiley stuttered, making Blaze's guard lower.

He sighed, closing his eyes for a moment, not noticing how Void was no longer sitting beside his sibling. "I know how bad you are, but I'm not as evil as you both. Run," Blaze commanded, and turned himself around to the exit of the zone.

Smiley stood up, before shaking his hand, signalling an attack. Void appeared from behind the two, and made his hands get swallowed up with a curling, morphing black aura. "Shadowed... Nightmare!" Void cast, sending out the hand-shaped attack.

"Think fast!" A female voice yelled, before a pink disc hit the hex and shot it back at Void, who dived to the floor to avoid getting hit.

Void jumped himself up, his hair messed up, and a scar on his hand from the rough landing, slowly dripping a pitch black, oozing liquid. "What!?" He gasped in shock, while his scar healed itself.

The duo turned around to see that around six different spirits had surrounded the two of them, and all had their weapons out. Lucy had a liquorice whip, which she currently had wrapped around her arm. A boy with a green and yellow retro-colour scheme, Lemmy, was using colourful water balloons that were bubbling due to magic energy. He also had a slingshot in a holster. The third person on the left, Shelly, was a girl with violet hair that trailed to her shoulders, and blue and pink eyes. Shelly was holding a giant sherbet disc shield, which glittered in the light. Another three were to the right, with one looking like bubblegum, another designed like chocolate, and the final looked like marshmallows.

The gum girl, named Charlie, had a giant bubble wand staff for a weapon. The smaller chocolate boy was wielding a spear made of different chocolate snacks. Finally, the marshmallow girl was using hardened marshmallows as gloves.

"Oh look, the candy crew is here. Let's chew them out, Smiles!" Void yelled.

Smiley pulled his dagger out of his hat, while Void summoned his deadly duel blades. "What are you cutie-pies going to do against us?" Smiley mocked, with an excited expression.

"Cutie-pies? Heehee! We'll make you regret that," Shelly yelled, before all of the candy land spirits, except for Lucy, started running towards the duo.

◇◇◇◇◇◇

Most were thrown away, except for Shelly, who tossed her shield out, for Charlie to use as a platform, and get into the air. "Looks like this's gonna be sticky!" She rallied, before sending out a barrage of sticky gum bubbles.

Smiley was just about to be hit by one, before Void pushed him out of the way, getting his leg stuck to the ground. Smiley's attention flicked to a bubble that was flying down. "Catch!" He jumped up, before using the bubble as a bounce pad. He bounced upwards, slashing Charlie in the arm, but nothing serious. She squealed in pain, before landing on the ground, shielding herself with a tough gum bubble.

Void smirked, before his legs shifted into mist, and reformed out of the sticky pink substance. "This might change their mood. Monochrome Corruption!" Void yelled, before making a grey, warping glow emanate from his hands.

"Wait...that's the same spell that made Lucy go black and white! Don't go!" Blaze warned, but it was too late.

Milo, the chocolate boy, was now rushing towards Void, his spear tip spinning like a drill. Void stepped to the side, making Milo's spear hit the ground and push him away. "Agh! Oh no..." Milo walked backwards in fear, before he tripped over his own feet, being caught by Void. "Thank...you?" Milo muttered in confusion, before feeling a surge of pain, like his soul was being torn apart. He yelled, seeing that his colours were being turned into black and greys, with hints of orange from the spirit.

"No! Milo!" Blaze yelled, as Void laughed cruelly, seeing Milo struggling to pull free from the man's grip.

He looked up feverishly, before seeing the spirit's face, which was cold and heartless. "You..." Milo managed to whisper out, feeling his energy being sapped along with his power.

Void looked at the boy, who now was lying limply on him, every drop of his normal colours drained. "Oh my, this one's tapped out. Let's see what I can do now." Void spoke to himself, before pushing off Milo, who crumpled to the ground without resistance. Void clicked his tongue while stepping away from him, twirling his gloved hand in a circle pattern while orange sparks coming from his fingertips. The sparks formed an aura, as a familiar spear appeared in his left hand. Milo tried to use his magic, but nothing happened. Void had taken all of his magic, even his weapon and powers. "Oh good…Maybe I could make this into something more my speed!" Void laughed, before the spear became metal, with crimson and amber streaks on the sides. The tip vanished completely, with one of Void's blades becoming thicker, longer and taller, transforming into the blade of the weapon.

"Oh my! A scythe. This is going to be easier than a knife cutting through butter." Void chuckled, seeing that Lemmy and the marshmallow girl, Marcie, were kneeling next to Milo, who was weakly shivering. He swung down his scythe, which slid against the pavement with a screech. The spirits gathered around Milo jolted, taking their direct attention from the boy. "So, does anyone want to try to stop us?" Void challenged, before getting a rock thrown at his head. Void turned around, seeing Samuel, Blaze and Stella standing in the distance. "Great. Sammy and the Goody-two-shoes crew have regrouped to ruin the fun."

Smiley smirked, spinning his dagger calmly. Stella pulled her blasters from thin air, along with Blaze summoning his flame blade, and Samuel taking the dagger he had stolen from Smiley from his pocket.

"Well, if it's a fight you want, it's a fight you'll get," Void threatened, then quickly blasting himself into the air and trying to hit someone from above with his scythe.

Luckily, Stella had jumped to the side, moments before the spirit impacted the ground and spun like a top, with Blaze pushing Samuel to the side and blasting the vampire with a lick of flame, making him recoil for a few moments to heal.

Smiley saw this, and appeared behind them, trying to stab one of them with his daggers, only to be blocked by Samuel, locking the daggers grip to grip. "Heh, smart." Smiley smiled slightly, before throwing his arm to the right, making Samuel lose grip on his dagger. Smiley picked it up, and was about to stab Samuel, before getting swiftly hit with a punch to the back, making him fall to the floor.

Marcie made one of her marshmallow gloves melt away, gently taking Samuel's hand and moving him aside. She spoke to him, protected from the combat. "Hey, are you okay?"

Samuel nodded, even though his arm was hurting. Marcie smiled, before going back into the battlefield. Void and Smiley were slashing at people with their weapons, with nobody being able to get close to them, without getting hit and thrown back. Stella flew upwards, shooting lasers down at the men, who easily evaded them, with Void even deflecting a few back at her. She pressed her headset, transforming into her attack form, before charging up her hand blaster.

Void saw the glint in the distance and had an idea, quickly making his hands glow. "Deflecto Surroundia," Void cast, making everyone around him fall to the floor, except Smiley.

He glanced at his brother, who heard him speaking in his mind. The golden man smiled back, as his face showed a mischievous determination. Void prepared himself, awaiting the girl's next move. Stella fired her arm blaster which rocketed out a teal beam of light. Void laughed, before sending out two portals and pushing Smiley into one, while disguising their movement with a mist cloud. Void dived to the side, making sure he wasn't spotted, with a glimpse of a yellow figure flying in the sky, barrelling towards Stella. She turned around, only to be grabbed by Smiley, who looked at her jokingly. "Dropping in? Ahahah!" Stella tried to break out of Smiley's grip, before she noticed that Smiley had hacked into her wing boosters and deactivated them, making them both start to fall to the ground at a rapid speed.

"Are you insane?! You're going to make us BOTH die!" Stella yelled, trying her best to reboot her suit's systems.

Smiley chuckled, looking into her eyes. "Nope. You, however, are a different story!" Smiley answered, before seeing the familiar glow of a portal, about a jump distance away.

Smiley looked down, and took the leap, making Stella start falling even faster. He fell through the portal, landing safely on the ground with a slight roll. Stella started spinning uncontrollably, getting closer to the ground, before she suddenly stopped falling. She looked around, before seeing that she was being levitated. She rebooted her system, before standing back on the ground, looking at the result of the fight. The candy land spirits were all on the floor but okay, Samuel was rubbing his arm, and Milo was sitting on a bench table and crying over his powers. In the corner of her eye, she spotted the familiar twinkle of Nebulus and Fawnia's teleportation auras in the distance, the figures of Nebulus and Fawnia appearing in their place.

She smiled weakly, then sighed and started to strut forwards to help her friends, before noticing that Smiley was arguing with Void. She listened in, trying to keep quiet.

"Why'd you save her?! We could've been two spirits down! I even risked my own life!" Smiley yelled, his eyes spinning to the point of being a blur, but Void seemed immune. Suddenly, Smiley was pulled off the ground, and was floating in front of Void.

His arm was raised, and was pointed straight at Smiley's chest. Black, distorting magic then began to flow from Void's hand into Smiley's chest like a flood of rushing water. Around the energy, even light itself was being corrupted, turning it shades of orange and red. Smiley tried to break free, but he couldn't move an inch. His smile was shattered, and in its place an expression of pain. He was crying.

"Do you know that Abyss Essence steals the life force of everything around it? It's a slow and painful process, and most people don't survive. It's like a poison, killing all around it and leaving nothing left. My magic is made of this energy. I wonder... what would sending my magic into your soul do? Corrupt it maybe? Or, maybe it would shatter it from the inside! After all, your incompetence to follow a simple task makes you worthless to me. At least now I can learn more about my powers," he explained. His eyes showed nothing but a vague sense of intrigue in whatever horrific things could happen if he continued.

Pain soon turned to agony and fear. He cried, begging to know why Void was doing this to him. Void just stood there, with a smirk on his face. "Because I can. You were meant to push both yourself and Stella into the portal. That was the plan. You broke the plan for your own goals. You may be the face of the Ministry, but I won't blink to retaliate if you do one more thing wrong. Got it, or do I have to use more Abyss Essence?" Void threatened.

Smiley winced, as he felt the hollow feeling of the essence spreading. He quickly nodded, before being dropped to the ground. He clutched his chest, seeing that there was now a small scar around the middle of it. There wasn't any essence in him anymore, but he still could feel pain coursing through his body.

He quickly nodded, before being dropped to the ground. "Fine," Smiley spat back with anger, before disappearing into nothing.

Stella started to step away from the scene, her heart pounding.

"I can tell that you heard us, dearie. You're welcome, by the way." Void spoke calmly, slowly turning around to face Stella, who was on edge at his glare. "Yeah, I saved your life! Now you owe me. I'm surprised that I was able to time it right! Hehe... well, I have to vanish. Bye bye, dearie!" Void smiled, before vanishing into mist with a click.

Samuel rushed up to Stella, hugging her tightly. "I'm glad you're okay! If whoever saved you had tried even a moment later, you'd have been on the ground!" He smiled, happy that his friend was out of harm's way.

"Who actually levitated her? I could've sworn that I saw..." Marcie started, before Stella butted in and answered her.

"Void. Void saved my life. He seems to value me over... anything. Even his own brother." Samuel glanced at his best friend, feeling like she needed some support. She saw his glance, sighed, and closed her eyes. "I heard the twins talking. I know that there's at least some good inside him, but for now, he's trying to hide it. He even threatened Smiley when he tried to hurt me," Stella explained, but started crying when she finished.

"You look heartbroken... I know what could cheer you up!" Marcie said, before holding her arms out for a hug. Stella accepted, with Samuel joining in too.

"Thanks for trying to make me feel better, guys." Stella thanked her friends, as the hug disbanded.

Samuel looked at the group in confusion, unaware of the situation. "Can someone tell me what has happened? For 1, Void's gone batty and is trying to kill us, plus he's teamed up with Smiles, and 2, I can't seem to find Florette anywhere, and..." Samuel continued to ramble, before noticing the heartbreak and sorrow in the rest of the main spirits eyes.

"Void made his choice. He chose to stay with his brother...by ending our friendships with murder," Nebulus uttered, coldly, with Samuel looking at him with awe and shock.

"Wait... He killed her?"

Blaze nodded, before looking down, sadly. "He killed her...and the Perfector victims. It was all him!" Blaze yelled, before Samuel stumbled back slightly in shock.

"What's next? He came here to kill me!... He did, didn't he?"

Stella nodded, her face tinged with regret. "Smiley wanted to get revenge after you stabbed him in self-defence and Void was desiring to...make you like him."

Samuel realised what this meant after a few moments, and glanced at the group. "So... what you're saying is that for nearly a month, I've been living with people that, at any moment, could've killed me. Does that mean…" Samuel uttered quietly, with Fawnia placing her hand onto Samuel's shoulder to comfort him.

"It means that… we need your help more than ever. Void was the strongest in our group and the smartest, and Smiley is cruel, deceiving and stealthy. They're a dangerous duo, but we have something they don't." Fawnia spoke in a determined way.

Samuel felt a piece of hope as he saw that, for the first time since Florette was killed, she was smiling.

"We have true happiness, freedom…and, as stereotypical as it is, friendship." Stella, who was keeping an eye on Milo, looked up. "After all… if you were able to go head to head against, and defeat, one sibling…why not the other? If you ever need one of my suits for it too, just ask! Don't break them though. The one you used to chase Smiley is still needing repairs!" Stella looked down at Marcie, who giggled, pleased to see her friends happy again.

Before she spoke, Charlie popped up behind her, along with Milo, who had managed to gain enough strength to stand up.

"It seems like things are getting better, don't you say, Nebulus?" Milo spoke, his cheerful tone back to its normal sound.

The alien looked down at the chocolate boy, a small smile appearing on his face. "Maybe. Are you okay? You all took a hit from them, especially you, Milo."

The Candyland spirits thought for a moment, before nodding, with Milo looking nervous.

"But, if she's…gone…where's her soul?" Milo wondered.

Stella placed a hand into her pocket, bringing out a silver locket, shaped like a heart, a rose symbol engraved in the middle. "I turned a gold locket that Void gave me into silver. He cannot touch it, or me, as it burns him on contact. Even magic is ineffective," Stella explained, before opening up the heart to reveal a green, shimmering crystal.

"You made her soul… into a crystal?"

Stella nodded, continuing her explanation. "Since it's now a crystal, it has time to regain its power easier, as well as being able to easily be stored, unlike how with a soul, only an entrapment spell works. Also, as long as it's not broken into shards, it's fine!" Stella laughed, with all of the main spirits agreeing and starting to leave.

"Hey guys, we're going now! Remember to be aware at all times," Nebulus exclaimed, Lemmy nodded at Nebulus and the Candyland spirits waved the group goodbye.

Meanwhile, Hypna was rushing around excitedly, ordering the lesser scientists around. "Jess, tell the new Head of Morale that we need some more posters, on the Minister's request. Emily, gather everyone you can when they're called! The election of a new Minister is a big thing, ya know! Tim, get the video crew from the Morale department, in case some people can't come! Can't have some people not in the know," Hypna ordered, with the scientists and workers smiling robotically and nodding, before rushing off to do their duties.

A young woman, wearing a cream dress and white cardigan, came in with a neat pile of clothes in her hands.

"Ah! Lily! I see you've got my new outfit?" A voice came from behind the door of a dressing room, in a happy tone.

"Yes, your joyness! I made sure it was both stylish and comfortable, like you asked." Lily exclaimed with pride. After a moment, the suit she was holding levitated in the air. It was a pale golden suit, possibly made of velvet or silk, ending with a triangular tail. Along with this drifted a gold ribboned bow tie, a pair of silver boots and a few gems, possibly yellow diamonds. They levitated towards the dressing room with a honey-coloured trail.

"Thanks Lily! This looks fabulous, you know!" The Male voice spoke, before a familiar spirit walked out with flair. He was smiling happily, a pinch of shimmering makeup on his cheeks.

"Is that makeup?... Not like I'm being rude, your joyn–"

Smiley, in his new shimmering gold suit, placed a finger on the fashion fanatic's lips, making her instantly stop talking. "I know,

Lily. Yes, it's a bit of shimmering makeup, but if me and Void can wear nail polish, I think a touch of shimmer is fine! Also, you can just call me Smiley, if it's easier!" He laughed, with Lily laughing as he removed his finger.

Hypna walked in front of Smiley, going to adjust his collar. "The outfit is fantastic! You've really got some talent, Lily!" Hypna complimented her, which Lily accepted with a smile. "I know you technically aren't the Minister until you say the speech, but it would be good to know anything you'd like to do before you do it!" Hypna blabbed, her tone showing her excitement.

Smiley chuckled, then shook his head. "I can't think of anything at the moment. I think we should keep what my... predecessor did. For the most part, of course," Smiley responded with a smirk.

Suddenly, a small, male scientist stepped into the dressing room, holding the door open for the group. "Everyone's ready! Are you ready...Minister?"

CHAPTER 18:
SECRETS OF THE PAST

S amuel lay quietly in Fawnia's guest bed, thoughts blurring in his head. It had been a short while since he'd learned the truth, and things were going wrong. Fawnia never speaks, or at least not in front of him, and Blaze has been prone to anger bursts. Nebulus has been acting meaner recently, and Stella has been busier, as if she was avoiding them. "So.. Void was the person who caused everything?...Can I trust anyone?" Samuel thought to himself, before he sluggishly got out of bed, and threw on one of Stella's violet dressing gowns, which had been cleaned and magically adjusted to his size. He sneaked over to the kitchen, before pouring himself a glass of orange juice.

"Nightmares?" The voice of Stella came from behind Samuel's back, making him snap around backwards, his nerves high from the darkness. "Be careful. Nightmares...He can manipulate them. And if you get trapped... you cannot resurface," Stella warned him, before going to leave.

"Hey. Why've you been ignoring us?" Samuel asked, before Stella walked closer to the boy, becoming more visible. She was in a pair of navy pyjamas, decorated with stars. She also had longer hair, obscuring her neck.

"I've...been busy. Setting up defences...making sure that Technoland and Candyland are lit at night, so that Void doesn't attack. Me and Blaze have even made sure that all of the weaker spirits have something made of silver on them at all times, like a necklace, or a bracelet." Stella rambled on about different things she had done, keeping her view away from the boy.

"Your hair. You never wear it out. Something's off here. Why're you wearing it that way?" Samuel asked firmly, for the woman to give in with a sigh, quickly making her aqua hair tie up in a bun. She turned her head left, before a mark became visible. Two scarred puncture wounds were on her neck, which Samuel could easily guess were bite marks from Void. "He bit you? When!" Samuel mouthed, trying to not wake anyone else up.

"It was...maybe five years ago. Void wasn't lying, for once, when he said I went to talk to him. But sometimes...when he'd gotten thirsty, I would let him take some of my blood. But one time, he lost control and tried to take more, which could've killed me. I fought him away, to force him to stop, but all it did was make my wound worse and as he got hurt in the struggle...put some of his own blood in the injury, which could've turned me like him. Luckily, he snapped himself out of his frenzy and gave me an antidote, but to this day, I've had this scar." Stella told the story, before taking out the bun, and her hair fell again on her shoulders. "Now... get back to sleep, okay? We might need your help in the morning." Stella spoke gently, before leaving Samuel in the kitchen.

He finished his glass of orange juice before returning back to the guest bedroom. However, before he pushed open the door, he felt a creeping cold chill and heard the growl of the wind outside coming from the guest room he was staying in. This would be normal and only unnerving, if it wasn't for the fact that Samuel had shut the door behind him, and the window was previously locked. He carefully shifted the door open so he could see inside the room, while trying to be quiet. The lights had been switched off, cloaking the room in an engulfing darkness. However, his eyes were drawn to a worrying sight. The window had been forced open from the outside, with the curtains floating weightlessly in the wind like a spectral dress. He scanned around the room in an attempt to try and find whoever had opened the window, dreading the answer. Stood in the corner of the room and staring at where he should be was the unwelcome figure of Void, almost blending into the darkness.

"Hmm...curious how he's not here. Maybe he's hiding? It's an adorable attempt, but it's futile at best, and a death wish at worst. Maybe I might make it quick, in the name of pity," Void mocked loudly, clearly uninterested in anything else.

Samuel flinched, realising the reality of the situation. This was like a game to Void, and he was caught in check. Movement would cause noise and get him caught, yet standing there would mean Void could sense him. Just as the teen was about to make a decision, he was returned to reality by amber eyes staring back at him through the keyhole. He panicked, and rushed into Fawnia's room, trying his best to not make a sound.

The room was barely lit besides the glow of a bedside lamp, which seemed to randomly flash and flicker. A canopy bed stood in the middle of the room, draped in delicate, white silk. He hesitantly inched towards the bed, hoping that the Queen could help him. She was lying eerily still as if she had been petrified, and she was covered in a blanket like a corpse in a morgue. As he pulled away the covers of her bed, he felt a shock jolt down his back like electricity. The queen was pale and gaunt like a ghost back from the dead. There were black, hollow abysses in the place of her eyes and mascara-like lines running down her cheeks. She was now wearing a laced black dress, and her face was frozen in a doll-like expression. Horrified from the sight of the deformed Fawnia, Samuel turned to leave. But from behind him, he could hear the sound of the bedsheets being shuffled, and feet touching the ground. With his heart in his stomach, he slowly looked behind him to see that whatever had replaced Fawnia had stood itself up, and was looking towards the window. He winced, hearing a slow snap. Fawnia's head had snapped backwards, and her stare was cold and dead, looking directly at him.

"He is here. You won't stand a chance. Give up. Give up. Give up…" She started to chant in a hollow voice, like she had transformed into a puppet.

"This has to be a dream… It's got to be!" Samuel said. He rushed to open the door, his pulse racing. When he did, he was greeted by the unwelcome sight of Void standing in the doorway.

"Found you, Samuel. It wasn't really that hard, either! Besides that, you might want to listen to her advice. I don't think you want to know how much pain you can tolerate, and I don't want to spend ages finding out. I've never been one for prolonged suffering, anyways. Now, would you kindly make this easy for both of us, kid? I want to see if Stella's still up for that Abyss offer," he said with a sinister tone. He inched closer to him, the flickering light obscuring his movements and making him appear like he was teleporting forwards.

Samuel stumbled backwards, failing to mask his terror. "Stop!" he yelled, trying to stop the demonic figures slowly enclosing him. On his word, the figure of Fawnia started to distort, her body twitching. Soon, she melted into a mass of black mist and retracted into the ground. As the teen had caught his breath, he was pinned to the wall by Void.

"You've worked it out… haven't you? This is just a nightmare. The saying is partially true, you know. If you die inside your dreams…you die in real life," Void explained coldly, with a sneer on his face.

Samuel managed to muster up all his bravery, and looked at the spirit dead in the eyes. "Then, were you expecting this?" he provoked, before pulling out a kitchen knife from his pocket and slashing the spirit's arm, making him let go in pain.

He dropped the knife and ran, seeing it get pulled into Void's hands by a long, black tendril. He ran down the stairs, making a beeline towards the palace's entrance. His heart was racing, hearing Void's footsteps, which always felt like they were only two steps behind him. "Gotta get out of here…" he thought. He pushed open the large metal door to the outside, before noticing how different the outside is. The pathways were shimmering, as if there was a thick layer of ice coating them, and there was a cloud of mist cloaking the surroundings; from the bare, claw-like trees, to the black shadows casting from the palace, barely illuminated by a blood crimson moon. Samuel left the Palace and hurried to the brightest place he knew, Technoland. The spectrum of lights were still glowing brightly, like a neon welcome sign. Stella was stood at the entrance, hugging herself with her arms.

"Stella! Please help! Void's chasing after me, Fawnia looked possessed, and everything's all messed up. I think that this is a dream!" he explained, his words barely getting out between each breath.

Stella turned around, her face filled with dread. "I'm not the real Stella. I'm imaginary, your reflection of her. But you're in real danger. This is your subconscious…a dreamscape, and it's getting corrupted. I can't say the source, but you probably know."

He nodded in reply.

"This is one of his most terrifying tactics. He can go into people's subconscious using his telepathy, and influence it like a plague. I was able to avoid his corruption by hiding, but the others weren't so lucky. It's a safe bet to say that everyone else is corrupted too. The good news is that everything should be fine by tomorrow," Stella finished. They started to walk into Technoland.

"Void…well, he'll not stop until either the night ends, or I die. I want the first option more," he said.

Her face lit up in realisation, with Samuel noticing quickly. "We could hide in my Ride Building! It's like a maze in there, he'll never be able to find us!" she said with energy.

He smiled in response, not noticing the figure walking towards the bridge of Technoland. As soon as she saw him though, she pulled Samuel down besides a barrier so Void couldn't spot them.

"Oh Samuel...playing with your imaginary friend now, are we?" Void laughed, while stalking through the streets of Technoland.

Stella peeked over to check if he had left, but quickly ducked down again.

"I commanded Fawnia to stop! Surely I can do the same with Void?" Samuel whispered to Stella, then stayed quiet following a shake of her head.

"You can command any character in your dreams, including me, as we're just figments of your imagination, even if we get corrupted. On the other hand, he's not a dream character like us. He's...the real Void. No amount of yelling to stop would get through to him, I'm afraid," Stella told him. After another check to see if the coast was clear, she gave a thumbs up. "Okay. He's gone... but not for long. We need to sprint to my building over there, without Shadows spotting us."

The two of them began to sprint towards the building, with Samuel in front, and Stella behind. Just as he passed through the Hyperspeed archway, however, the sound of Stella screaming came from behind him. He turned around, and was greeted with the unwelcome smirk of Void.

The Abyss Spirit was holding Stella in his arms, as she tried and failed to get away. "Well, look who's here. Found you, Samuel! You've done a good job escaping me so far, I'll admit. Surprised you even realised you could break my little...toys. Well, I have a little game for you. I'll be taking our little Princess in Distress somewhere here, and you need to find us. If you don't before the sun rises at eight, well, I win and you might end up never waking again. Let the game...begin!" Void explained, before laughing at the teen, as both he and Stella vanished into the mist.

Samuel glanced around, thinking for anywhere that Void could have taken her, before his eyes connected to the bright, amber light that shines from the drop of Abyss. "The Abyss! Of course. He's more powerful there, he can make it any way he sees fit, and is dark." Samuel sighed sarcastically, knowing he'd be at a severe disadvantage. He took a gasp of the cold, misty air, and began to sprint over to The X-periment Facility.

CHAPTER 19:
DUEL WITH THE NIGHT

After a minute or two of running, Samuel arrived at the entrance to the terrifying facility, which appeared more dominating in the crimson-tinted light in the nightmare. As he expected, the portal to the abyss was open, swirling in a shadowy manner, with a small humming noise coming from its ring. Samuel glanced for any way to get access to the portal, without much luck. However, he did notice that there was a statue in the middle, obviously from Void's corruption. It depicted the two siblings in detail, showing the dedication of whoever created it. The stone figure of Smiley was holding a detailed controller, mirroring Void, who held a dagger. From the way that the statue was built, the blade pointed towards the portal opening.

"I could climb it...but I'd need to be careful. The wind feels like it's got a mind of its own!" Samuel thought. He started to climb up the statue like a climbing wall, keeping his body close to the statue to reduce the risk of him falling or being thrown off by the wind. He had gotten to the shoulder of the Void statue when his hand slipped. He started to panic, hooking his foot onto a chipped chunk of rock, using it as a ledge. He paused for a moment to regain his grip on the stone surface, before he pulled himself up on to the arm. He stood there for a moment with his hand gripped to the cold, stone face of the statue, feeling the wind whip past him like a strong current of water. He put his arms out for balance, and cautiously walked across the arm, putting one foot in front of the other.

When he stepped onto the cold blade, he glanced down at the swirling blur of the portal. He readied himself to jump, but a thought passed through his head before he went through with it. He needed the mask, since the Abyss likely followed the same rules as normal. "This is my dream, even if Void is messing with it. I should be able to get the mask by thinking of it." When he locked the thought in his mind, a flickering blue light came from his hands. However, when the light glowed its brightest, an overpowering amber haze appeared and tried to absorb the light. The corruption seemed to even be able to block his will. However, he kept the thought in his mind, pushing against the power. The sky-like orb overpowered the corruption, summoning the mask in his hands.

He quickly put it on, before diving into the darkened swirls. He braced himself for the cold sensation, letting the icy feeling pass over him. When he felt himself on solid ground, he opened his eyes. For a moment he didn't know where he was, but he quickly recognised the place he was standing in as the apartment he had visited three weeks ago. However, it wouldn't take a genius to realise that something was wrong. The lights that normally gave the room a comforting, orange tint were now coloured a washed-out grey.

He winced, as a sickening smell was caught at the back of his throat. It was metallic, like iron or copper, but tinged with rot. The smell of dried blood. His eyes traced the room, finding the source to be a stain on the already damaged carpet. He was lucky the mask neutralised the smell, as without it the scent may have been unbearable. Clearing his mind, his focus was drawn to the walls of the room, which was dotted with notes and shredded pieces of paper. The notes that were still readable were a mixture of rushed scrawls and formal notes. The mad ramblings seemed to be from Void himself, with the messages commonly being about Smiley, the Ministry, and how they had betrayed him. Meanwhile the formal notes seemed to detail assessments and tests that the Ministry would perform on him. Samuel saw one detailing the ever-familiar Empathy Test, noticing how the document was never finished due to the scientist's untimely demise. The nightmare was true. Samuel's attention diverted to a specific note, which seemed to be singled out. "Test Subject 4B-725 'Void': Lethal and Violent. Emotionally numb. Permission to start subject on Assassination Program?" Samuel read from the small note, his eyes noticing the confirming tick next to the question.

He focused back on saving Stella, and the challenge that Void had given him. "Come on...where is she?" The boy said to himself. He looked to the side, seeing an open doorway near the kitchen. It seemed to be a normal bedroom door, though Samuel could only guess what really lay ahead. "Well, it seems like I'm risking it," he thought. He walked towards the door, opening it up wide. Instead of a dismantled bedroom greeting him, there was a thick darkness, with a winding staircase that appeared to float in the air. Samuel gathered his nerves, and ran down the stairwell, making sure to not trip or fall. He felt like he was running for hours, until it suddenly stopped. He paused for a moment in thought, but was abruptly interrupted by the feeling of the step shaking. He ran back up the stairs, as the steps behind him started to shake and fall into the perpetual blackness that was below him. He almost made it back to the doorway, but it slammed shut and unravelled into mist when he got close. Just as he slowed down, the step he was standing on fell below his feet, dropping him into the darkness.

He looked around frantically to try and find anything to grab onto, wishing that there would eventually be something to land on instead of the rapidly approaching ground. In the corner of his eye, however, he could see figures in the darkness. They had the form of people, but were made of curling mist and shadows. Their faces had been reduced to a pair of dimly glowing holes and gaps, and an empty hole was carved into their ghostly chests where their hearts would be. Some had limbs that were detached from their bodies, while others had the appearance of black, empty veins made of pure darkness. The thing that made Samuel afraid, however, was what they were doing. They all stared at him with blank, haunting expressions and reached out towards him with their wisp-like hands. They may have been victims of Void, or unlucky adventurers, but Samuel knew they were better left alone. Just as a dark, rocky platform came into view, his descent slowed almost to a stop to let him land safely. When his feet touched the ground, he saw the figure of Stella trapped in a diamond like crystal, with terror frozen on her face.

Void stood in front of the crystal, his focus glued onto the girl frozen in the crystal. Despite the fact he just trapped her in the crystal, he seemed to be calm and collected. He looked at the prism's surface, noticing Samuel in the reflection. He turned around towards him, his hands gripped together. The boy glared back at him, and realised something was off. He was wearing a pair of gloves that you would wear for climbing or parkour.

"Well, look who's arrived. Just on time, of course!" The man's tone was joke-like, but the context made it chilling, even twisted. "Where are my manners? You should at least be able to see where you are!" Void said with a click of his fingers. At the snap, the darkness retreated away.

The light revealed a large, stone arena, with the diamond prison hovering above it like a chandelier. "Well...I've been doing a few things while you were running around with your friends, both real and imagined. I grabbed a few things from The Smile Facility back from when Project Nightstalker was still ongoing. Since I'm back on contract with them, I could go in with no questions asked. I could've done that from the start, but it didn't seem fair for you to miss the fun." He took his hand out from behind his back, which revealed that he was holding a blaster. It looked like a crossbow made of ebony and quicksilver, and it was decorated with a pair of bat-like pieces in the middle. Void held it tight, holding it in the air. "Do you like it? This is Midnight, a blaster with two modes: A short range blaster mode, and a long range Sniper mode. One shot of the blaster mode, and you're frozen in place until I let you go. The other, well…it's for finishing targets off. Oh, just saying, you can take that mask off. I summoned oxygen in here for you to breathe, and I've prevented the abyss from freezing or draining you." He flourished the weapon with egotistical pride, before sliding it back to its grip.

Samuel cautiously took the mask off his face, and slid it in his pocket.

"Well, do you like the new look of this place? It's slowly bending to my will, and that isn't exactly good for you. After all, your subconscious is a part of your mind and, by extension, your consciousness. When this place falls, you'd be trapped inside your corrupted mind. That means not only would you be brain dead in reality, but you would become a drone under my will here. Not like you'd be around for long after that, but still. Tragic, I know. So, you're doomed no matter if you lose, or flee. What a twist!"

"Well, I'll win! I'm not going to give up!" Samuel yelled back, staying brave.

"Ah. Trying to be strong? Good for you! You know what? I have an idea. You saw those figures when you fell, right? I learned a while ago that souls can be collected and turned into other beings, like ghosts. Those figures are replicas of real souls which I've collected and sent to the Abyss. They were the victims of tragedies, murders and accidents from even centuries ago, which I brought to the Abyss to continue existing. Maybe they can be brought back to life one day, but for now, they're here with me. I think your friend is here too, kid. Eliza was her name, if I'm right?" Void said.

He brought his hand up into the air, making a holographic figure of one of the ghost-like beings appear beside him. Without most of the corruption, they looked more humanoid, although their blank faces still were discomforting to look at. "I found her body dead on the pathway, and in a gruesome way too. I could tell it was Smiley just by the way she was killed. Stabbing and running was always his thing. But her soul was still stuck in her body. It was a waste to leave it to flicker away, so I gave her another chance. The point is, death isn't the end when it comes to me. Not only can I take souls and make them ghosts, but I can also turn the living into vampires!

"I know you've probably realised that it's becoming harder to fight against the threats here. Smiley is becoming more ruthless by the day, and someone as calculative as me can predict someone's choices and actions easily. You prefer a more balanced route when it comes to conflict; you go for the attack when you can, and defend yourself if necessary. You also seem to have an understanding, although hit and miss, of when to run away. But mostly you try to resolve issues without conflict, since you know that a lot of people could easily overpower you. Am I right?" he said with a sneer on his face.

Samuel tried to hide his shock, but it was impossible. Void was right. He felt his stomach twist as he realised how out of his depth he truly was.

"I can sense your fear. I'm assuming I got it right! The point is, I know how you act, and you can't predict me. Ever since I first became an Assassin, I learned that you need to be one step ahead of your target. Like the fact that I stole the knife you got from the kitchen, to make you defenceless if I were to, say, lunge at you to try and slice into somewhere vital, like the neck. See? I plan things in advance. I know you will most likely fail and die in a full battle with me, and the corruption in your mind means stalling or running will also cause your death. So, I wish to offer you the chance to know you aren't going to suffer or be cut down. Stand down to me, and I will give you the mercy of a painless death, or continue fighting and face me without my restraint."

Samuel looked frozen, as he saw Void's blade pointed directly at his chest. He wasn't an expert in combat, but it was clear that Void could very easily strike him down where he stood with one word. He paused for a moment, before taking a breath to clear his mind. "No. I'm not going to give up, no matter what threats you throw at me!" he yelled, taking a stand for himself.

Void looked at the holographic soul of Eliza, who seemed to look upset. He shook his head in her direction, before recalling her away with a snap of his fingers. "Well, I'm done with formalities, and you seem to have a death wish. She and I both didn't want to make you suffer, you know. You already get the deal, so there's no use going through it. You win and live, or you lose and die."

They both were facing each other, with tension rising in the air. "Here." The man gave his blade to the teen, creating another shortly after. His blaster was strapped securely to his back, and ready to swap in during the battle. When he was near the other side of the arena, he pressed his gloves together. Samuel stepped back in dread, seeing the familiar glow of a forming techno-suit wrap around Void.

His body had been covered by a sleek, full body suit that was obviously made for vigorous movement. Most of the suit was coloured variations of black and grey. His hands and shoes had orange grip pads, and his face was covered by a crimson reflective visor. The suit was made of a Kevlar-like material that was sturdy enough to deflect damage, yet flexible enough to be able to withstand rapid movements and morphing. The light that Void summoned swam on the surface of the fibres, showing some sort of reflective layer over them. If the light hadn't been created, he believed that the figure of Void would be indistinguishable from the shadows. That, and Void's abilities of movement, would have made him an unseeable killer.

"You're lucky, kid. You're the first person in years to see my Assassin Suit. Not like you're going to wake up to tell anyone, though," he taunted, his voice turned robotic by the suit. He readied his blade, before starting his attack.

He rushed towards the boy, before swinging his blade down towards him. Samuel pushed his arm up, deflecting the blade with his own, and rushed to the left.

Void turned to mist, before catching Samuel off guard and knocking him to the cold, rocky floor.

"You don't stand a chance. I'm an Assassin. Trained to kill. You're delaying the inevitable!" Void yelled, staring down at the boy in contempt. He swung down, the blade slashing down at the ground as the rocks cracked at its strike, centimetres away from Samuel's head.

He looked up at the man, trying to remain calm. "You don't need to do this! What does my death mean to you?" he said, looking at the empty, red visor that blocked Void's face from view.

The visor slid away, revealing the expression of the man above him. "What does your death mean to me? Well, I get paid. Does half a million sound like a good amount?" A sneer was on his face, while his eyes were staring into Samuel's. Just as Samuel tried to escape, the visor slid back up again. He swung his blade down again, barely missing stabbing the teenage boy once more. Samuel kicked the man on the chest to move him away. He got himself off the ground. "I did want to be friends! With you, and them. But my lack of emotions and empathy made truly connecting impossible. I tried to change for so long, but it never worked!" he explained. With a swing of his arm, he brought his blaster out of its grip and fired away at the boy with projectiles that streaked through the air like fire.

Samuel spun the blade in front of him, sending some of the projectiles back at Void. "What?!" he said, as the beams slammed into him, sending him flying in the air momentarily. He shifted the firearm into its sniper mode with a pull of a switch, his piercing sight giving him deadly accuracy. Samuel caught the glint of the sights of the weapon, moving around to make himself a hard target. Void pulled the trigger, as a fizzing streak of amber light ripped through the air towards Samuel. He flinched, feeling the scalding hot strike sear his arm. He paused for a moment, holding his injured arm in pain. Just as Void fired at him, predicting a headshot, Samuel managed to swing the sword through the air, splitting the beam into harmless sparks. Enraged, Void launched himself higher using his dominion over the abyss, and slammed into the ground. The pound caused cracks to grow on the area near him, sending a rippling shockwave across the arena.

Samuel ran towards the wave, before jumping over the abyss-fuelled attack and landing safely down. Void looked at the scene with a burning fury, as both his blade and blaster melted into shadows and reformed in his hands, with Midnight getting slid back into its grip. "Ergh! Why can't I just win for once?!" Void spat venomously, before jumping into a portal, and coming out of another in front of the teen. Their two blades were locked together, with Samuel using all of his strength on his weaker arm as his injured arm would give him even more of a disadvantage. Void pushed against him, making Samuel step back. "This's my one chance. Nobody else cares about me now, anyways!" he explained, while aggressively fighting against the block.

Samuel knew he couldn't beat Void with strength, but he had a chance with his mind. "You don't need to do this... She cares for you!" Samuel spoke back, with Void seeming unfazed.

"No!... She made her choice when she said she didn't want to be near me. She abandoned me!" Void snapped back, trying again to push down the teen, with Samuel knowing that Void probably wouldn't miss a third time.

"She didn't! Stella still cares about you...she still believes in you, Void."

Void looked through the visor at him, before twisting his blade sharply left, trying to make Samuel lose his balance. "Even if she did...would you really think the rest could forgive me?" he answered back, his hands gripping harder on his blade's handle. The visor hiding his face retreated, revealing how he was scowling. "I've killed people in cold blood. Florette, countless guests, scientists, even Smiley, and innocent explorers like you. I've got blood on my hands, and you know it. Do you REALLY think I deserve forgiveness from her? I'm...nothing but a monster!" He yelled out, venting to Samuel, who stared back at him with a look of sympathy.

"...You need help, Shadows. If you stop trying to fight us, we could help you. Stella could help you!" Samuel offered him, trying to stop the duel. He looked down at his blue eyes, before relaxing his strength. Just as Void's pressure disappeared though, Samuel's blade flew forwards. He felt his stomach drop, as he realised what he had just done. The blade was stabbed straight into Void's shoulder. He howled in pain, which faded into groans. His blade unravelled to mist. He fell on his knees, as the suit glitched away. He held his shoulder, the wound intensely stinging on touch. With his teeth clenched, he tore the blade out and threw it to the side in one swift motion.

Samuel stood in shock, only able to mumble a quick apology. Void looked at his slightly shaking hand, which was dripping with his inklike blood. "...It's alright. You were in a life or death situation, and fought up your way out. I don't blame you. I've always been known to heal from these types of scenarios, anyways. Don't have a heart attack." He forgave him, and shakily stood up. "Well then. You won. You can go now, kid!"

Samuel quickly noticed a familiar locket hanging onto Void's neck, which he had tucked away into his shirt. "That's the necklace that matched the one you gave to Stella... If you didn't care about her...why'd you still be wearing it?" Samuel asked while pointing at the man, whose face froze in shock, as if he'd become a statue. "You care about Stella. That's your weakness."

Void looked surprised, and Samuel noticed how there appeared to be remorse in his eyes.

He flicked his right hand, before the crystal shattered and sent out a shockwave, knocking Samuel over. Stella was floating in the air, with gravity having returned to the Abyss's normal state. Samuel sprang over to the dream spirit, who looked back at him with a smile.

"Well done! You freed me. Wait... is Void okay?" Stella asked, gesturing to the man, who was floating by himself.

"Just go..." Void muttered quietly, causing them both to look at him.

"Are you ok?" Stella asked, before Void turned around, showing how he was crying.

"There. You win, Samuel. Just go!" Void screamed, before flicking his hand, launching the boy towards a portal.

As he entered the rift, he jolted awake in reality, with the real spirits crowded around him.

"Samuel! You wouldn't wake up... we thought something bad had happened and..." Fawnia panicked while hugging the teen.

"I...I need to talk to Stella," Samuel commanded slightly, taken aback.

"Why? What happened?!" Nebulus asked, panicked.

"...Void. Stella was right about him. He does have good in him. Stella is the one who can bring it out...She basically is his support," Samuel finished, before Nebulus was hit with a memory.

"I do remember Stella always taking care of him when he had... well, issues. Sometimes she came back tired, but she would brush it off as tiredness from a bad night's sleep. She has always been a determined worker," he said.

Samuel looked at him and sighed. "That wasn't fatigue from working hard. Remember that deal Florette made her take, about the blood? Well, she was the thing keeping the deal together. She'd let Void drink her blood, so he didn't die or become weak. And I can guess having fangs pierce your neck isn't the best feeling. She went through all that to keep him well, and kept it from you presumably to keep you all from worrying about her. She cares for him, and I just found out that he cares for her. Saying she'd be there for him was the one thing that got him to calm down." He got off the bed, and Nebulus charged a spell to allow him to swap back into his normal clothes.

Sally bounced on her feet, and laughed with a smile. "Oh my gosh! We gotta tell her!" The girl then sprinted outside, trying to find the Star spirit, with the others laughing at it.

"Still, I feel like there's something big going to happen. Be careful, Samuel. You're the weakest of the group, with or without your suit." Fawnia spoke up, her red dress sparkling, as she was sitting next to the window.

"We'll just need to stay alert for trouble. Void would be with him too, so maybe we'll get Stella to get him back? Just food for thought," Blaze mused, before the rest of the people in the room jolted, seeing a familiar golden glow, as well as a dark mist nearby, in Technoland.

"Looks like they're looking for trouble. Get Stella to call for the Technoland defences. We'll need as many hands as we can get," Nebulus commanded, before the group all started looking for Stella, knowing a fight was about to start.

CHAPTER 20:
THE FINAL BATTLE

The spirits searched around for the aqua girl inside the palace, from the main hall, to the entrance, to the ride shafts. "There's no sign of her. Where is she?!" Blaze had a small meltdown, his flame hued eyes sparking up like a bonfire.

"Blaze, dear, cool down and help here?" Fawnia snapped back, making the demon sigh and calm down.

"Maybe...she went to stop them herself!" Samuel theorised, before the spirits thought, then nodded.

"That sounds like something she'd do! We need to get there and help!" Nebulus asked, before handing Samuel a familiar pair of icy blue boots and their matching headsets. He smiled, before putting them on, and activating the armour, which formed around him seamlessly.

"Let's go, guys!" Blaze cheered, throwing up his arm and summoning his flame blade when he put his arm back down.

The group ran towards the entrance of the palace, eventually standing in the entrance plaza.

"Okay, we should do a surprise attack. If she gets in trouble, you guys attack on the ground, and I'll be in the air with Stella. Blaze could also use his demon form. Got it?" Samuel took command, with the spirits agreeing to the plan. Samuel smirked, standing up tall. "Computer, activate flight!" Samuel commanded the suit, before a similar pair of wings to Stella's appeared. Samuel kicked his legs, then he rapidly flew upwards, with Blaze in his demon form to his left. He looked down, seeing two familiar navy and pink beams following closely behind, and quickly switching right, waiting for command. In front of the group, the silver spires of Technoland shone with the hues of the colour spectrum. However, on the ground, the familiar figures of Smiley and Void were back-to-back, fighting off all of the Technoland spirits. The glints of laser fire and magic spells in the distance made Samuel pause for a moment from fear. In the corner of his eye, Stella was rising and diving in the air, avoiding attacks from the spirits. He took a deep breath, allowing himself to focus. "Now!" Samuel commanded, before the spirits joined the fight, with Fawnia and Nebulus defending the ground, while Stella, Samuel and Blaze attacked from the air.

"Oh great. THEY'VE come," Smiley said venomously, shooting out golden dagger-like auras from his hands.

"Looks like Samuel's with them, the idiots. Smiley, plan B!" Void commanded.

"Hey Stella. Want to throw them for a loop?" Samuel asked for Stella to laugh and call to his suit in reply.

"Let's do this, Sammy!"

The two of them flew downwards, before looping in a circle in front of Void and Smiley, with them both trying to swing at them, and missing.

They shot back up, before glancing down at the spirits, who were dazed for a moment.

"Yeah!" Stella high fived Samuel, before regrouping with the others, who were trying to hit the brothers.

"Hey kid, maybe try our plan?" Blaze said.

"Stella...I was in a dream. Everyone was all monochromatic and ghostly. Void challenged me to a game, but I won through my own emotions," Samuel started, with the two standing to the side.

"And, what's this got to do with me?" Stella said.

"In the game, you were taken by Void, and I had to find you before eight o'clock. But, then Void started a duel with me, my life on the line. When I managed to win, I noticed something...he was wearing the gold locket that you gave to him," Samuel continued, focused on swaying her to his idea.

"But, it wasn't protecting anything like yours, and he tried to make me think he didn't care...but he still wore the locket. The locket...that represents you."

Stella gasped and stepped back in shock. "You mean...he cares for me?" Stella said, drifting off for a moment, quickly snapping back to reality. "Woah woah, okay. If this isn't a lie, tell me something that'll prove it," Stella prompted him, doing a small finger point at Samuel.

"You have a scar on your neck from when Void lost control, and you try to hide it," Samuel said. He pointed back at her, mirroring her movements.

Stella smiled with a hint of surprise in her eyes, knowing inside that he was correct. Her hand brushed across her neck, revealing the faded bite mark in the same place as the dream. "It's true...I've always hated to see him suffering, even if I now know some of it was a lie. I'm lucky he even had an antidote! I'm convinced. What's the plan then?" Stella said, for him to smile in return.

"Show Void you care for him. If he sees that his fears are over nothing, he'll hopefully pick us over Smiley," Samuel replied with a commanding tone.

Stella responded with a nod, then launched into the air and rejoined the fight by firing down projectiles from above, while Samuel flew to help the Technoland Spirits who were hiding from the barrage.

Void glanced over at Smiley, before creating a mist ring around them to obscure their movements. Suddenly, both siblings appeared on the rooftops, clinging onto two metallic spires.

"Haha! How can you beat us...when you can't see?" Smiley said, giving his brother a sharp nod.

Almost in sync, they both summoned their weapons. They broke the lights on the roofs, lighting the area with strobe-like flashing. The spirits look around frantically, unable to track the spirits' movements. Samuel and Stella shot back into the air, scoping the scene.

Stella squinted, fighting against the flickering lights that cloaked the brothers' movements. She needed to make a plan, before her friends were overwhelmed. However, her suit's scanner picked up how there were still momentary shadows flicking from left to right. "Samuel, you deal with Smiley, I'll go for Void. Got it?"

Samuel nodded, as they both launched in the opposite direction. She landed carefully on the tiled roof, activating her visor to neutralise the flashing, to allow her to see. In the strobe she saw Nebulus and Fawnia trying to find a way to stop the barrage of light, while Defendia and Levi were lying on the floor. On the other side were Mesmerith and Twister, who had rushed in to help the Technoland Spirits once the fighting began. Void was battling fiercely with Blaze, their swords reflecting the light.

However, Blaze was soon thrown to the ground, his sword vanishing. "Easy. Don't try next time, or I might not go easy on you," Void said. He stood for a moment, before he saw Stella from the corner of his eye. "Oh, so you want to fight? I'd advise against that. The others didn't listen, so you have a chance." He strutted out of the blinding light, a summoned mist curling by his feet.

"No. I came because I miss you, Void! I want you back..." Stella said. She walked forwards, grasping him in a hug.

Void, however, pushed her away. "Forget about me. All I do is hurt people. You clearly didn't want anything to do with me before, so why're you still trying?" He grimaced, showing no emotion.

Stella paused for a moment and calculated a response, before stepping forward again. "How? I'd never forgive myself for letting you go! Just because you're different, doesn't make you more of a threat to me, or my friends!" she said, while raising her tone slightly.

His fists became clenched, as he growled under his breath. When he looked back at her, his eyes were red. "Are you an idiot? I'm a vampire. I have to focus 24/7 just to not kill you all! Isn't that in any way deterring you?" he stated, though his tone showed more annoyance than rage.

She shook her head after a second, as she would not back down.

"I respect your determination, but you need to go. I've already messed up enough, and I'm sure you and the others have some heroic things to do that don't include a half dead freak of nature." He started to say something else, but caught his tongue. With a sigh, he turned his back to Stella's pleading stare.

"I can help! You don't have to be alone. I will help you all I can, and you know it," Stella yelled, with tears now streaming from her eyes.

The man paused, turning his head towards her. The sight of Stella crying made Void freeze, barely able to speak. "Stella?...I...I didn't mean to..." He stumbled, while coming to comfort her.

But that comfort wouldn't come. As soon as he was an arm's length away from her, an overbearing pain blasted through his chest. His focus shifted from Stella's haunting stare to the source of the pain. Pierced through his chest was his own blade, now tipped in his darkened blood. Around the blade, he felt a rapidly constricting tightness, like his body itself was tightening.

"That was for Florette! Not so powerful now, are you?" Blaze said. The demon stood behind Void, holding the grip to the now bloodstained blade in his hand. Stella focused on him, her stare locked straight into his. The fire in his eyes was undeniable, and his anger was apparent. But while he had expected her to be thankful, or celebrate their half victory, she answered back with a stare of fury.

Blaze pulled his arm back to release the blade from the wound, limiting the force used to avoid straining himself. The rapid push, along with the shock in his system, caused Void to crumple to the ground with a crash. Unable to get up, he sank down and started to shudder from shock. Satisfied, the demon prepared to leave. Just as he had formed his wings, however, he felt Stella grab tightly onto his arm.

"Why did you think that was a good idea? Do you know how close I was to fixing this whole mess? The plan was to let me handle Void, not to run in and try to kill him!" she yelled, as the demon was forced to look at her. Despite sharing his pain, she was enraged at his actions.

"I know, but it isn't right. He's a cold-blooded murderer, Stella. He has killed 40 people, and admitted that with a smile. I'm not saying that you're wrong for trusting him, anyone would at first glance. But we don't know if he'll be good. I know you tried, you made that whole system to keep him from lashing out due to thirst. But, I couldn't just stand idly by while you let a known manipulator and killer back into our friend group," Blaze explained.

She returned his stare. "I understand your thoughts and hesitations. But I can't just abandon him. I promised to him years ago that I wouldn't give up on him, even through tough times! You don't know how many times I've woken up aching from being bitten the night before, yet still came to greet the morning with a smile! I was told that I needed to give blood to him, and it became something that I got used to. I spent time with him, I learned more about his personality than a spooky vampire. I can't waste all of that for revenge. I miss her too, but this is going too far."

For a moment, they stared at each other in silence. The demon looked at her in contemplation, before putting his hand on her shoulder. "Don't make me regret this, starlight," he said, before turning his back to the two of them and soaring into the air. She rushed back towards Void, getting down on the ground to get a closer look. His eyes were shut, and he had stopped shuddering a while ago. Her heart stopped, as her mind came to an obvious, but terrifying thought. She grabbed his shoulders in pure anxiety, trying any way she could to wake him up. "Void...can you hear me? Wake up!" Stella said to him, trying to find a way to wake him up.

After a few minutes or so, his eyes flicked open. "...Dearie? Why're...you still trying to help me? I'm just...a monster."

Stella sighed in relief, her heart pounding in her head. With her nerves more settled, she surveyed his situation. His clothing was torn and soaked in blood, though the worst damage was near the wound. While the outside was bad, she was still worried about the inside as internal damage could only be healed by the spirit itself.

"You're not a monster, Void. You've made mistakes and bad choices, I'll admit. I am still a bit upset about you lying to me, but I wouldn't leave you here, because I've always cared for you! It's definitely a bad time to say it, but...I love you," she asserted herself.

He smiled back, accepting her help. She fished through both her pockets and Void's, eventually finding some bandages and tissue. "I need to clean the wound, and get it bandaged. This might hurt, okay?" she reassured him.

He looked back at her with a sly smile on his face, despite the odds. "I've just been stabbed. I don't really mind some discomfort, dearie." He shrugged his shoulders.

She laughed for a moment, before focusing on the man in front of her. The clothes in front of the wound were now blocking the way, so she cut more of a hole using a plasma tool to get better access. Buying more shirts is better than death in any scenario.

With no time to lose, she pressed down on the wound while holding the tissue in her hand to stop the bleeding and quickly wrapped his chest up with bandages. While it wasn't the cleanest or healed, it was the best job she could do without any potions around.

With permission from him, Stella took his tailcoat off him and turned it into a makeshift headrest to keep his head up and off the ground. However, when Void turned his head to look at her, she noticed something that instantly caught her attention. His eyes were not his normal colour. They were nearly as white as snow. "No wonder you're not healing. You're parched. With this amount of starvation, I'm surprised you could even stand! But why are you doing this..." she said in shock. She sat on her knees, thinking of any possible explanation. When she realised the truth, her eyes lit up. "Wait. You're trying to sabotage his plan! You've been pulling a double agent, right?" Void looked up at her, before smiling. "I never should have doubted you. Sorry if that made you feel bad. I hope this covers that," she said with compassion.

She paused for a moment, before her view landed on the now abandoned blade that Blaze had dropped on the ground. Knowing what she had to do, she grabbed the sword's grip. With a fresh tissue, she started to clean the dark blood off the blade tip. He turned around weakly while looking at her, who was holding the now cleaned blade in her hands.

"What're you doing with my blade? It's quite light, and I don't want you to accidentally stab someone." He cracked a joke.

She carefully leaned him against a nearby ventilation system, slowly trying to make him upright. Once he was sitting at a somewhat normal position, she sat herself back down. "Why do I have your blade? Well, you need blood, right?" She gripped tightly onto the sword, and used the blade edge to draw blood from her hand with a muffled wince. He paused, his senses kicking in quickly after the cut formed.

He looked at Stella's hand, which had a familiar red liquid slightly dripping down the side. Despite blocking it out, he could hear the faint sound of a heartbeat in the back of his mind. Her heartbeat. He pulled himself away, knowing what could likely happen. However, her merciful expression kept him from ignoring her completely. She nodded at him, holding her arm towards him. "Go ahead. You can't be left like this, and I have plenty. Just, promise to not go overboard," Stella asked, her voice slightly shaking from the sting.

He held her hand in his own, tempted to bite it. He placed his hand onto the small cut, with Stella expecting him to numb it. However, when there was no numbness, she knew something was wrong. She looked down, and saw what he did. The cut was healed. She looked back at him, perplexed. But the sound of him laughing cleared her confusion. "Sweetheart. You don't need to do all this for me. All I need is a yes. Whether that yes is through words…or the colour red." He smiled, before holding her in a hug. When Void looked down again, he saw how Stella had purposely taken her necklace off, and sat in a way where her neck was out in the open. She had planned it. "…Thanks, Stella," he whispered. He shifted one of his hands to instead be on her neck, quickly chilling it to make it numb. He moved his hand back, then bit. Unlike what had happened with Florette, she felt no pain. Void's freezing touch and extra precautions to keep her safe made sure of that. She knew the feeling of getting bitten from the many times that she had donated for him. It was always a strange, yet comforting sensation, like a warm shower after a cold day. She smiled, wanting Void to be happy.

However, Void was different. He felt waves of adrenaline, though he toned himself down for her safety. He'd done this sometimes before in the past and knew the taste of her blood to be the taste of dark chocolate. The heat would make it taste like hot chocolate, so Stella would make some when she came over as an alternative, or as a simple drink to relax with. Ironically, it just made him like the taste more. For some reason, the heat was the part he loved the most, as he had none of his own.

He stopped when he had drunk enough, removing his mouth from the wound and quickly replacing it with his hand. "You alright? I'm worried I took too much," he said, healing the wound in a flow of magic.

Stella laughed, as they helped each other up. "Well, I'm conscious. So, you're in the green! You really need to relax." She joked with him, returning her necklace to her neck. Void quickly cleaned his mouth with his tongue, as Stella had used up his tissues.

She helped him put his tailcoat back on, then helped him stand up. He looked down, and recognised that the wound had now healed, though he would definitely need to rest after sustaining that much damage.

Blaze had flown back from helping the others, and was now sitting on the same ventilation system that Void was just leant against. He looked up at him, then down towards Stella. "I guess I know why you were so defensive of him. You have a crush! It's alright, I won't tell anyone if you don't want me to. I'll be alright with him, but he does need to have some sort of repercussion for what he has done. But, it would be better to discuss that outside of an active battlefield. Just, make sure to keep him from turning us into lunch if we say no." Blaze told a joke to lighten the mood.

Stella laughed, her hand in front of her mouth.

The demon turned towards the vampire, still keeping his cheerful tone. "I'll probably still be nervous with you, Shadows, but I can't hold a grudge forever. So, I forgive you. Go stop your sibling!" Blaze smiled, as the Technoland spirits were fixing the lights.

Samuel, on the other hand, was fighting Smiley, who was laughing darkly.

"Haha! Oh Samuel, we could've been friends!"

Samuel glared at him with bravery. "We could never be friends! You're insane, Smiley!" Samuel spat back, with Smiley faking a shocked expression.

"Oh my! Did I strike a nerve?" he said, spinning his dagger. Stella activated her helmet again and flew across the gap, while firing down a rain of bright, powerful plasma orbs at Smiley. He was jumping over and deflecting the attacks, with a mocking smile. He pulled his gun out of its grip, then clicked the switch, putting it to Bullet Mode. He aimed at Stella's wings…then fired. The bullets tore holes through her wings, launching the silver locket off Stella's neck and into the air.

"No! Florette!" Stella yelled out to the necklace, which contained the gem form of the Lime spirit's soul.

She slammed into the ground, as surges of pain blasted through her body. Weakly, she looked at Smiley, who was holding the necklace in his grip.

"Such a pretty little trinket, and what a stunning trick. Too bad I'm not an idiot, starlight," Smiley mocked the woman, who was sprawled on the floor, shaking in pain and fear.

"Please…don't break it!" Stella pleaded, tears now in her eyes, but Smiley didn't care.

"What? Do you mean…this?" Smiley responded emotionlessly, before he gripped the locket at the heart…and crushed it in his hand, as the lime glow flickered and faded.

Smiley threw the crushed locket towards Stella, who grasped at the locket's centre. The Soul gem of Florette was shattered, and was unfixable. She was truly dead. "You…you killed her!" Stella went to get up as her eyes streamed with tears. But, as soon as she had gotten on her feet, pain rushed through her body and caused her to crumple back down.

"No! Dearie!" Void gasped, as he transformed himself into mist, and appeared on the other roof, sprinting over to Stella. He held her protectively, keeping her safe, and unlatched her headset off her head with a hidden button. The headset was now bent and hanging on by a thread, so it was probably going to need to be replaced. He threw it away, focusing all his attention on Stella.

He focused his eyes to see her soul and bloodstream, which could act like an X-ray.

Her soul was cracked, and, without help, could risk shattering. "Luckily, it's not shattered...yet," Void spoke to himself, placing his hand on her chest. He focused, clearing his mind. "Soul Protectia," he whispered slowly. In his vision, Stella's soul was enveloped by a transparent amber aura, keeping it together. His attention was then drawn to her life force, which indicated to him that her left leg had been broken. "...Okay. Stay still, I'll get you help, okay, my dear?" Void comforted Stella, who looked up at him and smiled. Void brushed her face with his hand and gently placed her down to be safe. He stood himself up, as Smiley looked on, ecstatic.

"Oh look, is my dear sibling Void here to finish the job? Go ahead, strike her down!" Smiley laughed, with Void summoning one of his blades.

"Hey Smiley. Think fast!" Void sneered, quickly throwing his blade at Smiley, nearly impaling him to the spire.

"Ah! Why'd you do that?! You're on my team!" Smiley yelled, struggling to get the caught clothing out of the blade. He freed himself, falling to the ground.

"Oh, really? Why do you think I've been getting all my old tech back? Face it, Miles. I'm not on your side anymore, and I might not be fully ready to return to theirs. A Wildcard, per se." Void laughed.

Smiley stepped back, while his face looked like he was both going to explode in rage, and burst out in tears. "But we're brothers! The disaster duo! Were you lying to me about that too!?"

Void glanced at him with contempt. "I never lied. The Ministry did. They said that I was a failure, and you succeeded. Your ego grew larger, as did your belief in yourself. But you never lost that feeling deep inside you that screamed whenever I looked your way. You didn't think I noticed how your expression cracked when I walked by, or how you would back away when I got upset? That fear was made on purpose. I was created to kill, to instil fear into others. You were made to look friendly and keep people in line. You even have less power than me, because they were frightened to make another mistake! The only reason you got the popularity was because you had their colours. Face it, you have always been my lesser, but they were too scared to say it," Void explained.

He slowly walked towards his old brother, who was panicking at his glare. He stepped back again, and fumbled for his badge. "You won't come closer! I'm the Minister, and I command you to stop!" Smiley showed his new badge, which had a more modern design, and a crown at the top.

The older brother brought his arm up and snapped his fingers. Smiley's eyes widened, as he was pulled in the air towards him. "Pathetic. Do you really think some idiotic badge is going to make me bow to you? I want to tell you something here: I was never your brother. Now leave, before I repeat what I did back in 2018!" Void commanded with a frigid cruelty. He let go, and Smiley dropped to the ground. With a sneer, he returned to Stella and secured her leg in an enchanted bandage. It charged her leg with energy, allowing her somewhat limited movement in the leg. She could stand, walk and sit down, but she wouldn't be able to run or fight in it.

Smiley glanced nervously around the rooftop, fixing his eyes upon Samuel. He thought of a plan that would buy him enough time to escape with the Ministry in tow. "Fine... but I'm taking someone with me!" Smiley yelled, before his face became purely psychotic, as if he had lost his humanity. As Void snapped back around, Smiley threw his dagger out. Void tried to stop it, but he was too late. Samuel fell to the floor, as the dagger was stabbed through his chest. "Well, enjoy your friend's death!" Smiley laughed with an insane grin, before vanishing with a bright golden glow, that faded away to embers, like golden dust. Void rushed over to Samuel, trying to make sure he wasn't dead.

He was lying on the floor, his chest seeping with blood. Void screamed out for the others, who almost instantaneously arrived, with grave fear in their eyes. "Oh god...Samuel!" Blaze gasped, his hair flickering due to his fear. He paused for a moment, then turned back towards Void. "Well then, don't just stand there. Help!" Blaze yelled at the man, who shook his head back at him.

"And what could I do? The wound seems too deep for even me or Fawnia to heal, and it wouldn't clot quick enough to be safe to move him. There's nothing I can do! Unless..." Void thought aloud. He got down on his knee to survey the wound. It was a couple of inches deep: not too close to the heart or rib cage, but definitely a threat. He worked out the logic in his head, trying to not get distracted by the thick, suffocating scent of blood in the air. Just breathing in the lingering scent made his mouth fill with the taste of cinnamon. With all the information he needed, he stepped away to get the smell of cinnamon out of his system, so he could focus. After a few moments he sighed, realising what had to happen. As he turned to the group, his eyes were briefly flooded with red. "There is one thing I can do...but it's risky."

Samuel awoke in an abyss, filled with red, flickering warning signs. "Bleeding detected! Fatality risk is above 50%" Samuel read the warning out aloud, attempting to make sense of his situation. He looked down at his hands, noticing a faint, icy blue outline radiating from him. "That's not normal. Is this...my mind?" he said. He thought for a second, before he flew around the void-like space, trying to spot anything in the distance. In the corner of his eye, he saw countless grey orbs hanging in the air, like stars in the night sky. He carefully touched one, before it projected a picture of him and Stella having a race, from a few weeks ago.

They were his memories. However, the orbs were slowly breaking apart, with glitch-like static in the memory's cracks and splinters. Samuel floated down to solid ground with it in his hands. However, when his feet touched the ground, the orb cracked again.

In a panic, he dropped it and it shattered into static. He stumbled back, when his hand skimmed onto a small screen, which seemed to work like a keyboard. With a momentary flicker, the larger screen came to life with an image coming into view.

Void, Stella, Blaze and Fawnia were crowded around him, the tension between the group growing.

"Do you really want to do this? Not trying to be rude, but you have never actually done this. Are you sure you can save him?" Fawnia asked.

Void looked at her with a vague sense of sympathy. "Well, there's no time like the present. Anyways, I think we can all agree we'd rather him live, then for him to be dead. You all know what will happen, right?"

Blaze nodded, his casual demeanour replaced with worry. "Yes, you said. He'll be like you," Blaze said, as he was pulling at his wood bracelets like a stress toy.

Stella looked up at Void, feeling torn. "Please…don't hurt him. I'd hate to know he was suffering."

Void's eyes locked into hers, as he placed a hand gently down on her shoulder. "I promise he won't feel it. I'll do all that I can to make sure of it."

Stella placed her hand on Samuel's, which was becoming colder by the minute. "…What do we need to do then, Shadows?"

Void thought for a second, before looking at the group. "Okay. Fawnia and Stella need to heal the wound as far as they can. The wound needs to clot to make the bleeding stable. Then, Blaze will remove the dagger. Together, the wound should heal to the point where it's secure. After that, I'll use my powers to make sure that he won't…wake up during the process, and then the rest is up to me. Got it?" Void commanded.

The spirits nodded, and executed the plan. The girl's hands flowed with magic as the wound cauterised, while Blaze carefully removed the dagger. When they were done, the wound was now reduced to an obtrusive cut. Void placed his hand on the boy's forehead, as he cast a spell. In Samuel's view, Void's voice cast Dreamless Sleep from the darkness, which caused the screen to dissolve into thin air and multiple input opinions from the floating screens to be blocked by an inky blot.

Samuel tried to press them, but nothing worked. Then, the abyss-like area he was in started to crack and shatter, with a bright light pouring and leaking from the cracks. With a slam of his fist, the screen buzzed to life again. He looked at it inquisitively, only to notice something was happening. Void seemed to be holding him in his arms, while the view of what he would be seeing was tilted upwards. "...What is happening?" Samuel spoke to himself, his attention soon being dragged away by the glow of something behind him.

Samuel spun himself around cautiously, to be met with a transparent version of Void standing a few metres in front of him. Void stepped forward, his amber eyes glowing. Samuel stepped forwards and glared at him, trying to be intimidating. But, he could tell that it didn't work.

"Thanks for the kind welcome. I'm not trying to hurt you, I just want to tell you what's going on, as I think it would be malicious to leave you in the dark. As you know from experience, Smiley stabbed you with his knife. Ironically, it was the knife you used against him. Anyways, the wound's too deep for us to heal more than a clot and you'd quickly break the clot anyways. The only choice we have is for you to not be...mortal," the illusion of Void explained to Samuel, with a stern edge.

Samuel took a moment to figure out what he meant, with the realisation coming soon after. He gasped, staring back at the figure. "You...want to make me a vampire? I don't want to be immortal!" Samuel snapped back at Void.

He looked down at the boy, having expected that response. "Well, it's not like you have a choice! I've already started draining your blood for the transformation. You might as well spend whatever time you've got left accepting it, kid."

The hologram flickered and glitched into nothing, as the cracks filled a grand amount of the darkness. Before Samuel could try to prevent it, a large, gaping hole formed from the cracks. Samuel's dread soon turned to fear as he felt himself slowly getting pulled into the swirling vortex. He then noticed that small, blue sparks were breaking off of him and assimilating into the light of the rift. He flew against the strong, energy-sapping current and grabbed onto a cracked ledge, feeling a tingling sensation in his legs, as they were fading away.

Void's illusion again materialised in front of him, now flickering as the environment slowly broke. "Let go, Samuel. This is all for your own good, kid." Void spoke to him, calmly.

Samuel shook his head, afraid of what would happen if he did give up.

"You're dying, whether you fight or not. But if you trust me and go, you'll not be dead forever. Only three days, where it'll be like falling asleep on your end. On Halloween, you'll awake like nothing happened, except for your immortality. If you still reject this, I'll be forced to make you fall either way. If I don't take action, you'll be slowly absorbed by that rift. Unlike a Spirit though, there's no coming back from the light. You'll be dead. Game over! You just need to let go." Void hovered slightly, with what looked like tears appearing on his illusion form.

Samuel looked down at the large, gaping hole, as his legs were turning invisible with glowing glints of light breaking off of him at every moment, taking him with them. Samuel looked up again at Void, who was staring back at him with a serious glance.

"Void, I don't know if I can forgive you..." Just as Samuel finished speaking, the ledge he was clinging onto broke. The illusion of Void grabbed his hand to catch him, cooling it down from contact.

"Kid...I didn't want to do this. Believe me. But, it looks like your fate's up to me now. See you soon."

CHAPTER 20: THE FINAL BATTLE

Samuel looked up at the spirit in shock, unable to believe what was happening. Suddenly Void let go, causing Samuel to fall towards the gaping hole. He tried to fly away, but the strength of the rift's grip was too much. He closed his eyes from the blinding light while feeling himself quickly fading away. Void sighed, feeling bad for what he did for once, before glitching away. In a few moments, Samuel had vanished, leaving the darkness empty.

Back in reality, Void finished draining Samuel, and wiped the excess blood from his mouth with his hand, in his normal fashion. He took a few weak breaths after taking in so much, before turning around at the sound of Fawnia's voice.

"Is he...?" Fawnia asked Void shakily, with small tears welling up in the corners of her eyes, which were already dripping with mascara.

He looked at her with his now persimmon shaded eyes, which were so bright they were glowing, before silently nodding, as he knew what her sentence would've ended with.

Stella was leaning against him and crying, which Void noticed with a sigh and let her continue. "Transformation isn't just biting. Now this's the most painful part for me...a trade, per se. My blood, in return for his," Void explained to the group crowded around him, placing the boy down onto the floor. He sat for a moment, then turned his attention to his right hand. "This is going to hurt," he thought, before slowly pulling down his sleeve and biting into his own hand, making it drip and bleed his black blood. The blood now seemed to have a faint, amber glow, as if it was full of energy.

"Okay...that's frightening." Stella muttered and shuffled away, though she still was close by.

He placed his hand onto Samuel's bite wound and let his blood leak into it, causing the area nearby to be tinged with a black shade, which webbed and spiked around as if he was made of glass. He quickly healed the wound and his hand. "...One more thing. There's...an incantation that I've learnt which is basically a wish to the darkness for them to turn, kind of a respect thing to the Vampire culture...I recommend that you guys stand back."

The others stepped back, giving Void some space. He stood himself up, focusing his attention on the boy limp on the floor. Abruptly, his eyes were tainted with an ink black hue, with some of the black leaking out of his eyes like tears. As his hands radiated a translucent crimson mist, both he and Samuel floated in the air, almost effortlessly.

Void started chanting...but it wasn't English. It was a dark language, with a sharp edge.

"What's he saying?" Blaze asked.

Stella searched her mind, recollecting what Void had taught her during her visits to him while he stayed inside the Abyss. "I've got it! It's Umbrius. The language of the Dark Species. It originated from Vampires, but now all dark species speak it. Only they can fluently speak the language, as their mouth shapes are different from ours. They have fangs and sharp tongues, for example. While I can speak it, I can't speak it as well as him. It'll sound rough, but I could try to translate for you!" Stella explained to the others.

They nodded enthusiastically, wanting to know what was going on.

"Okay...He has a different dialect than what he taught me from the books that Fawnia gave him, but it's basically the same...I believe he's saying this..." She cleared her throat, as it helped her pronounce the inhuman sounds. She said what he was saying in a more clear and understandable way, while hoping it didn't also cause a magical effect.

Once she had finished repeating the chant, she went quiet for a moment, thinking inside her head. "...The translation in English is something like this..." she said, before focusing on the words. "Spirit of the Shadowed night, give this soul a new life. Though their heart won't beat, and their soul will be black...save them from the Reaper's scythe." Stella translated.

Fawnia looked at her, impressed at her knowledge. Void stopped chanting, then traced a symbol of a moon on the boy's forehead, with the symbol appearing and fading away where the wound was once situated, as both of them floated back to the ground. His eyes returned to normal, as he struggled to get back on his feet.

"It's done. He should...awaken... on Halloween." Void was clearly physically drained from the ordeal. Stella noticed his weakness on his feet, and caught him before he fell. She smiled, allowing him to lean on her for balance. He smiled back, as he gained his footing again.

"You two should get back to the X-Periment Facility. Samuel needs a safe place to stay, and I can assume you both may want to have each other for company. We'll be alright, we always are," Blaze said.

The group silently nodded, with Stella going with Void and Samuel.

EPILOGUE

The day was October 31st, 2028...Halloween. The sun was hanging in the middle of the sky, shining down upon the newly remade Magic Land. Structures had been rebuilt to their former glory, and the commotion of the larger battle from three days prior caught the attention of daring people from the nearby town.

This caused the sight of explorers to become common, although nobody believed the stories they told. Stella landed from a flight on a patch of grass near the X-periment Facility. "It's as if none of the past few years ever happened," she thought. She glanced about the new Facility, which had been given some TLC by the spirits of the area. The Perfector stood dormant, with Smiley and The Ministry having vanished without a trace. However, the newly remodelled land wasn't what she was looking for. She was headed for one place, hoping to see one person in particular.

She knocked on the orange door in front of her, and waited for a moment. Inside the building, the sound of footsteps came towards the door, which swung open to show Void. The scars that once sliced across his eyes had healed, leaving little to no signs of their existence. Because of this, he had moved onto contacts, which Stella herself designed for him.

"Hello there, dear! It's actually nice to see you today. Halloween already?" He chatted, before stepping aside to let her in, which she kindly accepted, shutting the door behind her. They both sat down, with Stella picking a single chair, and Void relaxing on a comfortable sofa. "I checked on him before. Nothing interesting right now. Fangs have fully grown…occasional movement…" Void rambled slightly, shaking his hand in the air, which Stella noticed had a small scar on the wrist.

"Your wrist. Still scarred, V?" Stella asked, a can of Fizz-e Cola in her hand.

Void looked down to the small scar, and nodded. "Guess I bit too hard. Doesn't really sting though, so I guess that's a plus?"

Void pulled his view away from the scar, but was still in his thoughts while Stella finished her drink. She tapped the can with her finger and made it vanish, keeping her attention on Void. As the atmosphere grew quiet, Stella saw how Void looked down and possibly upset, and decided to try and break the deafening silence.

"Are you alright, Void? Don't tell me you've skipped feeding these past few days. I know you're committed to your promise but you're draining yourself dry!" Stella grinned, trying to make him laugh.

Void looked up, before letting out a genuine chuckle. "I'll admit, you got me there. If knowing makes you feel better, I've been keeping myself from being too thirsty. Though some top ups wouldn't…suck." Void laughed, with a small wink.

Stella giggled at his sense of humour, with both of them smiling at the other. Just as the two of them were finishing their jokes, a loud crash thundered from below them, along with the sound of shattered glass. The sound sent a chill up Stella's back, though Void seemed more concerned than frightened.

"What was that?"

"Do you want the sarcastic answer or the honest one?" He got out a small silver coloured device, with crimson red patterns at its sides. Stella chose the latter. Both of them stood up, with Void turning towards her. "That is most likely Samuel awakening. Hopefully he still has memories of you, and has enough sanity right now to not see you as a walking, talking food source. Just in case he's not in the best mind right now, stick behind me. This device should stop him from getting too close, just in case. Any vampire that gets hit by it is stunned, like a taser," Void finished, before holding the device in front of him, like a gun.

He went down a stairwell while Stella stood behind him, with both entering into a group of rooms, which most likely were used to hold parts for Abyss and other rides around the area if they needed it. However, Void stopped at one specific door and sliced his hand in the air, signalling for her to stay quiet so the newly awakened boy wouldn't go to attack her.

"Hey...kid. Are you awake?" Void spoke, trying to get a response. He then peeked into the room, and saw a catastrophic mess. The pod, which was specially designed by Levi, had been thrown open by a superhuman force, the heart-rate monitor's freshly snapped wires strewn around. The monitor itself was bent on the tiled floor, its display cracked, glass shards sprinkled on the tiles like dust. "What even could've created this mess?" Stella gasped, before being stopped by the slow, unsteady echo of footsteps. A familiar teenager stood at the other side of the hallway, now wearing a black vest with blue shaded details, and boots that were similar to Void's. He stared at them, with a mix of confusion and rage in his eyes. He was different from what he used to be, and both Void and Stella could tell. His skin was icy pale, his hair now crimson, and his once inviting blue eyes...were tainted red.

"Samuel? What in the world happened!" Stella said, pained by her friend in such a state.

"...I'm no longer him..." The boy spoke, staring at the duo. "...I'm a monster," he cried out, before he disappeared from view.

The duo searched everywhere, but there was no trace of Samuel, or who he'd become, anywhere. They were now standing in front of Abyss's ride building, which Void had maintained throughout the years.

"He's vanished. But how?" She hugged herself in doubt, shooting panicked glares at Void.

"...Usually, a new-blood's powers aren't this quick to generate. Even then, I thought only I could transform into mist, and it took me ages to master it! Unless...he's more powerful than I'd guessed," he debated out loud, a detailed symbol of a crescent moon floating in the air in front of him. "He shouldn't be able to leave the park, as I hacked into the chip that the Ministry put on him. So, he'll be found by one of the others, if not us. Let's just hope he snaps out of it."

Both spirits glanced at each other, with a worried expression.

"I'll go back to Technoland, alright?" she said as she turned to go. He nodded in agreement, while she walked away.

Just as she was a few metres from the gate, a panicked scream ripped through the air. "What was that?" Stella rushed back towards him, pointing towards the scream's location.

Void had already turned in the direction, due to his enhanced hearing. "Well, it seemed to be Levi screaming. From the fact that Samuel just escaped, I think we should go as quickly as we can," Void theorised, with a collected tone. He looked at Stella, before having an idea. "Hold my hand."

Stella flinched for a moment at his command, taken aback.

"Just trust me," Void reassured her. Stella beamed back at him, before holding his hand. Suddenly, he took her towards the wall, which was in the shade. "Ever wanted to know what it feels like to be a shadow?" Void asked rhetorically, before the both of them seemed to melt into the darkness itself. For a moment, Stella felt like she was weightless, floating in the empty space. Soon, she was torn from this state, and now was in Fantasy Lane. Some of the buildings had fresh cracks crawling across their surfaces, with stone chips littered on the floor as debris.

Blaze and Nebulus were helping up Levi and Sally near the trail leading to the entrance, checking them for injuries. Nebulus saw the two appear from the corner of his eye and darted towards them when Sally had gotten up off the ground.

"Void! If you have anything to do with whatever that thing was, you better explain!" Nebulus piped up, looking at Stella and Void with both relief and anger.

"Calm down. Tell me what happened."

"Well...me and Blaze came to check up if these guys had seen any explorers around here, when somebody appeared out of thin air! I thought it was a spirit with their powers going crazy, so I stepped forward. He ran off!" Nebulus started off his story, as Sally was looking nervously at the pathway to the gate.

Void nodded, putting the pieces together in his mind.

"So, we followed them here, where he seemed like he wanted to leave. I, of course, told him he couldn't for his safety. He started yelling at me! Sally went to confront them...before getting thrown through the air like a toy, when the boy threw his arm forwards! He ran towards the gate, throwing Levi to the ground in the process."

As Nebulus finished recounting what had happened, Stella realised what was going on. "Did the boy have red hair, and act off?"

Blaze stepped forward. "Yes, He did! Acted kind of...wild. Like he couldn't be controlled," Blaze answered back, flicking a spike of hair away from his face.

Levi floated towards the conversation, using his holographic sketch pad he used for orders to draw an image. "Here. Look familiar?"

Void looked cold for a moment. "Then it's worse than I thought. He's actually trying to leave!" Void talked to himself, assessing the situation.

Nebulus looked at him with a blank stare, confused.

"If you want to know, that thing is Samuel. He's lost control of himself, from the looks of it. Has anyone been hurt, other than getting tossed out of his way?"

Nebulus flinched in shock, remembering what had happened three days earlier.

After a moment, the spirits looked at themselves for any injuries, and shook their heads when they found none. Void sighed in relief, then turned his head towards Stella. "Sweetheart, this could be dangerous. You need to head back home. Maybe you could take Blaze and the others somewhere safe, too."

But Stella was standing in opposition to his command, her eyes starting to glow. "I'm not having you throw yourself into danger! You said it yourself, that he's more powerful than you thought. What if he hurts you!" she argued.

Void placed a hand on the side of her face to comfort her. "I'll be alright. Even if he lashes out, I have the taser, remember? Do you really think I'll be defeated by an angry teenager?" Void reassured her with a joke, knowing how she liked to laugh.

She sighed, before giving him a hug. "Be careful, alright?"

Void nodded sincerely. She let go, following Blaze, Nebulus, Levi and Sally out of Fantasy Lane.

Void walked towards the entrance, ducking under some stray branches that tried to hit him. After a minute of walking, he came face to face with the gate. While the gate was tall and dominating to the spirits, it was only a few inches taller than him. However, the gate was the least of his concerns. The thing that he was interested in was the boy in front of it, who was focusing on his hands.

"How do I do it? I was using this curse's powers just a minute ago!" Samuel talked to himself, feeling stressed. He threw his arm out, but nothing happened. He sighed, slouching his shoulders. Just as he seemed to have given up, he noticed Void looking at him from across the pathway. "Why're you here? Do you want to torment me more!" Samuel growled; his guard now back up.

Void wanted to speak, but he didn't know a way that wouldn't escalate the situation. Instead, he silently shook his head.

Samuel rolled his eyes, and turned back to focusing on the gate. Just as he went to try to charge another spell, Void looked down to the floor. "I'm sorry. I'm sorry for whatever I did that made you upset! Was it that fight we had in your dreams? Was it when I went to my brother's side!"

Samuel turned to look at him, stepping closer towards Void. "You don't know what you did? You killed me! I'm never going to be able to return to my family, my life! Don't you get why that's upsetting?" he yelled. He stepped towards Void, shoving him away.

Void sighed, looking at the boy. "No, I don't. You're lucky in a way. At least you have a family! You have people who love you unconditionally. All I've ever had were scientists who broke me, or friends that I've always feared would turn on me!" he said, keeping his view on Samuel.

Samuel looked up to match Void's amber eyes, showing a faint sign of pity. But it soon faded. "It doesn't change what you've done. You're the reason I'm like this. Why should I even care!" he snapped, as a flicker of blue in his hands soon grew into a bright light shining around him.

Void started to run back to the street, seeing the luminous light grow brighter by the second. However, he didn't notice where he was rushing, and tripped on a jagged edge of concrete.

"Agh! Of course there were still some cracks!" he said, shuffling himself up.

But just as he had steadied himself on his feet, Samuel fired out the charge. The blue energy flung out like a shockwave, slamming into the unaware Void. The strength of the blast tore him off the ground, and sent him flying towards the trees, knocking him out cold.

◇◇◇◇◇◇

"Void? You told me you'd not hurt yourself! Are you okay?" Stella's voice rang out, as Void got back to his senses.

He rubbed his head, as most of the pain he was feeling was extinguished. "We really should stop getting into these situations, huh?" He cracked a joke, trying to make light of the situation.

Stella let out a brief laugh, before helping Void up. He looked back at the entrance, only to see the gate had been blasted open. Whatever spell Samuel had cast, he was gone.

Void paused for a minute, forming his phone in his hand. "Remember the chip? I should be able to track him." He swiped through his phone, only for the tracker to be inactive.

"Wait. Is that...the chip!" Stella said, picking up a small device and handing it to Void. "Well, it looks like we just have to hope he doesn't get into trouble."

Stella looked over towards Void, who was looking at the chip. However, she could tell from his expression that he was hurting. She panicked, wanting to make sure he was okay and wasn't hurt.

"I'm alright. Just aching from getting flung into a tree," he said with sarcasm.

Stella chuckled. She looked up at him with a small smile, happy he was okay. "You're lucky I spotted you! This time, I'm not leaving you to go rush off, alright?"

"Sure. What's the plan, dearie? You want to stay the night at my place or something?"

"If you want me to. Or, you could stay at mine. It would be better for both of us!"

They both started to walk down the street, avoiding the rubble dotted around the path.

"Alright, I'll stay at your apartment. You just need to ask if you need anything, okay?"

He glanced down, catching her briefly looking back at him. "I know you mean blood. I'm not thirsty for it all the time, sweetheart!" he said, his view on the surroundings. He noticed Stella shudder briefly, and put his coat over her shoulders. She looked up, only to realise that his eyes were red. Before she could confront him about it, he spoke up. "You don't need to act so worried for me. I'm alright, I promise."

She crossed her arms and stopped walking, keeping her glare on him. "If you're fine, you can stop keeping your eyes red! What're you trying to hide?" she said commandingly.

Void stayed silent for a moment and stopped walking. His eyes shifted to a pale orange. She asked why he hid his eyes, as Void looked at her.

"I don't like to keep on using you like some sort of blood bank! It makes me think that something could go wrong, that you could get hurt. It makes me feel like a bad person, even if I can't control it!" He raised his voice.

A few minutes passed, as a silence started to grow. Stella looked him in the eyes like what he would do to her. "Nothing can go wrong, you don't need to keep tormenting yourself with the day you accidentally went overboard. I've gotten over it, so it is up to you. If you constantly fear your own shadow, you'll just drive yourself crazy! Honestly, coming to me when you're thirsty is better than risking our friends' safety if they don't want to be bitten. You could say I'm like a Blood Donor. I'd never let you go without blood, because I saw first hand what happens. That was the whole reason I became your source, remember? If I had to get bitten a hundred times more to help you be happy, then so be it!" she vented, while looking up at him.

Void leaned down, brushing some hair away from her eyes. "You really want to keep me safe. I appreciate that, starlight. I admit, I am a bit of a doubter! But, it's hard not to be cold when you literally have no pulse. Anyways, I don't want to disappoint you. If you really want me to, I could have some later when we get to my place. Maybe we could watch a movie too. Does that make you feel better?" he said, with Stella nodding in response.

The two set off towards The X-periment Facility, holding each other's hands.

Outside the park, standing upon a hill, Samuel was looking down at them with a cold stare. "See you soon...Shadows," he said, just as Void and Stella rounded the corner. He placed his hand on the trunk of a nearby tree and left a faint, blue handprint. He looked at it for a moment, before turning away and vanishing into thin air. The secrets of what happened on the day of the murders and the truth of Samuel's disappearance remained hidden, with nobody from the outside knowing it. But, perhaps some things are best left forgotten.

-THE END-

Printed in Great Britain
by Amazon

11878910R00146